STORIES FROM SOUTH UIST

STORIES FROM SOUTH UIST

TOLD BY

Angus MacLellan

TRANSLATED BY

John Lorne Campbell

This edition first published in 1997 by
Birlinn Limited
8 Canongate Venture
5 New Street
Edinburgh
EH8 8BH

www.birlinn.co.uk

Reprinted 2001

ISBN 1 874744 26 2

British Library Cataloguing-in-Publication Data
A catalogue record for this book is available
from the British Library

Printed and bound by Omnia Books Limited, Glasgow

CONTENTS

Stories of Witchcraft

Ghost Stories

Humorous Stories

Adventure Stories

Notes

INTRODUCTION

I FIRST met Angus MacLellan, 'Aonghus Beag mac Aonghuis 'ic Eachainn, Mac 'ill 'ialain', at Lochboisdale, South Uist, in November 1949, shortly after I had begun making wire recordings of traditional Gaelic songs and stories in South Uist and Barra with the aid of a research grant from the Leverhulme Foundation, which I take the opportunity to acknowledge with gratitude here. He had come in by bus from Frobost, where there was then no electric light, to record stories for me in the hotel. Aonghus Beag tells his own story in the chapter that follows this introduction, and there is no need for me to elaborate it here; nor to describe the background of South Uist, the island where his family has lived for generations, as that has been most skilfully and sympathetically done in *Folksongs and Folklore of South Uist* by Margaret Fay Shaw.*

Aonghus Beag is a sturdy, cheerful man, with a very alert mind. He looks far younger than his ninety years and still conveys the impression of the bodily strength developed by his former livelihood, that of ploughman on mainland farms in Perthshire, Argyll, and Dumbartonshire, days about which he had recorded for me many reminiscences, which may some time become another book. He has the reputation of having been one of the most skilful sheep shearers in South Uist, and he is still capable of walking very considerable distances, and as a storyteller and conversationalist, he never wearies.

Loch Eynort, where Aonghus Beag used to live, is now considered one of the remotest inhabited parts of South Uist, but in the old days, before the evictions, and before Lochboisdale was developed, it was the main port of the island, and the scene of great comings and goings; it is from Loch Eynort, for example, that the famous Gaelic poet Alexander MacDonald

* Routledge and Kegan Paul, 1955.

(*c.* 1700–1770) portrays the Chief of Clanranald and his crew as setting sail for Carrickfergus in Ireland in his long poem called the *Birlinn of Clanranald* (*Biurlainn Chlann Raghnaill*). But after the Clanranalds sold South Uist to Colonel Gordon in 1838, Loch Eynort and the eastern part of the island, which contains the best hill grazing and the most sheltered land in South Uist, fell on evil days. A substantial population was evicted from this part of Uist to make room for big sheep farmers, and was dispersed to Eriskay, Benbecula, other parts of South Uist, or to North America*. In a statement made to the Crofters' Commission at Lochboisdale on 28th May 1883, Donald MacLellan, 'Dòmhnall Mór', Aonghus Beag's cousin, then aged about fifty-two, described how his grandfather, who lived at Glen Corradale, had a substantial stock of 600 sheep and 30 head of cattle impounded by a big farmer, how his father was later evicted and moved to a place three miles away, evicted again and forced to move by sea to Bàgh Hartabhagh with seven others, where they had to live in caves by the shore until they had made themselves turf huts, from which his father was evicted again six years later, to be given four acres of barren land on Eriskay.† Donald MacLellan told Mr. C. Fraser-Mackintosh, M.P., a member of the Commission, that 'I would return tomorrow if I were permitted to the land my father had. I would not give a snuff for the land which I presently occupy, if I were permitted to return to the land which my father tenanted—Uishnish or Glen Corradale'—where his grandfather had lived, and his ancestors from time immemorial. 'The chief of Clanranald sometimes spent nights in my grandfather's house.' Donald MacLellan's grandfather was Aonghus Beag's great-grandfather.

Only a remnant of the old population remained in the Loch Eynort district, impoverished by the loss of their traditional common hill grazings to the big sheep farms. Loch Eynort fell into disuse as the main harbour of South Uist; the entrance

* Their names were communicated to Alexander Carmichael by the late Fr. MacColl.

† Minutes of Evidence of the Crofters' Commission, Vol. I p. 740 (Question No. 11674).

is narrow with a strong tidal current, and there is a dangerous reef in it. Lochboisdale became the main port of the island. The Loch Eynort district was sufficiently isolated in Aonghus Beag's boyhood for school attendance to be difficult, if not impossible, and certainly not insisted on. It is, indeed, amongst persons like him who thus escaped the net of the Scottish Education Act of 1872, which made an English education compulsory throughout the Gaelic-speaking Highlands and Islands, that traditional oral Gaelic literature is now best preserved.

And what a literature we have here! The words of the late Dr Robin Flower are every bit as true of the Outer Hebrides, and particularly of Uist and Barra, as they were of the Great Blasket which lies off the coast of Kerry:

'I listened spellbound, and, as I listened, it came to me suddenly that there on the last inhabited piece of European land, looking out to the Atlantic horizon, I was hearing the oldest living tradition in the British Isles. So far as the record goes this matter in one form or another is older than the Anglo-Saxon Beowulf, and yet it lives still upon the lips of the peasantry, a real and vivid experience, while except to a few painful scholars, Beowulf has long passed out of memory. Tomorrow too this will be dead, and the world will be the poorer when this last shade of that which was once great has passed away.' Spoken Gaelic, Flower goes on to say 'is perhaps the liveliest, the most concise, and the most literary in its turns of all the vernaculars of Europe.'*

Only a portion of Aonghus Beag's stories belong to the oldest tradition, it is true. But he is a storyteller of consummate ability, the product of an immemorial oral tradition that is better preserved and more carefully cultivated in the Outer Hebrides than anywhere else in Western Europe. Often while sitting listening to Aonghus Beag and other storytellers, such as Dunnchadh mac Dhomhnaill 'ic Dhunnchaidh (the late Duncan MacDonald of Peninerine, South Uist) and Seumas Iain Ghunnairigh (the late James MacKinnon, of Northbay, Isle of Barra) or to their recordings, I found myself falling under the impression that they *must* have seen the events

* *The Irish Tradition*, pp. 105 and 106.

they described or have overheard the dialogues they reproduced in their stories. Aonghus Beag possesses to an uncommon degree the power of reproducing the conversation of his characters, and of varying his voice to imitate their tone, whether it be of an angry general, a disagreeable crone, a self-pitying drunkard, or the despairing mother on whom the fairies have inflicted a changeling for her own infant. He is also expert in the art of giving a spoken story form and climax.

We meet many well-known figures in his stories. In the older ones, Fionn mac Cumhail and his famous band (called in Gaelic *An Fhinn* or *Na Fiantaichean*) including Diarmaid, Oscar, Caoilte and Conan; Boban Saor, or Bobban the Carpenter, the famous joiner who invented the adze, so it is said, and for whom no task was too difficult; Kings in ancient Ireland, jealous stepmothers, cave-men or ogres, magic rings, escapes from dangers, feats of strength, persons under tabus or spells. It is of interest to consider the geography of the complex (non-Fingalian) Gaelic folk-tale. It seems to correspond to that of the Europe of about a thousand years ago. In these stories the Kings of Ireland, Norway, France, and Greece (*i.e.* the Emperors of Byzantium) are frequent figures; Kings of Scotland or England hardly if ever appear, which suggests that these stories must have been formulated before Scotland or England became united political entities.

Heroic and chimeric tales form only a small portion of Aonghus Beag's repertory of stories; this probably corresponds to the taste of his contemporary Gaelic-speaking listeners, who now prefer the simple folk-tale or the anecdote—humorous or adventure stories such as are well represented here. In Aonghus Beag's simple folk-tales we meet figures well known in international folklore: the shrew who is tamed and turned into a good wife; the 'clever peasant girl'; the magic mill that makes the salt that prevents the water of the sea from being fresh; 'clever Elsie' (No. 10); 'William Tell' (No. 15, in Uist attributed to Clanranald); the Old Robber who related his adventures to free—here not his own sons, but the sons of the King of Ireland (No. 5). This is here fitted into the framework of an old chimeric Gaelic story.

In the sphere of local traditions, Aonghus Beag has some

good stories about the MacDonalds of Clanranald, the ancient owners of South Uist and other lands, and their hereditary poets and historians, the MacVurichs of Staoiligearraidh. There is, or was, a wealth of such stories extant in South Uist, and a whole volume could easily be devoted to them and nothing else, but as far as I know, they have never been brought together.* They give a powerful impression of olden times—particularly of the seventeenth century. In justice to the Clanranalds, it should be said that their failings of pride and arbitrary violence were balanced by the virtues of fidelity to their ancient religion and to their legitimate sovereigns, the Stewarts.

The remaining types of stories translated here, the ghost stories and the humorous and adventure stories represent classes that have not received much attention from folklorists hitherto.† In the case of the last two classes it is not impossible that some of the stories derive from literary sources. No. 41 is clearly derived from a romantic novel called *St Clair of the Isles*, first published in 1803. There is interest here in showing how such a story can be taken into the Gaelic oral tradition and adapted to its conventions and standards.

I have continued to record stories from Aonghus Beag, and old songs and ballads from his sister, till the present time, since 1956 on tape instead of on wire. Up to date the total amount of material he has recorded for Mr. Calum MacLean and for myself comes to over 130 stories and a number of ballads, as well as many personal reminiscences of the days when he worked as a ploughman on mainland farms. The latter I hope to translate in due course.

There has been a good deal of argument amongst folklorists about the way that folk-tales are transmitted and about the relationship between literary and oral versions of the stories. So far as Aonghus Beag is concerned, he learned his stories orally from friends of his family who came to work or to call at his father's house at Loch Eynort. In those days the custom of the *céilidh* or informal conversational visit or

* The Clanranald traditions extant in Moidart were published by the Rev. Fr. Charles MacDonald in *Moidart or among the Clanranalds*.

† Cp. J. F. Campbell, *West Highland Tales*, IV, 428.

party was still in full vigour, and many winter nights were passed in playing cards, telling stories, and singing old songs; the *céilidh* would be in one house one night, and another the next. Aonghus Beag told me that he could learn a simple story by hearing it once, if it was well and clearly told. Longer and more complicated stories, such as the Fingalian tales, he would need to hear several times. He kept the stories as he heard them at first without alteration, except perhaps for a few words (I can imagine he may have given more vitality to the dialogues at times). He did not put together or mend stories by hearing different versions from different story-tellers. He is well able to remember who told him the stories. As a matter of fact, the forty-two stories in this book came to him from fifteen different persons; but two of these were the sources for more than half of them. Another person was the main source for his Fingalian stories and ballads.

I must now say a few words about the way these stories have been translated. This has been done direct from the tape recordings by writing down a fairly literal English translation in pencil while listening to the original on the tape. Aonghus Beag's diction is so good that very few words and still fewer phrases were inaudible and some of these occasions were due to outside noises. The stories were then typed from the pencilled draft translations and turned into idiomatic English in the process. This is the first time as far as I know that translations of Gaelic stories into English have been made for publication direct from tape recordings without the intervention and use of a transcribed Gaelic text. I hope it will be possible to print the Gaelic texts of some of these stories later. My model in presenting them in English has been the book *Tales from the Arab Tribes*, translations into English from Arabic made by the late Major C. G. Campbell, a masterpiece of translation of folk-tales from another language into readable English.

My object has been to put before English-speaking readers translations which will read naturally and which will convey something of the terse and vivid expression of the stories as Aonghus Beag tells them. I have therefore carefully avoided alike the pseudo-archaic and the Celtic Twilight styles as well as the closely literal type of translation. Purely modern English colloquialisms are also avoided. A good many translations of folk-tales from Scottish and Irish Gaelic were made between 1860 and 1914; some of these, particularly some of the Irish ones, were good; some are so painfully literal as to be almost unreadable, others are presented in a style that invests the stories with a false atmosphere. For, as Dr Robin Flower has said,* what characterizes the Gaelic way of thought and style is an extreme concreteness of language, an 'epigrammatic concision of speech, the pleasure in sharp, bright colour' which is the antithesis of the mistiness of the Celtic Twilight. However, the difference between the structures and the modes of expression of the Gaelic and English languages is so great that this cannot be conveyed by a purely literal translation; and my method has been to translate expressions by expressions rather than words by words. Anyone who wishes to study the method used can do so by comparing Peigi MacRae's account of Catriana nighean Eachainn which I printed in *Gairm*,† and the English translation of it I published in the *Scots Magazine* of October 1955.

My purpose then is to use words and expressions that would be naturally used by an English speaker telling the same story. Only in one or two places has it been seen fit to let a Highland accent come in, e.g. No. 35. The stories are not embellished in any way in the process of translation, but, as some of the devices of the spoken tale do not always answer when exactly reproduced in print, it has been advisable at times, for instance, to invert clauses and define the names of persons or places. Gaelic possesses emphatic forms of the personal pronouns 'he, she' (*esan, ise*) which are loosely used in stories to indicate the first of two persons the storyteller is referring to (a usage I have not noticed remarked on by any grammarian). English does not possess this device and it is necessary to use the name of the person meant. In a few cases I have bestowed names on characters in some stories who were only called 'a crofter' or 'a farm servant', for the sake of clarity. I have dropped scores of 'said he's', and I have

* *The Irish Tradition*, p. 110.

† III 58.

divided sentences which in the Gaelic are linked by the conjunction 'and', but which would not be so linked in English. I have been careful to assign the tenses of the verb that the context requires: Scottish Gaelic is poor in verbal tense-forms.

I have reluctantly translated the Gaelic *An Fhinn* and *Na Fiantaichean* by 'The Fingalians', because the word is familiar and pronounceable, although it wrongly implies that the 'Fingalians' were founded by Fionn mac Cumhail, whereas they existed before he was born (No. 1). *Rìgh na Gréige*, 'The King of Greece', I have rendered 'Emperor of Byzantium', because that is his correct title. *Fuamhaire* I have translated 'cave-man', because *fuamhairean* always live in caves, and popularly their name is connected with *uaimh*, a cave, in Gaelic. Though they are sometimes referred to as larger or even much larger than ordinary men, this distinction is not consistently maintained. 'Giant' is a misleading translation. They are nearly always portrayed as stupid cannibals, and may represent an extinct race of mankind.

It remains to say some words about the collection of Scottish Gaelic folk-tales and folk-songs in general. The first person who recognized the great interest of this material and attempted to organize its collection was that remarkable folklorist J. F. Campbell of Islay (1822–85). He was the first person, too, to see that Gaelic folk-tales had, in many cases, an international background. A selection of his tales was printed in four volumes in 1860–62 and was reprinted in 1893. Further volumes were published in 1940 and 1960, edited by J. G. MacKay. Towards the end of the nineteenth century, the 'Waifs and Strays' series was published under the patronage of Lord Archibald Campbell, containing many folk-tales collected by the Rev. D. MacInnes, the Rev. J. MacDougall, and the Rev. J. G. Campbell, minister of Tiree, the last a particularly able folklorist. Around the same time, the Rev. Fr Allan McDonald and Dr George Henderson collected many stories in Uist and Eriskay, most of which are still unpublished; the same applies to the folk-tales collected by, and sent to, Alexander Carmichael during the course of his long and active life as a folklore collector.

The invention of mechanical means of recording folk-tales, first the clockwork Ediphone of the 1920s, later the wire and tape recorders that came into use after the last war, has enormously simplified the task of preserving this material and the labour of collecting and transcribing it. But it can hardly be said that adequate use has been made of the opportunity these means of collection have afforded, at least until very recently. This has been due, partly to the mistaken impression that J. F. Campbell and his collaborators and contemporaries had exhausted the field, partly to the supine and obscurantist attitude that prevailed in Scottish academic circles towards Gaelic and folklore studies between the two world wars, and partly to what one cannot help feeling has been a tacit decision taken at a high administrative level, that no studies which tend to emphasize or perpetuate a distinct Scottish or Gaelic culture shall receive any official encouragement.* Thus millions of pounds of public money are available to construct a rocket range in South Uist that will probably be obsolete within a generation but unfortunately not before the influences it introduces will have done much to obliterate the traditional native culture of the island; hundreds of thousands of pounds of public money are available for the preservation and protection of plants and animals, some of which are in no particular danger of extinction, under nature conservancy; but not a penny is available for the recording and preservation of the uniquely interesting traditional oral and material culture of the Scottish Highlands, of which South Uist is now by far the most important stronghold, and which is in far greater danger of disappearing, than is the red deer.†

Academic recognition at least has been afforded since the

* Perhaps now the international nature of much of our Gaelic oral literature is beginning to be realized, the official mind may come to grasp that fact and divert itself of the fear that to encourage the preservation of Gaelic folklore might lead to a repetition of the Jacobite rising of 1745!

† The distinguished Swedish folklorist C. W. von Sydow drew attention to the importance of the Scottish Gaelic oral tradition and the urgency of recording it in a paper in *Béaloideas* in 1934, which was reprinted in his *Selected Papers on Folklore* (p. 59); but he made absolutely no impression on official or academic circles in Scotland at the time.

Irish Folklore Commission sent Mr. Calum MacLean as their collector, to the Hebrides in 1947, and since the School of Scottish Studies, of which Mr MacLean is now a Senior Research Fellow, was founded in 1951; but this institution is functioning on a mere pittance, while the cost of tape recorders and of tape put this method of collection beyond the reach of most private individuals.

If the publication of these translations succeeds in persuading anyone that research in this field deserves the support of governments, I shall feel that my labours have been rewarded. As it is, I hope the translations may give to others something of the same pleasure that listening to Aonghus Beag telling his stories has given to me.

It remains to record my gratitude to various persons who have helped and encouraged me in this work; to Aonghus Beag himself; to his niece, Mrs Patrick MacPhee, and her husband, and to the Rev. Fr John MacLean, formerly parish priest of Bornish, both of whom have made recordings of Aonghus Beag and his sister for me with my machine at times when I was not able to go to Uist myself to do so; to the Rev. Fr A. MacKellaig and the Rev. Fr D. MacDougall, parish priests of Bornish before and after Fr MacLean, for their help in many ways; to Mr Calum MacLean, who first encouraged me to record Aonghus Beag, in 1949; and to Major Finlay MacKenzie, owner of the Lochboisdale Hotel, a true patron of Highland music and folklore, who very kindly put a sitting-room in his hotel at my disposal to make these recordings in the days before electric light had reached Aonghus Beag's present home, Mr and Mrs MacPhee's house in Frobost. I am also obliged to Miss Annie Johnston, of Castlebay, Isle of Barra, to whom I am particularly indebted for notes on the old island houses, and to Miss Peggy MacRae, a contemporary of Aonghus Beag, for help in solving some difficulties in the texts of the stories, when visiting Canna.

Finally, I must record my indebtedness to the late Fr Allan McDonald of Eriskay. Not only do his collections afford a unique insight into the folklore of South Uist, but if it had not been for his labour in collecting unusual words and expressions from speech and old songs and stories between 1893 and 1897,* the task of making an accurate translation of these stories would have been very much more difficult for anyone who was not a native of the Isles.

J. L. CAMPBELL

Isle of Canna,
30th January, 1960.

* See *Gaelic Words and Expressions from South Uist and Eriskay, collected by Rev. Fr Allan McDonald*, 1859–1905. Dublin Institute for Advanced Studies, 1958.

POSTSCRIPT

SINCE these words were written, news has come of the death of Calum I. MacLean only a month before he was to have received the honorary degree of LL.D. from the University of St Francis Xavier, Antigonish, Nova Scotia, for his work for the preservation of Scottish Gaelic folklore. It is proper that tribute should be here paid to a scholar whose devotion to his subject and whose courage and cheerfulness in the face of a long and painful illness have been an inspiration to all other workers in this field. A version of the *Táin Bó Cúailnge* taken down from Aonghus Beag was published by Calum MacLean in ARV, Vol. 15, pp. 160-180, 1959.

Dr John Lorne Campbell (1906–96), scholar and farmer, dedicated his career to the recording, transmission and publication of the Gaelic song, literary and linguistic record of Scotland. His meeting with Angus MacLellan in Lochboisdale, South Uist, where he had gone to record waulking songs in the winter of 1948–9 led to the recording of Angus's stories, ballads and songs as well as his personal reminiscences. *Stories from South Uist* reflects the extraordinary nature of the literary Gaelic of an ancient oral tradition and of Angus' own skills. This had instigated a lengthy and successful phase of recording Gaelic song and story in the 1950s and 1960s and set the seal on Dr Campbell's pioneering collecting work which had begun in Barra in the early 1930s.

From his boyhood at Inverneill and Taynish on the mainland of Argyll, John Lorne Campbell went to St John's College, Oxford, where he studied agriculture with Professor Sir James Scott Watson, graduating in 1929. He had learnt some Gaelic from a Tiree man, Hector MacLean, Ground Officer of the Taynish Estate and at Oxford he began, in his spare time, the serious study of the language with Professor John Fraser. While at Oxford, he also began work on an anthology of Gaelic songs of the Jacobite Rising of 1745–6, which was published as *Highland Songs of the '45* in 1933 and republished in a second edition by the Scottish Gaelic Texts Society in 1983. In August 1933, John Lorne Campbell went to Barra to study crofting conditions and colloquial Gaelic. There he found a 'community of independent personalities where memories of men and events are often amazingly long; in the Gaelic-speaking Hebrides they go back to Viking times a thousand years ago.' His mentor was John Macpherson, 'the Coddy', whose lore has been preserved in *Tales of Barra* (1960). With Compton Mackenzie, then living in Barra, Campbell vigorously entered the economic and political life of the Hebrides by founding the Sea League, campaigning for the enforcement of fishing limits and the closure of the Minch to trawlers to protect the livelihood of the Islands.

In his approach to Celtic Studies, he recognised the importance of grasping a good dialect thoroughly and of learning the language from the inside. 'Book Gaelic' could be an obstacle to learning since, in his own words, 'all spoken Gaelic dialects differ from the literary language, in some respects consistently: the dialects of the Outer Hebrides are in fact more vigorous than the modern literary language, and contain many words and expressions that are not in the printed dictionaries.' He pioneered the use of mechanical and electrical recording equipment and took it acrosss the Atlantic in 1937 to record the descendants of Barra and South Uist emigrants in Nova Scotia. Source of the results of these efforts have been published in *Sia Sgialachdan* (1939), the three volumes of *Hebridean Folksong* (1969–81) and *Songs Remembered in Exile* (1990). Other topics developed by John Lorne have been the researches of the Celtic Scholar, Edward Lhuyd, the poetry and song of Alasdair MacMhaighstir Alasdair, and the incomparable folklore collections of Fr Allan McDonald, parish priest of Daliburgh and Eriskay. This original and outstanding work brought John Lorne Campbell honorary degrees from St Francis Xavier University, Nova Scotia, and Glasgow University, and a D.Litt. for his published research from Oxford.

In 1938 Dr Campbell bought the islands of Canna and Sanday and farmed them in the traditional manner until 1981 when he presented them to the National Trust for Scotland. In 1935 he had married Margaret Fay Shaw, an American who was collecting Gaelic song in South Uist and this longstanding partnership brought together her musical talents with his language skills to create a unique store in Canna and a lasting monument to their dedicated scholarship.

HUGH CHEAPE
National Museums of Scotland

THE STORYTELLER'S OWN STORY

I AM Aonghus Beag, 'Young Angus', son of Angus, son of Hector, son of Donald, son of Calum, son of Donald MacLellan.[1] My mother was Mary, daughter of John Wilson in Benbecula. I was born at Poll Torain on Loch Eynort, in South Uist, on 4th July 1869, and baptized at Bornish by the Rev. Fr Donald MacColl on the 13th. My forebears, MacLellans, lived at Loch Eynort and Beinn Mhór for generations. Some of them emigrated to North America about two hundred years ago.

My father was a landless cottar on the farm of the big farmer who had Bornish, John Ferguson. My father had to pay rent for every cow he kept. He was allowed to cultivate what he could dig with the spade, and that was not much. He was not allowed to keep a horse. He was paying two pounds a year for every cow he kept, and if he had a stirk, he had to pay a pound after the cattle sale to the big farmer, for having kept it.

I was the youngest of his four sons. My brothers left home, but I stayed on after they had gone away. School was far away, and I did not get much of it. I was very young then. When I was about fifteen, my brother Hector, who was sailing, came home and gave me a gun. I used to go out with it pretty often. The world was a hard place in those times. One day I went to the hill to try to get a rabbit, and I shot one rabbit. Charles MacLean the big farmer at Gearrabhailteas had a fool of a shepherd who reported me to the gamekeeper, and not only to the gamekeeper, but to the factor as well. I was taken up to Lochmaddy* and fined two pounds or fourteen days in prison for the rabbit.† The Exciseman was at the

* Lochmaddy, in North Uist, the administrative centre of the Inverness-shire Outer Islands, where court cases are heard.

† Probably it was for trespass in search of game rather than for the rabbit itself.

court, and waited at the foot of the stairs until I came down, and when I came down he said to me: 'That rabbit was pretty dear for you.' 'Indeed it was.' 'Well, they treated you very badly, they might have left it at ten shillings. They couldn't have fined you more for a first offence. The best thing you can do is to take out a licence and give them their fill of work.'

'Very well, give it to me.'

The Exciseman took me into his office and gave me a licence, and when the steamer came to Lochmaddy I went aboard, and who was on board but my brother on his way home with a new gun for me, a double-barrelled gun. I was very pleased to see him. We were put together in the steerage, and when we reached Lochboisdale, I put the gun on my shoulder and walked down the gangway and up the pier with it; the lad who had been taken to Lochmaddy to be fined returned to Lochboisdale with a new gun! After that I used to go out in a boat on Loch Eynort not caring who saw me, killing plenty of shags, and though I had been fined two pounds at Lochmaddy, I took in what would pay it within the year!

There was no work to be had, so I started fishing lobsters with two others, Allan MacMillan and Donald MacLellan from Snaoiseabhal. Some days we did middling well, and others we were working at a loss. Then I enlisted in the Militia. The night I went to join the Militia was the first night I ever spent away from home. We took the steamer to Lochmaddy, myself and six others, and when we reached Lochmaddy we had only a very little money between us, which we put together to buy tea and biscuits, hoping to make tea in some house or other. Behind the prison there was a neat little house with its door open, and we went over to it. A young woman came to the door. We asked her if we might brew a kettle of tea as we had had nothing to eat since breakfast at home that morning. (By now it was late in the afternoon.) She said we might, and asked us to come in. We went in, and put the kettle on the fire; but it wasn't long on the fire before an old woman appeared, the worse for drink, swaying from side to side. She turned to the girl and asked her who were these men who were in the house? 'Oh, only people who've come in to make some tea.'

'They can't make tea here!' said the old woman. 'If they want to make tea they can easily find somewhere else to make it.' She took hold of the kettle and took it off the fire and put it on the other side of the room. 'What brought you in here?' she asked us. Not one of us was saying a word, only listening to her. The oldest of us, Duncan MacDonald, said:

'Well, it'll take someone stronger than you to put us out of here.'

'What sent you here rather than to any other house in Lochmaddy?' said the old woman.

'This was the only house we saw with its door open. If you had kept the door shut we would be outside yet.'

'Well, the door that let you in is the door that will let you out,' she said.

'We won't go out,' said Duncan.

'Oh, it won't take me long to find someone who'll put you out.'

I didn't care for the way things were going, so I got up and went out to the end of the house without a word to see if there was any other house we might go to to make tea. Then I saw the old woman come out of the door and go to the other end of the house. The girl had gone into the small room* in the middle of the house to go to bed. I thought I would slip in and ask her where we could make ourselves tea, and I did so.

'Oh,' she said, 'if you go a bit farther on, about half a mile, you'll find plenty of places where you can make tea, and somewhere to stay. I'm very sorry I couldn't make tea for you.'

'Is that your mother?' I asked.

'Oh no.'

At that moment whom did I hear coming into the house but the old woman. I was terrified she was coming into the small room, so I blew out the candle. She went into the kitchen. 'Aren't you the most useless men I ever saw?' she

* Gaelic *clòsaid*, the small room in the middle of a three-roomed thatched house. It can open off either of the main rooms or off the passage inside the front door, as presumably it did in this case. See p. 208.

said. 'Why didn't you go away along with the lad who's with you to the house over there where he's by himself?'

When they heard this, they all got up and went out. When they had gone out, the old woman slammed the door and locked it. 'Ho, rascals!' she said, 'that'll keep you out to-night. What did you let them in here for?' she shouted to the girl.

'Oh, they only came in to make tea; they had their own tea, they only wanted somewhere they could make it.'

'Upon my soul,' I said, 'is she coming in here?'

'Oh no, she's going to another room,' said the girl.

'How shall I get out?' I asked.

'I'll let you out when she goes to sleep.'

The old woman was a good while at the fireside before she went up to the other end of the house. The girl was waiting to let me out. When she thought that the old woman was asleep:

'Come into the kitchen now, and I'll see if I can make you a cup of tea.'

'I'm afraid she'll get up.'

'She won't get up, she's asleep.'

I went into the kitchen. The girl put a chain on the fire, and I got tea. Then I went off to see if I could find the others. I went on to the pier. There wasn't a sign of any of them,[2] until I heard a noise[3] over at the back of the pier in an old carpenter's shed. I went over, and there they were. It was a frosty night and they were lying on planks in the shed there, white with frost. Then they started damning and cursing me, 'Where were you, we were looking for you since night came!'

'Where was I but in the small room along with the girl!'

'You were *not*!'

'Yes I was. Why did you heed the old woman when she told you I was in yon house by myself?'

'Doesn't Providence protect you! We were looking for you since nightfall, and you in the small room along with the girl!'

The steamer came at six o'clock in the morning, and we got tea when we got aboard her. I went to the Militia then, and when camp broke up, I engaged with a farmer near Inverness.

My brother had been near Inverness himself, and had engaged with a farmer, and had had to leave him at half-term.* I found this was the same farmer I had engaged with! He had given me half a crown as airles money, but when I found that this was the man I had engaged with, I'd sooner have jumped in the sea than go to him! I didn't know how in the world I could get clear of him. He had promised to meet me at seven o'clock in the square,† and I didn't go! I and some others decided to take the train and go to Oban by Perth; if there were enough of us it was likely we would get to go at half fare. We went to the station and asked the stationmaster what it would cost to go to Oban. 'Twenty-one shillings.‡ But if there were fifty of you you'd get fishermen's tickets at ten and six.'

'Oh, we'll be here, and more than fifty of us!'

'Very well, be here at ten to ten, and you'll get them at ten and six.'

We went to the station when it was near the time, and when the office opened, we crowded round the window asking for the tickets. Everyone who got a ticket ran to the carriage. There weren't many more than twenty of us altogether! But alas when I got to the carriage whom did I see in the station but the farmer I had engaged with looking for me, to catch me! I hid until the train left. That's the only time I ever kept something that belonged to another man, the farmer's half-crown!

After we reached Oban, I engaged there with a farmer to go back to Perth. The farmer whom I engaged with lived four miles out of Aberfeldy. I spent two and a half years with him. During that time I never saw a day that kept us indoors. It made no difference if it was wet or dry or what weather it was; when there were snow showers and the wind was so cold

* Farm servants then engaged by the six-months' term, starting at Whitsuntide or Martinmas. Something must have gone wrong if Angus's brother left at the half-term.

† In Inverness the square is in front of the station.

‡ They could have travelled to Oban on the boat that went through the Caledonian Canal for eight shillings, but it would have meant staying in Inverness overnight.

it would take the nose off a monkey, the farmer would come to the stable and say:

'It's cold, cold today, lads.'

We would say it was, very cold.

'Oh yes, it's a good thing it isn't wet,' he'd say.

The day it was pouring with rain, the farmer would come out with an oilskin on:

'It's wet, wet today, lads.'

'Yes, indeed it's wet.'

'Oh yes, it's a good thing it isn't cold!' he would say. It was never going to be cold and wet on the same day!

I left him at the end of two and a half years, and I engaged with a farmer nine miles outside Pitlochry. I spent a year with him. He wouldn't let us out on a bad day at all. We sat at the same table as himself, and were a lot better off there. Then I heard the news of the death of my brother Hector who was sailing; he died of smallpox at Dunkirk in France. My father and mother were alone at home, and I thought I would go home to be with them for the winter. I came home for that winter, and left again in the spring. There was very little work to be had at the time. I went to Oban and started working with some stonemasons, building a church. The wages were low, the pay was only fourpence ha'penny an hour,[4] a few men were getting fivepence an hour; sixpence an hour was the highest rate for a labourer. I couldn't save much to send home.

Then I engaged with a hotelkeeper at Loch Lomond, an Irishman called Edward Kane. I spent two and a half years with him, and then came home for another winter. Then I had to go away again, and I engaged this time with another hotelkeeper, at Dalmally, a man called Fraser, who was a good master. I spent two years with him.*

Then my father got a croft from the Congested Districts Board, and I came home, and helped my father work the croft, and started at the fishing. I got a boat, and my neighbour John MacAskill and another man John MacDonald, worked together steady. We fished herring and mackerel, ling and cod and lobsters and every kind of fishing. Sometimes

* Aonghus Beag was on this farm when the Boer War broke out.

we were doing very well and sometimes we were working at a loss. Often we were in danger of losing our lives. One night MacAskill and I were out by ourselves in a little boat, sixteen feet long, and it came on bad at sea. We tried to get into an anchorage where we could shelter. When we were only twenty yards outside, it came on a hurricane against us, and we were likely to be blown out to the open sea. We were going past a promontory and staying as close to the shore as we could, and we managed to put down an anchor as we went past the point of the promontory. The anchor held, and we managed to put another out. We sat in the boat all the winter night, and neither of us could see the other for spindrift. That was the longest night I have ever spent.

Another time John MacAskill and I were returning to Loch Eynort from Lochboisdale by sea. It was at the beginning of the summer. It was very calm, and we were rowing.

There is a bad place in Loch Eynort where there is a tidal current—the *Sruth Beag* or 'Little Current' it's called—which runs at seven knots at spring tides. When we arrived from Lochboisdale, the current was so strong that we could not get into Loch Eynort against it. There is a submerged rock outside the place where the current runs into the sea. We let out our anchor at the outside end of this rock, to wait until the current should slacken at low tide. We had a lot of meal and salt aboard. We were tired out, and we stretched out and fell asleep. John MacAskill was sleeping below aft, and I was lying amidships. When I awoke, my two feet were above my head as if they were up against a wall and my head at the foot. I looked round, and saw that the sea was level with the gunnel and just about to come in amidships; the boat had gone dry on the middle of the rock, and was about to turn upside down over our heads! Things looked ugly.

John MacAskill was lying below aft on the other side of the boat, and was now standing straight up against her side! I was too frightened to say anything. I got up and crawled up on the high side of her. The anchor was at the bow. I managed to let it run out and to throw it out on the rock, and I threw another anchor out behind the rock and managed to tie the rope to the boat's tholepins, and made it as tight as I could to keep her the way she was. Then I woke MacAskill up. When he opened his eyes, 'God save me,' he said, 'where are we?'

'Never mind where you are,' I said, 'but see you get out of here before she turns upside down over your head.' He dragged himself out of her on to the rock, and we held her there. Luckily it was low tide. Well, we kept her from turning over with the anchor until the tide came in and raised her. The sea was up to the top of our knees above the rock before she floated on an even keel. Then we got aboard her and came home. The sun had risen, and we were very glad to have escaped from the danger in which we had been. I never saw such a miracle as when the boat stayed on top of the rock and didn't turn upside down over us!

As long as Charles MacLean had the farm of Gearrabhailteas we had leave to keep some sheep on the hill. I used to work for him. When he gave up the farm, Mr MacDonald came there from Barra. He had had Vatersay.* Well, the order was that no one was to have sheep on the place but himself. All the shepherds had some sheep of their own, and they had to get rid of them. My sheep were on the hill, and I would have no chance to keep them unless I got someone else to keep them on his land for me.

Anyway, MacDonald had a shepherd out at Loch Eynort called Christie, and when there was to be a gathering, Christie used to give me a warning to take my sheep off the hill to my house so that they would not be taken into the fank. I used to do this, and MacDonald didn't know I had any sheep on his hill! He had a half-wit of a manager from the Isle of Skye, called Neil Beaton, who was a lot worse than his master, if he got up against you. This time I was sent for to go to shear at Gearrabhailteas. It was the old sheep off the machair we had to shear, and it was difficult to shear them, as some of their fleeces were full of sand. Beaton thought there was no one as good at shearing as himself. This day he came out in good trim; I was sitting on the shearing-stool opposite him, and the first sheep he got, he said, 'Get a move on, Mac-

* Which was broken up into crofts in 1908.

Lellan.' I didn't think anything of it, I thought he was joking at first; but when he had shorn the sheep, 'That's one!' he shouted.

'Well, it won't be long before this one's done too,' I said. My sheep was put out, and we got two others, but before he was half-way with his second one, mine was done and away. 'That's two,' I said. 'He'll have to hurry.' Before he had put out his second one, my third one was ready to go along with her.

'Oh,' I said, 'there isn't a man on the island who can beat me at this. You may as well give up now.'

He didn't say a word, but he got so red in the face! He got up and jumped over the shearing-stool. 'Let me see your shears,' he said. 'There they are.' He took hold of them and tried them. 'There isn't a pair like them here,' he said. 'Haven't they fallen into good hands?' I replied. He had to agree.

We were going to finish shearing the old sheep early. Beaton came out and said to Christie, 'Go and bring down the ones across the road this side of the hill-top, and the ones around the mill, and we'll have less to do tomorrow.' He turned to me:

'Have you got your dog?' he said.

'No.'

'Why didn't you bring him with you?'

'I didn't need a dog here.'

'Well, you'll have to go to gather in the morning.'

'All right, isn't the dog out there already? Where are you going to gather?'

'The hillside above Loch Eynort,' he said.

My word, when I heard this, with my own sheep out on the hill! Every one of them would be in the fank tomorrow!

I didn't let on, but when Christie was going off, I said to him:

'Don't bring in any more than you can help. Give me a chance to get off early. Put them off to the hill with the dog.'

'I will if I can,' he said.

Christie went off, and came back with two hundred sheep!

I could have boiled him when I saw what he had brought in. The sun was getting pretty low. Well, I said to myself that if there was a chance to get away, I would have to go tonight! it would be no use trying to get my sheep in the morning. I began to shear for all I could. Beaton said I had gone mad! The sun had just set by the time we had finished. I asked what time would they be starting to gather.

'Oh, I'm sure they'll wait until they've taken their food.'

'Well, though they went there right away, I'll be there before you.'

'Well!' he said, 'there's steel in MacLellan!'

I didn't make for my house, but for the hill. I got all my sheep in except one, without a dog or anything else to drive them except pieces of turf! I drove them to our house. When I arrived, my mother, peace to her soul, was waiting for me. By then it was one in the morning. I lit the lantern and hung it in the cowshed and put the sheep inside, and shut the door. I had to take off every stitch I had on and put dry clothes on! Everything I had on was soaked with sweat.

When I had had something to eat, all there was for it was to go back to the hill. I was only just sitting down to light my pipe after reaching a hill-top when I heard Beaton's shout from the hillside above me. My dog began to bark. He heard it. 'Ha, there you are!' he said. 'Yes,' I replied, 'you haven't got the better of me yet!'

When I had got past this time I said to myself that the day would come when he would get the better of me, and that the best thing I could do would be to report my sheep myself, rather than have anyone else do it. I went to Gearrabhailteas. One of the farmer's daughters met me outside. I asked her if her father was in, and she said he was. 'Come in,' she said. I went in. He was in the parlour. She went and brought him. 'Well, my good fellow? What are you doing at Loch Eynort, Angus?'

'Not much.'

'Is that what you've come to see me about?'

'Yes.'

'What is it?'

'A few sheep I've got out on the hill there. If you can't let them stay there—they were born and reared there—I'll have to send them away, I haven't got a place for them myself.'

'Are there many of them?'

'There are twelve ewes with lambs and a few eld sheep with them.'

'Oh, well, Angus, as for that number, it won't make any difference to the hill. Leave them there since they're there.'

'Well,' I said, 'whatever you're asking me for keeping them, I'd be ready to give you.'

'Oh, indeed, you're doing a lot for us. Leave them there.' I got leave to keep the sheep there, when no one else in the township was allowed to keep a single sheep!

When the Land Bill was passed,* we got some hill ground for sheep. I was then working on the land more than at the fishing; I was fishing every summer and working on the land the rest of the year. When my father died, I was alone with my mother, and I kept on with the croft; we kept sheep and were doing well enough. After my mother's death, I kept on alone for a year or two, but I wasn't keeping my health very well, and I had to part with my stock, except my sheep, and it was then that I retired and came to live at Frobost.

Most of the stories that are translated in this book I learned from three men; Alasdair Mór Mac an t-Saoir, 'Big Alasdair MacIntyre', a shepherd behind Beinn Mhór; Dòmhnall mac Dhunnchaidh mhic an Tàilleir, 'Donald, son of Duncan, son of the tailor', a MacDonald from Peninerine, a stonemason who built a house at Loch Eynort for us,† and Ailein Mór mac Ruairidh, Allan MacDonald, my brother-in-law, a crofter at Peninerine; they, and others, used to come to my father's house for conversation and stories on the long winter evenings, and we used to go to pay such visits at other houses ourselves.

* In 1911.

† This Donald MacDonald was the father of Duncan MacDonald, Peninerine, the famous storyteller, a younger contemporary of Aonghas Beag, who died in 1954 aged 71. See *Scots Magazine* of September 1954, p. 473. Duncan himself was a stonemason in his young days, and recorded his method of building a black house, see *Gairm*, Vol. V, p. 313. Five of his complex tales were printed by K. C. Craig in 1944 under the title *Sgialachdan Dhunnchaidh*. Duncan made many recordings for the writer and for the School of Scottish Studies.

FINGALIAN AND OTHER OLD STORIES

1

HOW THE FINGALIANS WERE FOUNDED

IT WAS a King of Ireland called Cairbre Ruadh who first raised the Fingalians. Many invaders were coming to Ireland and imposing tribute, as there was no one to resist them. It looked as if Ireland would be destroyed. The King made a proclamation that all the biggest men and women in the kingdom, must marry, whether they were in love with each other or not, in order that he might have strong valiant men in the kingdom to repulse the blackguards that were invading it. So it fell out. But the Fingalians became so numerous that the King, who was supporting them, couldn't do it, as they ate an enormous amount. The Fingalians plotted together, now they had grown so strong, that they wouldn't be ruled by the King of Ireland at all, but would make one of themselves King, and would rebel against the King of Ireland, as they could keep themselves well enough. So it happened. They made one Cumhal* King, and rebelled against the King of Ireland.

After that, they were taking every deer and cow and animal they could get, and were leaving nothing. The King of Ireland wished he had never raised them! He wanted to put them to death, if it could be done. He had never been despoiled like this! So he and the King of Norway made a plan, that the King of Norway should come to Ireland, and that they should

* Pronounced *Cu'al, u* nasal.

make a big feast, and should invite Cumhal to it to see if they could find a way to kill him, as if their king were killed, they would go to rack and ruin,[1] and return to his obedience as they were before. This was done. The King of Ireland made a proclamation (that there was to be a feast and that) no one who came to it was to carry arms; only nobles were to attend it. He invited Cumhal.

The Fingalians were not willing to let Cumhal go at all, as they feared he was being invited in order to be put to death, as they had been so much against the King of Ireland.

'Well,' said Cumhal, 'if I don't go there, they'll say I was afraid to go. I'll go, and I'll take my arms with me, and if they won't accept me with them, I'll come back.'

So it happened. Cumhal went off, taking his arms; when the King saw him coming he went out to meet him. 'Oh, Cumhal,' he said, 'I thought I told you no one was to carry arms tonight.'

'If I'm carrying arms, they won't do any harm to anyone who does no harm to me,' said Cumhal. 'If you won't accept me as I am I'll go back.'

'Oh no, you mustn't go back. Come in.'

Then the nobles began the drinking and the feasting within. Afterwards, they began to dance. Every time Cumhal got up to dance, the daughter of the King of Norway was his partner. The King of Norway said to him:

'I think you'd like to keep my daughter in Ireland; I don't think you want to part with her at all.'

'Well, it was in my mind,' said Cumhal, 'that if I didn't get her by consent I'd take her by force.'[2]

'Oh, indeed, you don't need to take her by force, you're welcome to her. Of course you'll get her.'

That was all right. Cumhal prepared to marry her then and there, and the ball turned into a wedding feast. The King of Ireland had a man, called Arca Dubh whom the Fingalians had expelled for some crime he had committed. Arca Dubh was hidden in the room to which Cumhal and the daughter of the King of Norway went to sleep, to kill Cumhal when he slept. When Cumhal fell asleep, Arca Dubh arose and thrust his sword through Cumhal in the bed, and killed him.* This was all right for the King of Ireland; but he wouldn't let the daughter of the King of Norway go until the end of nine months, for fear that she might be with child by Cumhal. If she was with child and it was a boy, he was to be killed at once for fear that he would try to avenge his father. The King of Norway's daughter remained in Ireland, and it was seen that she was with child. A midwife was got to attend to her, and when she was delivered, when the child was born it was seen to be a boy. She asked what the child was.[3] 'A boy,' said the midwife. 'For heaven's sake, hide him, before they find out.'

The midwife put the child in a basket and put a lump of fat in his mouth for him to suck to keep him quiet. The King of Norway's daughter was then delivered of a girl child; she had twins.[4] This made things all right, it was announced that the child was a girl; no one was displeased with her, as a girl wouldn't seek vengeance. The midwife came out. Her brother was the King of Ireland's carpenter.† She went to see him. 'Come with me as quickly as you can,' she said, 'I've just done wrong; make me a shelter out in the forest before they catch me.'

Her brother went with her into the forest, and started to make a shelter for her, beside a river. She was sitting with the child in a basket, rocking to and fro. When he had finished making the shelter, he turned to her.

'What have you in that basket?'

'Never mind what I've got in it!'

'I suspect it's the son of Cumhal. If it is, he won't live long.'

'Go and cut the branch that's across the door of the shelter, it will hit my head as I go in and out.'

He went and got his saw and began sawing the branch. She arose and got his axe and came up behind him and struck him on the top of his head with it, and split his head. He fell dead there.

*** From other versions it is clear that Arca Dubh killed Cumhal with Cumhal's own sword, Mac a' Luin, which, along with Cumhal's dog Bran, he then stole.**

† Elsewhere said to have been Boban Saor, see story No. 6.

The midwife and the child stayed in the shelter. She used to visit the castle to see the daughter of the King of Norway; she got plenty there to take back with her. No one heeded her; she used to be going back and forth anyway. The child was coming on very well. Her way of washing him was to take him out to a deep pool in the river; she used to push him under in the pool, and he would come to the surface like a seal. This was his play! She was telling his mother how able the child was, and how he was coming on.

'I swear I won't go back to Norway before I've seen him,' said his mother.

'Maybe you'll get a sight of him,' said the midwife.

One time the midwife was at the King's palace. The King had a big dog, and when she went away it followed her to the shelter. When her rations ran out, and it was time for her to leave again, it was her custom to leave a lump of meat for the boy to suck until she returned. She forgot to take the dog with her. After she had gone out, she thought the dog might destroy the child if they fell out about the meat. She turned back; and when she got back she found that the dog had been torn to pieces by the boy when he and the dog had fallen out when the dog had tried to take the meat from him.

She went off, and when she arrived at the castle she told his mother of the boy's feat of strength. His mother was pleased.

'Well, I'd like to get one sight of him before I leave.'

'You'll get that. He's growing very clever.'

Next time she took the boy to the town, so that his mother might see him. By now he was growing big. It happened when they arrived that some schoolboys were playing, swimming in a lake. The boy had never seen anyone except his foster-mother. When he saw the schoolboys he went down out on the lake along with them. To each of them he came upon he did what his foster-mother used to do to him, pushed them under—and knocked their brains out on the bottom! There was a bishop looking out of a window watching them.[5] The bishop shouted, 'Who is the crop-headed, white-haired (*fionn*), tough-eyelashed boy[6] knocking out my scholars' brains?'

'Oh, may he be happy in his name, may he be happy in his name,' said his foster-mother, 'Fionn mac Cumhail,

"White-hair the son of Cumhal".' It was the bishop who had baptized him!

When they heard it was Fionn mac Cumhail, they began to gather together to catch him and kill him. His foster-mother shouted to him to come in, that they were coming to kill him. He came back and off he went. His foster-mother could not keep him in sight. He came back and caught her and threw her on his back. He was going through woods and briars and over stone walls, and when he stopped he had nothing of her but her two shanks, which he threw out on a loch, and ever since that loch has never been called anything but Loch nan Lurgann, 'The Loch of the Shanks'.

Fionn was then alone on the hill, very hungry, as he wasn't getting much. But he saw a man fishing in a river, and went to him to see if he could get a trout from him. He asked him if he would give him a trout.

'I won't,' said the man, 'but I'll put out my rod for your luck now, and if I get a trout you'll get it.'

'Do that, then.'

The man put out his rod, and a trout took the bait, and when he landed it, it was the finest he had ever caught.

'Will you give it to me now?" said Fionn.

'No, I won't. I've been a long time fishing for the King of Ireland, and I never took him one like this. But if you were lucky then, you'll be lucky again. I'll put the rod out again. If I get one now, you'll get it.'

'Go on, do that, then.'

The fisherman put out his rod again, and another trout took the bait. When he landed it, it was much finer than the first one.

'Will you give it to me now?' said Fionn.

'You can have it, but you must cook it without putting a mark of burning[7] on it, and you must give me my choice portion of it.'

'You'll get that,' said Fionn.

Fionn went and put the trout on a flat stone and collected wood, and made a fire before it, and the trout began to cook on the stone. Then a red-hot splinter jumped out of the fire and fell on the trout and raised a blister on it.[8] Fionn put his forefinger on it to burst it, and burnt his forefinger, and put his forefinger in his mouth. That is when Fionn got the power of divination,[9] from the trout. Then he learned that the man was Arca Dubh, who had killed his father, and that his father's sword was buried under the floor of Arca Dubh's house, and that his father's dog was there.

When the trout was cooked, Fionn ate it, and then went to Arca Dubh's house. His wife was at home. Fionn told her that someone had sent him to look for Cumhal's sword: 'Well, if the like is here I don't know where it is.'

'I was told it was buried under the floor,'* said Fionn.

'Oh, if it is, I can't get it out, you must do that.'

'I will,' said Fionn. 'Give me a spade.'

He got a spade and began to dig up the floor. He went down a good way without finding the sword. Then he put his forefinger under his tooth of knowledge[10] and found out that the sword was there yet. He kept on digging until he found the sword, which was in a lead chest buried below the floor. He took the sword out of the chest. Cumhal's dog Bran was lying beside the fire, and when Bran saw the sword that had belonged to his master being taken away, he got up and shook himself; he shook out seven pecks of ashes,† and the first jump he made, he was at the door.

Fionn went off (back to the river). When he arrived, Arca Dubh was fishing in the river where he had left him.

'Did you cook the trout?' asked Arca Dubh.

'Yes, and ate it,' said Fionn.

'Have you eaten it without giving me a piece of it, after I gave it to you?'

'I think I needed it more than you did,' said Fionn. 'Wasn't it you who killed Cumhal?'

'It was,' said Arca Dubh.

'What sort of death did you give him?'

'Upon my word,

'He squealed like a pig,
'He bellowed like a boar,

* A clay floor, presumably.

† *i.e.*, fourteen gallons.

'He broke wind like a gelding
'With his own sword impaling him,'[11] said Arca Dubh.

'O well then,' said Fionn, 'I'll give you the same death you gave him.'

He turned on Arca Dubh and killed him then and there.

Fionn was all right now. He had the dog Bran, and the dog used to catch deer. One day when Fionn was on the side of a hill he looked out over the ocean, and what did he see but a boat coming, with two men in it. They came ashore below him and came up where he was. He had never seen men as big as they were. They asked him what he was doing there, and he said he was herding goats. 'Do you know where Fionn the son of Cumhal is?' they asked.

'No,' he said, 'but if one of you will come behind the knoll there, I'll tell you where Fionn the son of Cumhal is.'

'Come along then,' said one of them.

Fionn went over behind the knoll with him, and when he got him behind the knoll he turned on him and killed him. Then he came back and killed the other one.

A year passed, and then what did he see but a boat of the same kind coming to the same place. There were only two men in her, and they came up to where he was, and asked him if he knew where in Ireland was Fionn the son of Cumhal.

'No,' he said.

'Do you know where the men are who came in that boat a year ago?' said the man. 'We recognize the boat.'

'Oh, Fionn the son of Cumhal killed them,' he said.

'If Fionn killed those men, we needn't go any farther. We may as well return.'

'What do you want Fionn mac Cumhail for?'

'There's a monster in one of our lakes in Norway that takes a man every day. It has been told to us by seers that only Fionn mac Cumhail can kill her.'

'Aye, aye!'[12] said Fionn. 'Well, I'll be willing to go along with you, if you'll take me with you.'

'We will," said one of them. 'Come here, then.'

He had a big coat on. He caught hold of Fionn and put him in a pocket on one side of the coat, and put Bran in a pocket on the other side. They waded out to the boat, and got into it. When they reached Norway, no one knows how pleased the daughter of the King of Norway was to see him.* No one there had ever seen such a fine handsome little man. He was seen nowhere but along with her. The next day when Fionn got up, the King of Norway's daughter was weeping.

'What's wrong with you?' said Fionn. 'Are you ashamed because I slept with you last night?'

'No, indeed.'

'What is it, then?'

'There's a monster in the lake down there, which takes a man every day. People are getting so scarce now that lots have to be cast who will go to her. The lot has fallen on my brother.'

'Oh, if it has, don't let that worry you; it isn't your brother that will go to her today, but me.'

'Oh, you won't go to her today whoever does.'

'No one will go to her until I've gone first.'

Fionn came out and told the son of the King of Norway that he would go to the monster in his place today. That was all right. 'See you tie up my puppy-dog,' Fionn said. He had found out that if the dog went before him, he would not come out of the encounter alive, but if he encountered the monster before the dog did, he would survive. He went and caught Bran and put three chains on him. Many people collected to see them. Then the monster came to the surface. The first time she drew (her breath) she pulled Fionn down to her a bit, she nearly took him off his feet. She came to the surface again and this time (when she drew in her breath) she pulled Fionn down to the edge of the lake. The third time, she sucked him into her mouth. Bran jumped up and broke every chain on him† and was inside her mouth behind Fionn's foot. It wasn't long before the monster submerged, and when she

* In other versions of this story the country to which Fionn goes to fight the water monster is *Rioghachd nam Fear Móra*, the 'Kingdom of the Big Men', not Norway. It is obvious that the daughter of the King of Norway here is not the same person as his mother.

† It is clear from other versions that the monster's method of dealing with Fionn was to inhale him; also that Bran's chains broke at each inhalation, one by one, not all at once at the last one when Fionn was swallowed.

surfaced again she began tearing madly through the lake, and nearly splashed ashore every drop of water in it. At last she thrust herself on land, dry. Then they saw Fionn emerge from one of her sides without a single hair or shred of clothing on his body, and Bran emerged from her other side, red and hairless. Then they understood that he was Fionn the son of Cumhal.

The son of the King of Norway thought that he would go down and kill him when he was so weak coming out of the beast's belly, and that he would proclaim throughout the kingdom that it was he who had slain the monster, seeing that the lot had fallen on him. When Fionn saw him coming, he put his forefinger under his tooth of knowledge, and discovered his intention. Before he reached him, Fionn said to him:

'Where are you going? Weak as I am I still won't be long in putting an end to you, if this is the way you're going to repay me for having saved your life.'

They gathered together then and took Fionn up to the castle, and I'm sure they got doctors who attended to him.

'Now see and go and put hair on my puppy-dog,' said Fionn. The doctors took the dog away with them, and he came back looking like a big white hairy mop.[13]

'Ho, ho,' said Fionn, 'that wasn't the colour I wanted him to be at all.'

'What colour do you want him to be?' said the doctor.

'Yellow legs on Bran,
White belly, two black sides,
A green back for the hunt,
Two pointed blood-red ears,'[14] said Fionn.

They took Bran away again, and came back with him coloured as Fionn wanted.

When Fionn got well, he prepared to return to Ireland. The King of Norway sent a vessel with him laden with gold. When he reached Ireland—there were then no banks to put it in—he put it in a cave by the shore. That's the gold Fionn used to give away (afterwards) when there was a war, and he wanted to make peace; he kept it in the cave.

When Fionn returned to Ireland, he kept on going to try to see if he could find one of the Fingalians. The Fingalians, those who survived of them, were working for the King of Ireland, digging peats, and at every kind of exposed outdoor work; they were enslaved. Fionn came upon them, and talked with them. He asked them:

'Have you any hope of being better off than you are?'

'Yes, we believe that someone will get us out of this yet. We heard that Fionn mac Cumhail was in Norway. If he came, we might still get out of here.'

'Couldn't Fionn come without your knowing anything about it?' he asked.

'Oh, we would know. The Hammer of the Fingalians[15] is on the shoulder of yonder mountain. No one can strike it before Fionn mac Cumhail does. When he strikes it, it will be heard throughout the five fifths of Ireland, and then we'll know he's come.'

'Oh, indeed,' said Fionn. 'I'm surprised that you're hungry when there are so many deer out on the hill there. Are you killing them?'

'Ho, ho, we were once, but we mayn't do it today.'

Fionn went and let Bran into the deer. The first deer Bran came to, he tore out its throat and left it there, and went after another one. He killed three.

'My word, isn't that dog like Bran?' said one of them, 'but that's not the colour he was at all; but that's how he used to catch the deer.'

They collected the deer, and skinned them.

'Where, now, shall we prepare them?' asked Fionn.

'The cauldron in which we used to cook the deer is down there. We buried it there in case the King of Ireland should get it.'

They went down. There was a green cattlefold there, and the cauldron in which they used to cook the deer was buried in it. It was dug up. They made a fire, and put the three deer in the cauldron; they let out their belts[16] the day they ate the three deer.

'Come now,' said Fionn, 'and show me the Hammer of the Fingalians, after the good dinner I've given you.'

They went with Fionn. When they reached the Hammer, it was hanging on a cliff-face.

'Is this the Hammer of the Fingalians?' asked Fionn.

'Yes,' they said.

Fionn went over and caught hold of the Hammer. When he struck the cliff-face, every mountain and crag in Ireland resounded. Everyone in Ireland heard it, and the survivors of the Fingalians ran to each other and gathered together, and Fionn became King over them, as his father had been, and there I left them.

2

HOW THE FINGALIANS LOST THEIR HUNTING AND RECOVERED IT

AS LONG as the Fingalians remained together, no kingdom could get the better of them.

Garry and the Women

On this occasion, the Fingalians were close to starvation. They lived on deer, which they hunted; and through witchcraft the hunting had failed them. They were so hungry that they were holding their bellies in with seven oaken pins. But their women were getting fatter and fatter, while the men were dying of hunger. They were going every day to the hill and getting nothing in the hunt. Fionn did not know what in the world the women were getting that made them grow fat; it couldn't be the little the men were able to give them. The women had a house to themselves. One day Fionn made a plan to leave one of the Fingalians called Garry in the house to keep a watch on the women[1] and find out what they were getting.

When the Fingalians had gone out, Garry saw the women tidy themselves and go to the shore and collect shellfish. Every one of them came back from the shore with a lapful[2] of shellfish; and when they had cooked the shellfish and eaten them, they buried the shells for fear the Fingalians would see them. When Garry saw this, he went and lay down and fell asleep. He used to snore terribly when he slept. The women heard him snoring in the house, and they looked in, and saw him asleep on the floor. They saw that they were betrayed; there was nothing for it but to try to put Garry to death, because, if he told the other Fingalians that the women were going to the shore for shellfish, the men would destroy the shore in two days, and the women would be done for.

The women went into the house. Garry had long hair; they made nine plaits of his hair and they put nine pins on each of the plaits pinning them to the floor, and then they went out and raised a shout together around the house. Garry jumped up and left his scalp pinned to the floor, and came out bald and bloody, without hair or scalp. He didn't know what he should do to the women, but he began to chase them until he got every one of them inside the house, and when he had got them in he went and shut the door and set the house on fire over their heads.

He knew then that it was death for him at any rate when the other Fingalians came home and found the women burnt, and he thought he had better flee. Now it happened that snow had begun to fall, and Garry started walking backwards from the house until he reached the shore; and he found a cave in the bank of the shore and went inside it.

When the Fingalians came home from the hill, they found nothing but a bare ruin and the women burnt before them. They saw Garry's footsteps coming to the house, but none going away from it. Fionn swore by the edge of his sword, by Mac a' Luin,* that he would never rest until he had beheaded the person who had done this, with Mac a' Luin. He told the Fingalians to follow the tracks to see from where they came. They followed the tracks until they found Garry in the cave in the bank of the shore; then they brought him before Fionn. Poor Garry told Fionn what had happened to him, and everything he had done.

'Well,' said Fionn, 'you only did to them what they deserved. If I had not sworn by the edge of my sword that I would not rest until I had beheaded the person who had done

* The name of Fionn's sword.

it, with Mac a' Luin, I would not put you to death; but now you must be put to death.'

'Then,' said Garry, 'you must give me the death that I chose.'

'You may have that,' said Fionn.

'The death that I chose,' said Garry, 'is to be beheaded with my head on your thigh, by Mac a' Luin, wielded by my son Aodh'—Garry had a son called Aodh, than whom there was none of the Fingalians more valiant. He was only a young man.

When Fionn heard that Garry wanted to be beheaded on his thigh, he feared he would lose his leg, because his sword could not make an uncompleted blow,[3] it must cut what was before it, or else it would lose its magic virtue and be no better than any other sword. But he had to keep his word. So he got seven oaken beams, and seven hides of old leather, and seven sods of tough turf;[4] and Garry's head was put on his thigh, with the seven beams and the seven hides and the seven sods of tough turf on top of it. Garry's son Aodh was brought in and the sword Mac a' Luin was given to him and he was asked to 'cut that'. Aodh did not know what was underneath, but he drew the sword and cut through the seven beams and the seven hides and the seven sods of tough turf, and he cut off his father's head; and the sword stopped at the top of Fionn's thigh. When Aodh saw his father's head fall, he raised the sword and turned to Fionn and asked, 'On whom shall I avenge my father's death?'

'Go,' said Fionn, 'and avenge it on the high tide down on the shore.'

Aodh went and took a paddle[5] and got into a boat, and kept out the high tide for three tides after that; then he grew tired, and put the paddle under his arm, and fell asleep; and the tide came in and drowned him as he slept.

The Re-tempering of Mac a' Luin

Fionn's sword Mac a' Luin was then no better than any other sword, since it had not cut through what was before it. It was then that the Fingalians went to the fairy smithy to temper it; and it was then that the Ballad of the Smithy was composed. For of them went with the sword, and:

One day when the Fingalians were on the plain of rushes—
There were four youths in the company—
Myself and Oscar and Daorghlas,
And Fionn himself, the son of Cumhal.

We saw, coming from the hillside.
A tall dark man with one leg
With a hood of dark grey skin,
And a purse of the same material.

Fionn spoke—he was on the hillside—
To the person who was going past us:
'To what land do you journey,
O man of the skin covering?'

'My name is Lunn Mac Lìobhainn
If you want to hear my story,
I was a while herding goats
For the King of Norway in Gailbhinn.

'I am descended from the daughter of Mac Asgaill
Who was good in charge of children;
Happy the woman who was mother
To me and to my only brother.

'I impose on you as tabus,
If you are attending at the smithy,
To go to a dark glen at the west of the world
Far from the door of the smithy.'

'Where, o smith, is your smithy?
Or would we be the better for seeing it?' said Fionn.
'If I could, you would not be the better for it;
Why should you be the better for seeing it?' said the smith.

They then set out to walk,
They went with a fifth band
Until they reached the green mound of the judges,
Then they went in four companies.

One band was with the smith,
Another was with Daorghlas,
Another was with Dearg mac Breithimh,
Fionn was last and by himself.

The smith only took one step
Westwards on each empty valley;
(He went so fast) I could hardly see
The edge of his dress on his backside.

'Open, open!' cried the smith,
'Don't shut the door before me!' said Daorghlas;
'I would not leave you in the door of the smithy
All alone in a place of danger,' said the smith.

They'll get there a bellows for blowing
They'll get there equipment for the smithy;
Then there came four fellows,
Four smiths, repulsive and misshapen.

Each smith had four arms,
A claw hammer, and iron pincers;
The one who was answering them spoke,
And no worse did Daorghlas answer.

Daorghlas the man heating the smithy,
Who was wont to remain standing;
Redder than charcoal of oak
Was his face from the fruit of his labour.

Then one of the smiths spoke
Dreadfully and angrily—
'The right hand of the thin (*caol*) fearless fellow
Has spoilt my steel anvil and broken it.'

Fionn spoke, while standing—
He was attending to the pincers—
He called Daorghlas 'Caoilte',
'We'll leave it a widespread nickname.'

They would get there, beaten out,
The straight, bright swords—
The company that was filled
With the enchanted swords of the green.

With 'Fead' and 'Faoidh' and 'Eibheach'*
And 'Conalach' son of the smithy
The twelve swords of Diarmaid,
Many a man had they slaughtered.

I had 'Geur nan Calg',
Useful in time of battle
'Mac a' Luin' was in the hand of Mac Cumhail
It never left flesh unsevered.

Do you remember the day of the tongues
In the smithy of the sons of Mac Lìobhainn?
Tonight I lament my condition,
After recounting the company.

(After having been heated, the sword Mac a' Luin had to be tempered in human blood; Fionn did this, killing the smith's mother by a trick. Aonghus Beag did not recite this part of the ballad.)

The Fingalians recover their Hunting

After the Fingalians had had the sword Mac a' Luin re-tempered at the fairy smithy, some of them were going to the shore (to get shellfish) every day, and they were going in turn by couples to the hill to see if they would have any luck at

* The names in inverted commas in this and the next verse are the nicknames of the swords.

hunting. One day those on the shore saw a cave high up in the bank of the shore, and the cave looked as if someone was living in it. They were afraid to go inside the cave as they had grown so weak[6] through lack of food. But there was one of the Fingalians, called Conan, who was the weakest of the band. He alone of them was under these tabus: any opportunity he saw, he must take; any door he saw open, he must enter; if he saw a table with food on it, he must sit down there; any chance he saw to give a blow with his fist, he had to give it.

Diarmaid went down and took hold of Conan by the back of the head and turned his face towards the mouth of the cave. Conan was on his knees on the shore, and he called down seven thousand curses on Diarmaid for having turned his face towards the south of the cave, so that he had now (under his tabu) to go inside. He went in; and when he had gone in, he found a big cave-man sitting at a table on which was a roast deer which he was about to eat. When Conan saw the food, he went to the other side of the table and began to eat the deer. The cave-man paused and put his elbow on the table and his hand under his cheek while he considered the most painful death he might inflict on Conan for being so impudent as to start eating the deer that was before him. Conan looked up at the cave-man and thought he had never seen a better chance for his fist than the cave-man's ear above him, and he swung around with his fist and struck the cave-man on one ear and knocked out his brains through the other. The cave-man fell dead, and Conan went down to the entrance of the cave. The other Fingalians were watching outside to see what the outcome would be.

'Well,' said Conan, 'you can now come in. The one you were afraid of before you needn't fear any longer.' But they thought that Conan and the cave-man had made a plan to lure them inside and put them to death, weak as they were. So they paid him no heed. Conan went back inside and got a rusty old sword that was hanging there, and began to saw with it until he had cut the arm off the cave-man at the shoulder, and then dragged it down to the entrance of the cave.

'If you don't believe me,' he said, 'perhaps you'll believe this.'

Then the Fingalians went and ate the rest of the deer. It was this cave-man who had been depriving them of their hunting by witchcraft.

Next day Oscar and Caoilte went to the hill, and when they got there, they had never seen such a number of red deer and roe deer. They began to kill the deer and they killed eighteen stags. These they collected on a mound in the evening to carry them down. But what did they see coming down the glen but a big lump of a carle,[7] a man like a shepherd; he came up to them and said:

'You have had good hunting.'

'Yes indeed,' said Oscar, 'though we didn't have for a while.'

'Well, I'm only a poor man, and wherever I'll be tonight, I won't be thought much of if I'm empty-handed. I would be very glad if you would give me some of the deer.'

'You can have what you can carry,'[8] said Oscar.

The carle went and took a withy from under his arm and began to put the deer on the withy, until he had all the eighteen stags on it.

'My word, Oscar,' said Caoilte, 'I'm afraid you've made a hopeless blunder.'[9]

'It can't be helped,' said Oscar.

'Come over here and put it on my back,' said the carle, preparing the burden.

'Oh,' said Oscar, 'though I promised you what you could carry, I didn't promise to lift it on to your back.'

'I don't know if I'll need help,' said the carle, and he went and swung the withy on to his shoulder.

'I impose tabus on you,'[10] he said, 'as the nine fetters of the wandering fairy woman, that every little layman who is weaker and more timid than yourselves may take your heads and your ears and your livelihoods from you, unless you find out where I'll prepare these deer tonight.'

The carle went away with his burden, and Caoilte went after him. Caoilte was the fastest of the Fingalians; he could go so fast that they would see seven heads on him when he went at full speed. When Caoilte was climbing a hill, the carle was at the top of it descending on the other side; it was now dusk, and he was going down a glen, and there was a big river running down the glen; when the carle was down at the river, Caoilte lost sight of him. He was walking here and there to see where the carle had gone, not knowing whether he had gone up in the air or been swallowed by the ground. Oscar arrived then, and asked Caoilte where the carle had gone.

'I don't know, I lost sight of him around here,' said Caoilte.

There was a cliff-face there, and what did they see but a big ring in the face of it. Oscar went and caught hold of the ring, and gave it a pull, and a door opened in the cliff-face, and the carle (he was a cave-man) was inside with his burden.

'You have come, lads,' said he.

'Yes,' said Oscar.

'Well,' said the cave-man, 'there's a cauldron over there. See you have the two best deer ready cooked for me by the time I awaken. I'm going to sleep now. Unless you have the deer ready cooked for me when I wake up, I will kill you.'

Oscar and Caoilte flayed the two deer and put them in the cauldron. Then they went and began to collect sticks and everything that was best for making a fire, and started the fire beneath the cauldron. The water in the cauldron began to freeze! The hotter they made the fire beneath it, the thicker the ice grew on it. The enterprise went against them altogether, and at last they went out of the cave, with only death to expect, and were lamenting face to face outside. But what did they now see but a tidy little red-haired man climbing up from the river that ran down the glen. They went down to him.

'You are in difficulties, lads,' said the little man.

'Yes, we are,' said Oscar.

'Will you tell me, Oscar, the greatest difficulties you were ever in, and I'll boil your side of the cauldron and I'll kill your share of the cave-man?'

'Why, you wretched apparition,[11] if you've come to make fun of us,' said Oscar, 'go away, or though I am as I am, I'll knock your brains out on the cliff.'

'Hunh!' said the little man. 'Will *you* tell me, Caoilte, the greatest difficulties you were ever in, and I'll boil your side of the cauldron and I'll kill your share of the cave-man?'

'I might as well,' said Caoilte, 'as to go on lamenting here.'

'Very well, what were the greatest difficulties you were ever in?'

The Greatest Difficulty of Caoilte

'The greatest difficulty I was ever in,' said Caoilte, 'was when I was at school. We were playing outside that day, swimming. We saw a little currach[12] coming with a man in it. He came ashore, and he began to chase us, and he caught me and seven others. And he put us on a withy (like fish) with the withy through our mouths coming out at the back of our necks. He tied us together and threw us into the stern of the currach' He set out and reached an island away out in the sea, where he dragged the currach seven times its own length up on to the grass; then he went up with us on his back. He had a cave on the top of the island, and a wife there, and when he went in, he threw us down at the far end of the cave.[13]

'There was a red-haired old woman inside the cave along with his wife. He asked if his food was ready, and his wife said it was. She put meat before him. (He ate it and) every time he had picked a bone he hit the red-headed old woman in the face with it. When he was full, he said to his wife: 'Have the best one on yon withy cooked for me by the time I awaken!'

'His wife came down to the far end of the cave. I was the biggest and sturdiest of them, and I was at the top end of the withy, and I was alive, but the others were dead. She told me she must kill me. I beseeched her to let me off the withy and spare me, and not to kill me, but to cook one of the others for him. This she did. When the cave-man woke up, she had another one ready for him. He asked her if that was the best of them.

'"Yes," she said.

'"Why, there was a better one there than that," he said, "see that he's ready cooked for me when I wake up again."

'She came back to the end of the cave. By this time I was

getting a good deal stronger. She told me that she had to kill me this time, any way; and I told her that I wouldn't let her kill me now. I asked her who was the old woman who was with her there. She said it was her sister.

'"I'd think she'd prefer death to the way she's being treated," I said. "The best thing you can do is to bring her down here and we'll kill her together and cook her, and then we'll both try to escape from here.'

'So she did. She called to her sister that there was still one on the withy who was alive and that they should kill him. Her sister came down, and when we had got her at the far end of the cave, we turned on her and killed her together. When the cave-man awoke, the red-headed sister was ready cooked for him.

'"Is that the best one of them?" he said.

'"Yes," said his wife.

'"Oh, very well, keep on with them like that until they're finished."

'(After he had eaten her) he fell asleep again; and when he was asleep, I went up and put the poker[14] in the fire, and when it was white-hot I went and thrust it into his one eye—he had only one eye in his forehead. The first jump he made he struck the ceiling of the cave! His wife and I managed to escape outside. We made for the shore, and when we reached the currach, we started to put it out. Every scrape the currach made (when being dragged down) could be heard throughout the five-fifths of Ireland.* Anyway we launched the currach and went away in her. We had not got far when we saw him coming. He took a black ball of yarn from under his arm and threw it at us, and the yarn struck the stern of the currach. Fast as she had been going forwards, she was as fast then going backwards! There was an axe in the currach, and I got up and tried the axe on the yarn, and it only made a clang, as if I had struck an iron bar[15] with it! The cave-man's wife told me to see if I had two pieces of silver[16] on

* The division of Ireland into five-fifths takes us back to the time of Cù Chulainn and the Ulster cycle. 'Already in St Patrick's time the Five-Fifths were only a memory of the past.' See the chapter on this subject in Eoin Mac Néill's *Phases of Irish History*.

me, and if I had, to put one piece below the yarn and the other above it and try the axe on it again.

'It happened that I had, and I tried the axe then, and cut the yarn with the first blow. When the cave-man felt that the yarn had broken, he jumped[17] down on to the shore and knocked his brains out. That was the greatest difficulty I was ever in.'

'Go and look at the cauldron now,' said the little man. Caoilte looked in the cauldron; one side of it was boiling and the other had three feet of ice on it.

'My word, Oscar, my side of the cauldron is boiling,' said Caoilte.

'Is it?' said Oscar.

'Yes,' said the little man. 'Will you tell me now, Oscar, the greatest difficulty you were ever in, and I'll boil your side of the cauldron, and I'll kill your share of the cave-man.'

The Greatest Difficulty of Oscar

'Well, as Caoilte has told you, I may as well tell you,' said Oscar. 'The greatest difficulty I was ever in was on the night of my wedding-feast. I came out of the house as it was hot inside with dancing and drinking. What did I see but a ship coming towards the shore. A woman came out of the ship, with two men, and they came up to me. The woman had a shoe in her hand. She was the daughter of the King of Norway, and she had dreamt that she should marry the man whom the shoe fitted. She made me try on the shoe; and when I tried it on, it fitted as well as if it had grown on my foot.[18] She said that I must go away with her and marry her. I said that I was married already.'

'She said that didn't make any difference, I must go. I said to her that I wasn't going to go at all, as I had just come out from my wedding-feast.

'"Well," she said, "you must see me on board, anyway."

'I went down with them, and I went aboard the ship, and they took me below deck.[19] When she had got me below, she turned to me and said:

'"I impose a tabu on you, that unless you will be my

husband before the morning, you will die." I tried to catch her, and she turned into a mouse[20] and went at once behind a coil of rope. I lifted the coil, and the mouse went to the other side. I chased the mouse until I lost it altogether. When I came up to go ashore, I could hardly see Ireland in the distance! I was taken to Norway. This was the plan that the Kings of Norway and Ireland had concocted to destroy us, the Fingalians; that we should be taken to Norway one by one (in this way) and hanged there.

'When I reached Norway, I was put in prison. The Fingalians were looking for me everywhere, until they found out I had been taken away to Norway. Then they went after me. The day I was to be hanged, I was brought out to the scaffold of the gallows;[21] and when I was standing on the scaffold, whom did I see coming but Diarmaid, and my heart rejoiced at the sight. He came up and tore the gallows apart, and took me away with him. That's how I escaped, and that was the greatest difficulty I was ever in.'

At the moment, who came out but the cave-man. He looked around and turned to the little man, and said:

'Are *you* here?'

'I am,' said the little man, 'and since I am, narrow will be your share of the green glen tonight!'

The cave-man didn't wait to hear more, but jumped down to the river (at the foot of the glen) and knocked his brains out on the bed of the river.

'Well, go in now,' said the little man. 'If I have been of use to you, you have been of use to me. I was under spells for ever, until you and Oscar told me the greatest difficulties you were ever in.'

The Fingalians got their hunting back as it had been before, and that is how I left them.

3

THE FINGALIANS IN THE ROWAN MANSION

ONCE THE Fingalians were invited to a big feast (in the fairy Rowan Mansion). When they arrived, the food was on the table before them. When they sat down at the table, their feet stuck to the floor and their backsides stuck to their seats. They were unable to move. This was a plan that had been made to put an end to the Fingalians.

Diarmaid was not with them. They heard him coming. Fionn mac Cumhail found out—he had the power of divination—that nothing could loosen them but the blood of the three children of a king. He called to Diarmaid to stay outside, and to go and see if he could catch the three children of a king and kill them and bring their blood, which was the only thing that would loosen them. He was to rub some on his own feet first, before he came in.

Diarmaid went and caught the three children of a king, and killed them, and brought their blood with him. Before he arrived at the mansion, he rubbed some of the blood on his feet. He went in, and first freed Fionn. Then he started on the others, and freed them all, until he came to Conan, who was the worst of all the Fingalians. By then, the blood was used up, and Diarmaid could only leave Conan as he was. When Conan saw he was going to be left, he said to Diarmaid:

'Oh yellow-haired, generous[1] Diarmaid, if I were a big plump[2] female, you would not leave me.'

'Do you say that?' said Diarmaid. He came back and caught

Conan under his armpits and plucked him up, leaving the skin of his backside on his seat and the skin of the soles of his feet on the floor! Diarmaid lifted him up in his arms, and put him down on a mound outside. 'Go and walk now,' he said. This was the greatest danger the Fingalians were ever in while they were together.

4

THE DEATH OF DIARMAID

DIARMAID WAS the third strongest of the Fingalians, and a very handsome man. No woman ever saw his face without falling in love with him. Very often he used to hide his face. But once when he was washing himself, Fionn's wife (Grainne), saw him. She fell so much in love with him that she insisted on eloping with him. They fled together. When the Fingalians came, there was no sign of Diarmaid or of Fionn's wife. The Fingalians went after them, and looked for them for three days and nights; they could find no trace of them. But the third night they came to the edge of a wood where Diarmaid and Fionn's wife were. When they heard the Fingalians coming, they climbed up into a tree. The Fingalians made a fire at the foot of the tree, and while they were at their supper, Oscar said:

'I'd like to know where Diarmaid is now.'

Diarmaid felt around and found an acorn on the tree and threw it at Oscar. He was very accurate. He hit Oscar between the eyes with the acorn, which fell to the ground. Oscar bent down and picked it up.

'Well, wherever you are, Diarmaid, it's your right hand that threw that at me. Whoever is on your side, I'll be with you,' he said.

When Diarmaid heard this, he jumped down and embraced Oscar. They were all right then; Fionn was afraid to say a word to him. With Oscar at his side, Diarmaid was the strongest of the Fingalians. But Fionn had a spite towards Diarmaid ever after, because he had fled with his wife.

There was a wild boar[1] in the mountain. The Fingalians went out to see if they could find a way to kill it. It had a (poisonous) spine on its back. No matter how Diarmaid was wounded, he would be all right unless he was wounded in a mole[2] on the sole of his foot. So long as nothing entered that, he was safe enough, no matter what was done to him. Fionn knew this; this was the reason he had for hunting the boar.

When the boar heard them, it set off; and it was then that the ballad was made:

The monster wakened from its sleep
And ran swiftly down the glen
When it heard the sound of the Fiann
To east and west it turned its head.

The boss of the shield[3] met the boar,
Into its belly the spear went
The shaft was broken into three,
The toughest end was on the pig.

He drew from its sheath his ancient blade
With which every fight he won,
The son of Duibhne[4] killed the boar
And he himself came back unhurt.

(Aonghus Beag here omitted three verses which describe how Fionn was disappointed at this, and then asked Diarmaid to measure the length of the boar with his feet, hoping that the poisonous spine on its back would enter Diarmaid's mole. When Diarmaid did this unharmed, measuring the boar in the direction its bristles lay, Fionn asked him):

'Diarmaid, arise again,' said Fionn,
'Measure it from the back with care,
And you'll get what you ask of the King
Your choice of spears and of sharp swords.'

Diarmaid arose—unlucky step—
To measure again for them the boar,
With great pain went the poisoned spine
Into the valiant hero's heel.

'Give me a drink, Fionn, from your hands
Ideal son[5] of my King, help me!
For my clothing and my food
Alas, woe's me if you won't give!' said Diarmaid.

If Fionn were to give him a drink from his hands, he would be healed.

'I'll not give a drink to you,' said Fionn,
'Neither will I quench your thirst;
You never did anything for my good,
But that you did increase my hurt.'

'In the Rowan Mansion* when you were caught
Then I came to set you free,' said Diarmaid.
'When you were in danger of death
I came to help you cheerfully.'[6]

Diarmaid died. They Fionn repented, and said:

'Evil the thoughts that came to me,
To kill my sister's only son†
For any wife in the wide world;
I shall stay with her no more.'

He put away his wife.

The mound that last night was the greenest
Tonight with Diarmaid's blood is reddest;
To the Fiann a cause for sorrow
If Fionn himself had not sought it.

Diarmaid, charmer of womankind,
Son of O'Duibhne, of comely shape,
Wooing has not raised her eye[7]
Since earth was laid upon his face.

That is how poor Diarmaid was put to death.

* See preceding story.

† Fionn's twin sister. See Story No. 1.

5

THE BYZANTINE BRIGAND

ONCE THERE was a King of Ireland; and the King was married. He hadn't been married long before his wife died. She left him one child, a boy. The King didn't want to get married again as he was afraid that, though he might get another wife, she wouldn't be good to the boy. But the King was only a young man; and he thought he would put his son where he could lack nothing, in a high summer-palace with a single tree,[1] where he could come and go to visit him, and that he would go to ask for the daughter of the King of Spain and not let on that he had been married at all.

So he did; he went to ask for the daughter of the King of Spain, and they were married, and he had two sons by her. The King used to go to the mountains every day to hunt, and one day when he was away in the mountains, who came in but a witch called the 'Eachlair Urlair'* while the Queen was preparing food for the King when he returned.

'Here you are,' said the witch. 'You poor fool, preparing for his return, while you're thinking that it's your own children who will inherit the kingdom, but far from it; he has an heir of his own who has a better right than either of your sons. You think the King was never married until he married you; but he was. And he has a son in a high summer-palace with a single tree, where he can see everyone and no

* The 'Eachlair Urlair' was a particularly evil witch who specialized in aiding cruel stepmothers. See *Eriu*, IX, 15; M.W.H.T., I, p. 492.

one can see him. That's where his hunting begins and ends. You only have the worse part of it.'

The Queen's crown fell from her head[2] at the insult.

'But if you pay me well,' said the witch, 'I'll make a plan for you so that he won't trouble you any more.'

'I'll do that, if you tell me what you want.'

'I want enough wool to fill my two ears.'

'How much will that be?' said the Queen.

'The fifth part of what Ireland produces.'

'Well, you'll get that, then.'

'Well then,' said the witch, 'when the King comes home, you take to your bed and pretend that you're dying. And when he is going up to ask what is wrong with you, take a mouthful of red wine, and spit it out, and tell him that you are spitting out your heart's blood because you have found out that he was keeping his son hidden from you all the time you've been here, thinking that you wouldn't be as good a mother[3] to him as you were to your own children. He'll go to get the lad then, and when he brings him home, it will be easy enough for you to get rid of him. You'll only need to put a tabu on him to go and get the palfrey of the Emperor of Byzantium. That's something he'll never get.'

So it happened. When the King returned home, the Queen had taken to her bed. She had filled her mouth with red wine. When he went up to ask how she was, she spat it out.

'Oh, what's this, what's this?' said the King.

'Oh, leave me, leave me, you evil man, my heart is broken, I'll never be good for anything again!'

'What wrong have I done you?' said the King.

'What wrong have you not done me? Keeping your son hidden from me ever since I came here because you thought I wouldn't be as good a mother to him as I was to my own children!'

'Tut, tut,' said the King, 'if that's what's wrong, I'll go and get the lad and bring him home.'

'Away with you at once,' said the Queen, 'I'll never put foot on ground until I see him here.'

The King went to get the lad, and brought him home; and the Queen got up. (That day) the lad was made to sit at the table between herself and the King, and she put her own sons on the opposite side. On the next day, she put one of her own sons between herself and the King at the table, and put the lad at the opposite side from her. On the third day she put one of her own sons on each side of herself and the lad at the other end of the table. The lad stopped eating—he wasn't taking anything—and his father said to him:

'Aren't you going to take your food?'

'No,' said the lad, 'I'm not going to take food or drink until I find out what this business means. The first night I came here I was put in a place between you and my stepmother. The next night I was opposite my stepmother, and today I'm put by the door.'

'Yes, you are,' said the Queen, 'and you'll go farther than the door. I impose tabus on you[4] as the nine fetters of the wandering fairy woman, that every little layman who's weaker and more timid than yourself may take your ears and your head and your livelihood from you, unless you come to me with the Emperor of Byzantium's palfrey[5] within a year from today.'

'Oh, take your tabus off me, you evil woman,' said the lad.

'No, I'll not,' said the Queen.

'Well then,' said he, 'I impose tabus on you that you must stand on the highest pinnacle of my father's palace until I return with the palfrey.'

'Take your tabus off me and I'll take mine off you,' said the Queen.

'No, I'll not,' said the lad.

He got up and went out on his way. He hadn't gone far before he heard a shout behind him. He looked back, and who were coming after him but his two half-brothers!

'Oh, go back, children of an evil mother,' he said, 'it's enough for me to have to go without your coming too.'[6]

They would not go back, but 'where you are, we'll be!'

They travelled on until they reached Byzantium. When they got there, they didn't know their way around, and they were asking for the Emperor's palace. Then a big red-headed man met them on the road, and asked them where they had come from like that. They told him they had come from Ireland.

'And where are you going?' said he.

'We're going to get the palfrey of the Emperor of Byzantium.'

'Ho, ho! If that's so, you've gone far enough! I am the Byzantine Brigand, and I'm sure I'm as good a thief as any of you are; and I've never failed to steal anything I've tried to steal, except that, and you won't succeed at it.'

'Well, there's no help for it,' said the lad. 'My stepmother has put tabus on me to steal the palfrey, or else to die.'

'Well then, my lad, die you will. You won't get the palfrey. But as you find it such a difficult business, you'd better follow me tonight, and some plan may occur to us by the morning.'

So they did. They went along with the Brigand.

'Well,' said the Brigand, 'four men take corn to the palfrey every day, and this is the road they go on. They usually stop to take breath on that knoll up there. Sometimes they take a nap on it. Suppose they take one tomorrow, if we can manage to let some of the corn out of the sacks and get inside them ourselves, we might get into the stable in them, and find some way to get the palfrey. Unless we get in like this, there's no other way; it's guarded night and day.'

The next day, they saw the corn-carriers coming, each with a sack on his back. (When they came to the knoll) they put down the sacks to take a breath, and lay down in the shade, and fell asleep.

'Come on, now,' said the Byzantine Brigand.

He went and put the King of Ireland's three sons, one in each of three of the sacks, and he went inside the fourth sack himself. When the carriers awoke, they put the sacks on their backs and went on. The one who was carrying the Brigand kept falling behind.

'My word, how heavy this sack feels beside what it felt before,' he said.

'Why,' said another, 'mine feels heavier, too!'

'Oh, that's because the sun has taken our strength,' said the third. 'We've slept too long today.'

When they reached the stables, they opened the sacks and poured the contents into the corn-bin; and the first thing that appeared was the big red head of the Byzantine Brigand.

They shouted for the guard, and in the guard came, and seized the Brigand. When the other sacks were opened, there was a thief in every sack. They were bound hand and foot and thrown into prison, till they should be burnt.

The Emperor of Byzantium sent for all the notables in the Empire to come to a great feast[7] to see the death of the Byzantine Brigand whom he had taken prisoner, and who had left nothing unstolen in the Empire. A great multitude collected at the palace; they were dancing with delight and drinking and making merry inside. They became so excited that they broke into the place where the prisoners were, in order to tear them apart before they were put on the pyre, which they preferred to burning them. The prisoners were knocked down on the floor, with some pulling their hair and others their beards, some kicking them and others spitting on them. The Byzantine Brigand could only suffer.

'Well, Brigand,' said the Emperor, 'I'm sure you were often in danger, but you were never in such danger as you are tonight!'

'Oh yes I was,' said the Brigand, 'I have been in greater danger than you have me in yet, and I escaped.'

'Go on, then,' said the Emperor, 'tell us about it.'

'You are not worthy to be told about it, but I will tell you on conditions.'

'What conditions?'

'On condition that you free the eldest son of the King of Ireland from his bonds and let him go with the rest. He isn't used to being kicked around and spat upon.'

'Do you tell me that I have a son of the King of Ireland tied up here?'

'Yes,' said the Brigand.

'He can go free then,' said the Emperor. The eldest of the lads were untied.

'Go on, then, tell us what greater danger you have been in than this.'

'Well, once I was hunting in the mountains, along with twelve others. A snowstorm came on us, and we got lost. One of us would say "that's the way" and another would say "no, this is the way". At last everyone took his own way, myself included. The snow was heavy, and I didn't know where I was going, I just kept on. At last I found a highway, and I said to myself that it should take me to some house or other.

'Then a man met me on the road, a big strong man with a basket on his shoulder. I was surprised that anyone who had a home would be out at such a time. The man asked me where I was going. I said I didn't know.

'"Well, you'd better come with me. I've come out to get a basket of coal. If you'll fill the basket for me, I'll put you up for the night."

'I went back with him until we reached a black hole going down into the earth. He said that that was where his coal was, and that if I would get into the basket he would lower me down, and when I had filled the basket with coal and he had brought it up, he would let it down again and bring me up myself.

'I went down in the basket—I don't know how deep it was—and when I reached the bottom, there was a crowd of men down there before me. Some of them began to lament, and some of them began to rejoice. I asked them what was making them lament, and they said that it was because some of them were frightened of me, and that they were going to kill me. I asked the others why they had started rejoicing.

'"Because when we saw how able you looked coming down, we thought that if we were ever to have a chance of getting out of here, it might be you who would get us out."

'"How did you get down here?" I asked.

'"We came as you did, to fill the coal basket."

'"Well, this is what you'll do; I'll get into the basket, and you put enough coal on top of me to hide me, and when he lifts it up and goes away, I'll get you all up again."

'So they did. I went into the basket, and they put plenty of coal on top of me, and then shouted up that the basket was full. When he had pulled up the basket, he put it down on the edge of the hole and went away. When I thought he had gone away, I emptied myself out of the basket—and where was he but a little way off from me! When he saw me getting out of the basket, he turned back and came to grips with me. I was tired and hungry, and even if I hadn't been, the odds against me were too great. He was likely to do for me. But it happened that his foot struck the basket and he fell, and I got on top of him, and before he could get up (I did for him). I took out the people who were in the hole. And I think I was in greater danger that night than you have me in so far.'

'Well, Brigand, so you were, but you escaped; but you won't escape from here.'

'I don't say that I will,' said the Brigand.

They continued beating up the poor Brigand for another while, while a big fire was made outside in front of the palace.

'Well, Byzantine Brigand,' said the Emperor, 'the fire is lit, and it won't be long until you're in the middle of it; and you won't trouble me or anyone else in the Empire any more; and though you were in the black hole itself, you were never in such danger as you are now.'

'Yes I was,' said the Brigand, 'I have been in greater danger than you have me in yet.'

'Go on, then, tell us about it.'

'You are not worthy to be told about it, but I will tell you on conditions.'

'What conditions do you ask now?'

'That you loose the second son of the King of Ireland and let him go free with the rest.'

'Do you tell me that I have two sons of the King of Ireland here?'

'Yes.'

'Well, I'll do that.'

The second son of the King of Ireland was unloosed and allowed to join the company.

'Go on, now,' said the Emperor, 'tell us about it.'

'Well, once there was a great bishop in our district, and he died. Many people were at his funeral. I was there myself. When they had buried him, they put a big flat gravestone on top of his grave. There was a lot of gold around his body, and he had his gold ring on. When night came, I thought it would be a loss to let all that gold remain beneath the earth, as it couldn't be of any use to the bishop. So I went to the graveyard to see if I could open the grave. The gravestone was so heavy that I couldn't manage to lift it, but with every device I knew I got it standing on edge on the bank of the grave. I went down into the grave, and I broke open the coffin, and took away the bishop's ring, and the gold around his body. When I was ready to come up, what happened but there came a puff of wind which blew the stone back on top of the grave as it had been before. I was in the grave, with no hope of getting out of it.

'But it happened that there were other people who had had the same idea as myself, and they came to open the grave, and when they lifted the gravestone, I saw the sky, and jumped on to the bank of the grave; and they scattered here and there, thinking that the one who had been buried was arising. That's how I escaped. And I believe that I was in greater danger then that night than I am in your hands yet.'

'Well, you were,' said the Emperor, 'and you escaped; but you won't escape from here.'

'I don't say that I will,' said the Brigand.

By now, the fire was well alight, and they went to put the Brigand on it.

'Well, Brigand, the fire is ready now,' said the Emperor, 'and you and that other thief are going on it, and you won't trouble me or anyone else in the Empire again. Even if you were in the grave itself you were never in such danger as you are now.'

'Yes, I was,' said the Brigand. 'I was in greater danger than you have me in yet, and I escaped; I have been in greater danger than I've told you about.'

'Go on,' said the Emperor, 'tell us about it; we will let you tell it.'

'Why, you are not worthy of being told it, but I'll tell you on conditions.'

'What conditions are you asking for now?'

'That the youngest son of the King of Ireland be freed. I think that if their father knew the way you're treating them, the highest stone in your palace would be the lowest.'[8]

'Do you tell me that I have three sons of the King of Ireland here?'

'Yes.'

The third son was set free.

'Go on, tell us, then,' said the Emperor.

'Well, one night—it wasn't very long ago—I was on my way to see what I could steal. I came to a big cliff that I knew very well, where I had often sheltered. What did I see but an open cave in the face of this cliff. I went to the entrance of this cave to see if anyone was inside. There was a woman inside with a boy-child on her knee, and a knife in her hand. She lifted the knife to thrust it into the child, and the child began to laugh; the woman uttered a cry, and the cliff re-echoed it. I spent some time watching her, surprised at what she was doing. At last I jumped into the cave and asked her what she was doing. She told me that the cave-man who lived there had brought her and the child to the cave, and that she was now compelled to have the child cooked for him by the time he returned.

'"I haven't the heart to kill him," she said, "but here he is, you kill him."

'"Have you anything else at all you can cook for the monster instead of the child?" I said.

'"Yes."

'"If you have any fresh meat, go and put it in the pot, and we'll cut off the child's little toe, and you put it in the pot along with the meat. If he argues that it isn't the child, show him the toe to prove it is."

'That was done. I put the child's little toe on a block of wood,[9] and cut it off with one blow. The child began to bleed and to cry. We stopped the bleeding, and when the child had finished crying, it fell asleep. I went to the far end of the cave, where there was plenty of meat, and I wasn't there long before I heard the cave-man coming. When he came in, he pulled a standing stone against the door,[10] and when I saw him shutting the door, I said to myself that I was inside and inside I would remain as there was no way of getting out. He asked the woman if the food was ready, and she said it was. The first bite he took of the meat, he said:

'"You fraud, this isn't the child!"

'"Yes it is," she said, "look at its little toe; I put it there for fear you wouldn't believe me."

'"Well, it's certainly tough," he said.

'When he was full—he ate plenty—he lay down on the floor opposite the fire, and he was sending the draught up the chimney with his breathing like the bellows of a blacksmith. I went up and put the poker in the fire. He had only one eye, in the middle of his forehead, and when the poker was red-hot, I took it out of the fire and thrust it into his single eye. The first leap he made, he struck the ceiling of the cave with the back of his head, and the second time he leaped, he was on his two feet. He was jumping here and there, trying to catch me with his hands; he couldn't see me. I was jumping out of his way, back and forth. Then he stopped and said:

'"If it's anyone in the world, it's the Byzantine Brigand who's done this to me."

'I answered him and said I would never deny my own name, that it was I who had done it, and here I was.

'"Well," he said, "I'm done for, anyway. I've a gold ring; you can have it, so you won't forget this night."

'He gave me the ring, and the ring would have fitted my arm.[11] I told him the ring was too big for me.

'"Put it on your finger," he said, "and ask it to get smaller."

'I put the ring on my finger, and asked it to get smaller, and it got smaller, until it fitted me as well as if it had grown on me.

'"Does it fit now?" he said.

'I told him that it did.

'"Where are you, ring?" he said.

'The ring answered, "I'm here."

'He jumped at me. I was never in such danger[12] until then. He was likely to murder me, though he was blind! I was doing my best to avoid the woman and the child. One time I thought I would try the door, and I managed to push the standing stone out of the door, and I got to the knoll. He shouted, "Where are you, ring?" and the ring answered, "I'm here", and he came after me. I was as badly off as ever except that I had more room. I had no knife with which to cut off my finger, and the ring wouldn't come off. I started working on it with my other hand, until I got it over the joint, and I was cutting my sinews with my teeth until I got the ring off. When I had got it off, I went to the top of the cliff that was above the shore, and I threw my finger with the ring down over the cliff. He was above me, and he shouted, "Where are you, ring?" and the ring answered, "I'm here!" He jumped over the cliff, and knocked his brains out on the shore. That's how I escaped, and I believe that I was in greater danger that night than you have me in now.'

The Empress was standing in the door with a fair-sized boy beside her. She jumped forward and said:

'I'll not live twenty-four hours unless you free him at once, even if he has stolen the whole of Byzantium. He saved my life and the life of my son, every word he has said is true,' she said, taking off the boy's shoe, 'look at his foot, where his toe was cut off!'

'Well, indeed,' said the Emperor, 'though you've done to me what you've done, I'm glad I didn't put you to death. Though you've done harm, you've done good. You saved my wife and my son. I'll give you anything you ask, and let you go free.'[13]

'Well,' said the Brigand, 'I won't ask for much. I don't need gold or silver. What I ask for is your palfrey, so that the son of the King of Ireland, who has been put under tabus by his stepmother until he brings it back to her, can take it—that is what brought me here, to try to get it for him; I wasn't after it for myself.'

'For your sake,' said the Emperor, 'he'll get it.'

The Byzantine Brigand got his freedom, and the son of the King of Ireland got the palfrey; and when he returned with it to Ireland, his stepmother was dead; and there I left them, well enough off.

6

BOBBAN THE CARPENTER

ONCE THERE was a famous carpenter called Bobban Saor. He had three sons. One day he said to his wife that he wanted to make his sons carpenters.

'Aren't the lads carpenters already?' said she.

'Oh no.'

He sent for his eldest son, and when he came Bobban asked him:

'Son, what can be done about the river that runs beside the house here? I didn't get a wink of sleep all night with the noise of the river.'

'I don't know,' said his eldest son. 'I believe that if a wall were built between the house and the river, it would help.'

'Oh ho! You won't make a carpenter,' said Bobban.

He sent for his second son and asked him the same question.

'Oh,' said his second son, 'I think that if a wooden partition were put up there pretty high, it would deaden the sound of the river.'

'You won't make a carpenter, either,' said Bobban.

He then sent for his youngest son, and asked:

'What can be done about that river beside the house? I haven't had a wink of sleep[1] from its noise all night.'

'I don't know what can best be done about the river,' said the lad, 'except to move the river from the house or else to move the house from the river. The river can't be moved from the house, but the house could be shifted farther away from the river.'

'You'll make a carpenter,' said Bobban. 'Well, now, there are a hundred of my sheep here, go and sell them and bring me such and such a sum of money for them, and bring me back the sheep as well.'

The youngest son went off with the sheep. Everyone who met him asked him where he was going with them, and he would say he was going to sell them.

'What do you want for them?'

He would tell, and:

'I'll buy them.'

'Oh, right enough, but I must have the sheep back with the money. I have to get the sheep back.'

'Take the sheep where you like, then!'

Bobban's youngest son next saw a young woman going to the well. She asked him:

'Where are you going with those sheep, young man?'

'I don't know,' he said, 'I'm trying to sell them.'

'What do you want for them?'

He told her. 'Well, I'll buy them from you.'

'Oh, right enough,' he said, 'but I have to get the sheep back along with the money.'

'You'll get them back, too,' she said. 'Come this way with them.'

The sheep were put into a shed, and she got two men and they sheared the sheep. She paid Bobban's son the money, and let the sheep out.

'Take them away,' she said. Bobban Saor had only been asking for them the value of their wool! His son returned with the sheep.

'Well,' said Bobban, 'here you are, did you sell the sheep?'

'Yes.'

'Did you get the money?'

'Yes.'

'Have you brought back the sheep?'

'Yes, I have.'

'Who bought them?'

'A young woman I met on the road.'

'Go and marry her then,'' said Bobban. 'She's the wife for you.'

His youngest son went and married the girl, and brought her home.

One day Bobban Saor was working with an adze shaping wood. His son was as good as Bobban himself at everything except the adze. His son said to his wife, 'You wait, maybe we'll learn the secret[2] of it from him yet.' His wife went and boiled some eggs and took the shells of them, and put them before Bobban Saor next morning.

'Who has been shelling the eggs like this?' asked Bobban.

'Your son shelled them with the adze,' said she.

'Oh, hasn't he kept his arm close to his side,' said Bobban. That was how his son learnt the secret of Bobban's skill with the adze.

Now Bobban and his son got a message from the King of France asking them to go over to do the joiner work on a big castle the King had built. The King sent for Bobban Saor as there was no more famous carpenter than he for the castle. Bobban Soar and his son got ready to go; they had everything ready, and their tool-bags packed, when Bobban asked his son:

'Will you carry me today if I carry you tomorrow?'

'Well,' said his son, 'I have enough to carry myself without carrying you too!'

'Oh well, if you have,' said Bobban, 'we'll go back.'

They returned. The son's wife said to him:

'What made you come back?'

'My father wouldn't go unless I would carry him today, and then he would carry me tomorrow. I have enough to carry myself as it is.'

'Tut,' she said, 'that wasn't what your father meant at all. Your father meant that if you entertained him with stories today, he would entertain you with stories tomorrow, so that you would both feel the way shorter.'

'Is that what he meant?'

'Yes.'

The next day Bobban Saor asked his son:

'Will we go today, son?'

'Yes.'

'Will you carry me today if I'll carry you tomorrow?'

'Yes.'

'Very well, then, we'll be going.'

'If you're going now,' said the son's wife to him, 'take care that you are not a night without a sweetheart until you come back to me again.'

On the way to France, Bobban Saor said to his son:

'Now, you'll be the carpenter, and I'll be the apprentice.[3] Anything you have to do, you only need to ask me to do it.'

This was agreed. When they reached the castle, and had opened their tool-bags, the son took an axe-head out of his bag, and passed it to Bobban.

'There,' he said, turning to him, 'put a haft on that.'

Bobban Saor caught hold of the axe-head and looked at it; then he began to shape a haft. He was looking from the axe-head back to the haft again. Then he threw the axe-head up, and when it came down it landed in the haft, and the haft fitted it as well as if it had grown on it! When all the French joiners saw this, they wondered what the (Scottish) carpenter could do, when his apprentice could do a thing like that. What happened was that they picked up their tool-bags and went off and left the job to Bobban Saor and his son.

Bobban and his son worked until they had put the castle in order, and it took them a long time. Eventually the King of France was afraid he could not afford to pay them for the time they had worked on the job there. Bobban's son had been making up to one of the King's maidservants. Their work on the castle was finished, and they were to leave the next day. Bobban's son went to see the girl. When he came, he found her weeping.

'What's wrong?' he asked her.

'Plenty. The King's preparing to have you killed, because he's afraid he can't afford to pay you.'

'Don't let that trouble you,' said he.

The next day the son told Bobban Saor about it.

'Take it easy,' said Bobban Saor, 'maybe we'll get the better of him.'

He went and got a piece of silken thread, and he and his

son started to measure the castle with it. The King came in and asked if everything was ready now.

'Nearly everything; I wouldn't like to leave with anything wrong, or in case anyone else found anything wrong after I'd gone; I'm sorry I haven't brought the tool I need for it with me. I must go and get it.'

'Oh, you're not going at all,' said the King. 'I'll send someone for it.'

'If I can't go to get it myself, the only one you may send to get it is your son,' said Bobban.

'Well, I'll send my son for it,' said the King. 'What kind of tool is it?'

'It's "a turn with a turn, and a turn against a turn, and the little gadget",'[4] said Bobban Saor.

'Oh, indeed,' said the King.

The King's son went with a party, and reached Bobban Saor's daughter-in-law. He told her why Bobban had sent them over, to ask for 'the little gadget and a turn with a turn and a turn against a turn'.

'Oh yes,' she said, 'Come in here.'

She showed the King's son into a room, and when she had got him inside, she locked the door.

'You go back,' she said to his companions, 'and say that the "little gadget" won't go over to France until the "big tool" comes back over here; unless my husband and my father-in-law[5] return to me, the King will be without a son.'

That is how Bobban Saor got his wages and came home, and the King of France's son got back to France.

SIMPLE FOLKTALES

7

THE WEDDING-FEAST AT HACKLETT

THIS WEDDING-FEAST was at a place called Hacklett. The house was some way from the church. The bridegroom had left for the wedding, and everyone in the house wanted to go to it, but they didn't know who should be left in the house; someone had to stay there. There was a brother of the bridegroom there; he was only a simpleton, who didn't go to social gatherings at any time. The people in the house thought that the simpleton could look after the house all right until they returned, as he was very careful about everything to do with the house, though he was only a simpleton.

They went to the wedding, leaving the simpleton to cook the goose so that it would be ready for the wedding party on their return. The simpleton was cooking the goose, very pleased he had been left in charge of the house. He tasted a piece of it, and liked it very much. Then it occurred to him that his sister would have given him half of the goose, and that the other half would do for the in-laws, so he ate half the goose. He was still hungry; and he thought then that his in-laws would have given him their half of the goose just as soon as his sister would; so he ate the whole goose.

Then he realized he would be in a terrible fix if the wedding party were to come back and find nothing ready for them to eat after having left him in charge of the house. There happened to be another goose sitting on eggs in the barn, and he thought he could kill the goose that was sitting and have it cooked before the wedding party returned. This he did; he killed the goose and plucked it and put it in the pot.

Then he realized that he had made a mistake by killing the goose that was sitting on the eggs, because the eggs would become useless now that there wasn't any creature to sit on them. But he thought he might hatch the eggs himself, as he was always at home; so he went and sat on the eggs himself. When he had been a while on the eggs, he remembered that the goose used to go to wet herself in the pond beside the house; and he thought that he himself would have to do everything the goose used to do, if he were to hatch the eggs. He went into the pond for a short time, and then came back and went to the eggs; when he had been a short time on the eggs, he had to go out again, as he thought it was to keep the eggs damp that the goose used to go out so often.

He found it very tiresome to keep going between the pond and the eggs, and it occurred to him that it would be a good thing if he could have the pond indoors. There was a big tub full of water in the house ready for washing the dishes after the party returned, and he went and poured it on the floor. He had a big enough pond then! He was a while in the pond on the floor and a while sitting on the eggs in turn; and when the wedding party came back, the house was in a fearful state, nothing but a sea of water, and the housekeeper was brooding eggs and wouldn't let anyone near him! They had to lure him off the eggs with the wedding-cake, so that they could put the house in order before more people came, or they would have been put to shame! That's what happened at the wedding-feast at Hacklett!

8

GEORGE BUCHANAN AND THE DOGS

ONCE THERE was a drover in Scotland who used to go at times to England with cattle and sheep and sometimes with pigs. He had a very good dog. An Englishman took a fancy to the dog and wanted to buy it; he was willing to pay anything the drover asked. The drover sold him the dog for five pounds; the Englishman would have paid more if he had been asked to.

The drover then regretted he hadn't taken plenty of dogs to England; he thought that if he could get five pounds apiece for them there, it would pay him better than dealing in cattle and sheep. He started to collect dogs all over the place, until he had collected five hundred of them. He then got a ship and took them to London. When he arrived he didn't dare to tie up at the quay with them; he anchored offshore. He himself went ashore to see if he could sell the dogs. There was no one there who would buy a dog, people didn't need them.

But whom did he happen to meet but George Buchanan.[1] The drover told him what had happened to him. 'Well,' said George, 'I don't know how the matter will turn out for you at all, but take it easy, perhaps I can make something of the business.'

George then went off and started shouting, 'Who will buy five hundred dogs at five pounds a dog?' Two Englishmen were standing near by. One of them said, 'What are you thinking of, today, George?' The other said:

'Isn't he a smarty! It wouldn't take much to send him scurrying![2] Where can he get five hundred dogs?' The Englishman started towards him. 'Leave him alone,' said the other. 'No,' said the first, 'where can he get five hundred dogs? Even if he collected every dog he could find in England, he wouldn't have five hundred.'

The Englishman went to George Buchanan. 'Have you got the dogs, George?' he said.

'Yes.'

'Well, I'll buy them. But you must deliver them to me here at ten o'clock tomorrow morning.'

'All right,' said George. 'You be here then, and I'll deliver them to you.'

The Englishman went off.

'Go on, now,' said George to the drover, 'and have your ship in here at the quay tomorrow at ten o'clock in the morning.'

Next day George Buchanan came at ten o'clock, and the drover's ship was brought in and tied up at the quay. The Englishman arrived. When the ship's hatches were opened, the dogs were out and up the quay and off out of sight through the town; they were ravenous with hunger and had been eating each other! The Englishman had to pay George Buchanan for the five hundred dogs and then send men after them throughout the country to shoot them before they ate every creature in England.

'Off with you now,' said George to the drover, 'and never come here with dogs or cattle again!'

9

THE REASON WHY THE SEA IS SALT AND NOT FRESH

YOU ALL know that the water of the ocean is salt and not fresh. I am going to tell you the reason why. It was, and still is, a custom for everyone to have ham[1] at Easter. This time it happened that ham was terribly scarce, as it was with us during the war. There was once a crofter[2] called Donald, whose wife sent him out to see if he could get ham for them to have at Easter. He was trying to buy some everywhere, and he couldn't get any. But one evening he found a little shop which had ham, and he got what his wife needed. On his way home he met one of the fairy folk. The fairy asked for the ham, saying it was just what he had been looking for and hadn't been able to get. Donald replied that it wasn't to give it away that he had been looking for it himself.

'Well,' said the fairy, 'I'll give you anything you ask me for, if you'll give me the ham, so I won't go home empty-handed. I have a mill, which I'll give you for the ham; there is nothing you can want that the mill won't make for you.'

When he heard that, Donald agreed to give the ham to the fairy. He went off with the fairy, and when they reached the fairy mound, the mound was open. Donald went inside with the fairy, who was then ready to give Donald anything but the mill, but Donald would only take what had been promised to him.

The fairy gave him the mill, and taught him the verse that made the mill make anything, and another verse to make it stop when it had made enough.

The crofter went home with the mill on his back. When he got home, his wife took a look at it:

'Is this the ham you've been looking for since early this morning?' she said, 'the whole village thinks you're a fool. If I'd gone I'd have been back with ham long ago.'

Donald didn't say a word, but put down the mill and recited the verse. Ham began to flow from the mill! When he had got enough, he recited the verse to stop the mill, and the mill stopped.

'Have you enough ham now?' he said.

'Yes, indeed, we can give ham to everyone in the village now. You've brought fortune and happiness![3] Will the mill make anything else besides ham?'

'Oh, it'll make anything. Are you satisfied now?'

'Indeed I am,' said she.

After that Donald set up as a merchant selling things, and he was selling cheaper than any of the others, as well he might, as he didn't have to buy anything, there wasn't anything the mill couldn't make for him; until at last he became a millionaire![4] But there came a very bad year, just like this year itself, and the farmers lost their crops; one of them lost the whole of his crops. He had heard about the mill, and he went to see the mill's owner to see if he could get it for a while to make seed to sow his land, or if Donald would sell it to him, as he had plenty of seed himself.

Donald agreed to sell the mill to the farmer. He sold the mill for a great sum of money, and he taught the farmer the verse for starting the mill, but he didn't teach him the verse for stopping it! He wanted to get the mill back again. The farmer went off with the mill on his back, and went into his barn and recited the verse. Seed began to flow; the lads began to take it away and fill all the granaries[5] with it, until every place was full. The mill was producing seed as busily as ever. It began to look as if the village would be submerged with it! Too much was worse than none at all! The farmer ran to Donald who had sold him the mill, to find out what should be done. Donald came back with him and recited the verse to stop the mill, in his mind, and the mill stopped. The farmer didn't dare to make anything with it again, as he couldn't stop it.

But there happened to come around a ship that was looking for salt, and the captain heard about the mill, and went to look at it. He asked the farmer if he would sell it to him. The farmer agreed, as he wasn't doing much with it. He thought it would be enough if he could get as much for it as he had paid for it. He sold the mill to the captain, and the captain went off with it and took it aboard his ship. The farmer had taught him the verse for starting the mill, but he hadn't taught him the verse for stopping it, as he didn't know it.

When the captain took the mill aboard and recited the verse to start it, the mill began producing salt. The men began to stow the salt on the ship. At last the ship was fully laden, and the mill was still producing salt as busily as ever. Eventually it sank the ship! The ship is there on the bottom yet, and there she will remain, with the mill producing salt with no way to stop it, and no word of the verse! However much fresh water goes into the sea, the sea will be salt from the work of the mill. There you have the reason why the sea is salt and not fresh!

10

THREE MORE FOOLISH

ONCE THERE was a young man who went to ask for a girl in marriage. When he arrived, the girl was at home with her father and mother. He told them what he had come for. After a while she got up and went out to the peat stack to get peats to make a fire so that they could cook a meal. While she was at the peat stack she said to herself that if she were with child by the young man, and the peat stack were to fall on top of her, it would be a shame. She began to cry beside the peat stack. When her mother got tired of waiting for her to come back, she went out and found her crying beside the peat stack.

'What's wrong with you!' said her mother.

'I thought that if I were with child by that young man, and the peat stack were to fall on top of me, wouldn't it be a shame!'

'By Mary, it would be a shame for me, not for you!' said her mother. The two of them started to cry beside the peat stack. The father and the young man were alone in the house. When the father got tired of waiting, he went out himself and found his wife and daughter crying beside the peat stack.

'What's wrong with you?' he asked.

'Well,' said his wife, 'we thought that if your daughter were with child by that young man, and the peat stack were to fall on top of her, it would be a shame for us!'

'By Mary, it wouldn't be a shame for you, but for me!' said the husband. He began to cry along with his wife and daughter. The young man was left in the house by himself. At last he got up and went out.

'What's wrong with you that you're acting like this?' he said.

'Oh,' said the husband, 'if our daughter were with child by you and the peat stack fell on top of her, it would be a shame for us!'

'Well, she isn't and she won't be. I'm not coming back until I find two that are wiser or three that are more foolish than you are.'

He went off, and followed the road. He was going past some fine fields when what did he see but three men walking there with a big black dog in front of them. When the dog stopped, they stopped. Not one of the men was saying a word to the others. The young man went over to them. Not one of them spoke. But when dusk came, they stopped, and one of them said:

'Well, if what is indoors were outdoors, I would invite the stranger in.'

'Well,' said another, 'if what hasn't been done had been done, I would invite the stranger in.'

'Well,' said the third man, 'since I have neither of these things to do, I'll invite the stranger in.'

He took the young man home with him. When they arrived, his wife came into the room. When the young man saw the wife, he thought he had never seen such a fine woman, and that it would be a good thing if he had a wife like her.

'It would be a good thing,' said his host, 'if it were without gossip or shame or scandal.'[1]

The young man looked at him; he had only thought and not spoken.

The daughter then came in; she was much prettier than her mother. The young man said to himself that he would be happy if he could have her.

'That would be a good thing, with her relations' consent,' said his host.

The wife then got up and put a small pot on the fire. When the young man saw how small the pot was, he said to himself that whatever she put in it would not be enough for him, as the pot was so small.

'That would be a good thing, by the grace of God,' said his host.

The meal was now ready and they were asked to come up for it. The young man sat down at the table.

'Go on now, take your food,' said his host.

'I'll not take food nor drink until I find out what you mean by the words you've said to me since I came to the house.'

'What is that?'

'When you said "that would be a good thing, by the grace of God".'

'Well, I'll tell you. You thought when you saw the pot, that as it was so small, what was in it would not be enough for you. I said then that it would be good, by the grace of God. When you saw my wife, you coveted her for yourself, you said to yourself that it would be a good thing if you had one like her. I said it would be a good thing if it were without gossip or shame or scandal; but there was no way for you to get my wife without that. When you saw my daughter, you said to yourself that you would be well off if you had her. I said then that you would be well off if you had her with her relations' consent. Now take your food.'

'What was the meaning of the business which you and the other two men were at today?' asked the young man.

'Well, I'll tell you that too. We were dividing my father's land. Our father had ordered that none of us should speak to the others while we were dividing the land. The plan we made was to take the dog with us, and that we would accept the boundaries as the dog designed them. We never spoke a word to each other all day. That's what we were at today.'

'What did the man mean when he said that if what was indoors were outdoors he would invite the stranger in?'

'His mother-in-law's body is in his house, so it's a bad place for a stranger. The one who said that if what hadn't been done had been done, he would invite you in, has a wife who beats him every night when he gets back home; when that's over, she's a good enough wife. That was a bad place to invite a stranger also. As I had neither a mother-in-law to bury nor a wife waiting to beat me, I invited you in. Now take your food.'

The young man took his food; and afterwards he asked for the daughter, and got her in marriage. Then he returned home; he had seen three people quite as odd as the three he had left crying beside the peat stack!

11

THE PRIEST, THE MINISTER, AND THE TWO HENS

ONCE THERE were a priest and a minister who lived near each other. The minister used to go to call on the priest, and the priest used to go to call on the minister, as they were very friendly. One day when the priest was calling on the minister, he asked the minister to promise to come to dinner with him on a certain date.[1] The minister promised to come. The day the priest expected the minister he went to see his housekeeper. He told her to make a good dinner because he expected the minister to come to dinner that day.

'Well, I haven't much for him. If only I had known before.'

'Tut, you've plenty. Haven't you got ducks and hens? Kill a hen or two, that'll make a good dinner.'

'All right,' she said.

The housekeeper went and killed two hens and put them in the pot. She had a young man[2] who used to come round to see her; who came in, but he!

'Are you alone?' he said.

'I am just now,' she replied.

'What have you in the pot there?'

'Two chickens. We expect the minister for dinner today. The priest often calls on him. He's a real gentleman.'

'I'd give anything for a bit of chicken. Won't you give me a piece for myself?'

'It won't do to break them.'

'Why not?'

'The priest would kill me.'

'What could he do to you even if I ate them both?'

'What but dismiss me!'

'What do you care? Aren't we getting married anyway?'

'Oh, even so, I'd sooner leave in the right way.'

'By the Book, I'd give anything for a bit of chicken meat!'[3]

'Wait then,' she said, and she went and lifted one of the hens out of the pot. 'Here, take a wing of that one.'

He started on it, and he ate every bit of it!

'Well, well! that was good! Let me try a little piece off the other one to see if it's as good as the first.'

'Oh, you won't stop until you've disgraced me!'

'Oh, you needn't expect the minister today; I saw him leaving home in the morning.'

She went and lifted the second chicken out of the pot. 'Well, then, try a little piece of it.'

He began on the second hen, and he left nothing but the bones![4] Just then they heard a knocking at the front door. She went down. Who was there but the minister! He came in and went down to the room where the priest was. The housekeeper went back to the kitchen with her head in her hands.

'Oh, I'm done for,' she said.

'Don't be afraid.'

The priest came down and asked if the dinner was ready.

'Yes, but I can't find a sharp knife. The knives here are so blunt.'

'Give me the knife, and I'll sharpen it for you.'

She gave the priest the knife, and he went down into the passage and got a steel sharpener[5] and began to sharpen the knife.

'Go down now and tell the minister that the priest is going to crop his ears'[6] (said the young man). She went into the parlour, taking the dish with her. The priest was sharpening the knife in the passage.

'Who's there?' said the minister.

'The priest.'

'What's he doing there?'

'Well, you won't like it. He's sharpening the knife in order to crop your ears!'

'God save us! Is he off his head?'

'He hasn't been well in his head for some days.'

'Oh, what will I do? How can I get out of here?'

'You can get out this way,' she said. She went and let the minister out by the back door. Then the priest came into the kitchen.

'Where's the minister?'

'Oh, the minister went off, and he's taken the hens with him!'

The priest thought the minister was having a joke, as he was a humorous sort of man. He went out after the minister with the knife in his hand, and saw the minister leaving the house at a full trot.

'Hey, hey,'[7] he said, 'hey, leave one of them!'

'If I leave one of them, I might as well leave both,' said the minister, running harder than ever!

12

HOW A BAD DAUGHTER WAS MADE A GOOD WIFE

ONCE THERE was a rich farmer who had three sons. When he died, he left his farm to them to carry on for as long as they chose to stick together. Each of them had a right in the house and in the land.

The eldest of them married a gentleman's daughter, and was well off; and the second married a wife who was as well born as his brother's. The youngest of them, who was a carpenter, was then the only one of them left unmarried. He decided to marry. His brothers told him that if he got married, he must get a wife who was just as well-born[1] as theirs were.

'No I won't,' he said. 'I'll get the daughter of a bad mother, as bad as I can find.'

'Well, she mustn't come here!'

'Yes she will, she has as good a right to come here as your wives had!'

He took his pony and his dog, and went away, not knowing how far he would go. The day was bad, and snow was falling. What did he see on his way but an old man at work ploughing in a field. He went over to him, and said:

'Oh, oh! you've got a bad day for ploughing!'

'Well,' said the old fellow, 'indeed, it isn't good!'

'Why do you have to work outside on a day like this?'

'Well, there's no one else to go out but myself, and the work has to be done, and I must keep on with it.'

'Is there no one but yourself?'

'Oh yes, I have my wife along with me at home, and my daughter.'

'Well, indeed, I'd think they wouldn't let you work outside on a day like this.'

'Well, my good lad,' said the old man, 'and you look like one to me, you are right enough there. If there was a way I could stay at home, I wouldn't come out myself; but I'd rather to be outside, than indoors listening to the women-folk.'

'Indeed,' said the youngest son, 'is that the way of it?'

'Yes, it is,' said the old man.

'Well, I'd think your own daughter wouldn't want you to be out of doors (in weather like this).'

'If her mother is bad, my daughter is seven times worse.'[2]

'May I marry her?' asked the young man.

'I never saw anyone on whom I'd wish her, but if you think you can bring her to heel, I'll not keep her from you.'

'Oh, I'll take her right enough, if you'll give her to me.'

'That's just what I'll do,' said the old man, 'but if you're going to ask for the girl, keep on to the house, and when I come home, don't let on you've ever seen me. If *I* say you can have her, her mother will never let you have her at all,[3] but if I say you can't have her, her mother will let you have her at once.'

The young man went on to the house. Only the mother and daughter were there. Oh, they made him welcome enough! At nightfall the old man came home. He was asked to join their meal in the kitchen, and when they were at their food, the young man asked for the daughter.

'Well,' said the old man, 'my daughter's my only help, and the day she leaves me I'll be utterly done for. I don't want to part with her or give her to anyone.'

'Listen,' said his wife, 'shut your mouth, you shameless fellow! Little trouble you had rearing her! What have you to do with her? Yes, my lad, of course you can have the girl!'

They agreed to get married; and the daughter of the old man became the wife of the farmer's youngest son. Then they left for his home. The pony was their only conveyance, and the girl was put behind him on the pony's back. Her mother came out with a bundle of canes and held them out to her daughter.

'Here,' she said, 'take these with you, I'm sure there'll be many a day you'll need them.'

They left, and they hadn't gone far before the young husband's dog went off after a hare. He shouted at the dog, but the dog paid no heed. When the dog did come back, he took a revolver[4] out of his pocket and shot the dog and killed it.

'Goodness,' said his wife, 'why did you kill the dog?'

'Why should I let him live, a worthless creature[5] that wouldn't heed me?'

A little later he heard a noise behind him. He looked, and saw she had dropped the canes!

When they were getting near to his home, they came to a river which ran between them and the house. He put the pony at the worst bit of the stream, and began to lash the pony to make it go across the river. The pony only backed and would not go near it. He asked his wife to dismount, and he got off the pony himself, and took out his revolver, and put it to the pony, and killed it.

'My God, why did you kill the pony?' she said.

'Why should I let it live, a worthless creature that wouldn't do what I told it?'

He went and took the saddle off the pony.

'Here,' he said. 'You carry that.'

'Indeed I'll not carry it; you might have let the beast that was carrying it live; the saddle would be fitter on it than on me.'

'Are you saying you won't carry it?' he said.

'Oh, of course I'll carry it, but you really might have let the pony live, it would have been more suitable on her.'

'Well, if the pony had done what I told her, I wouldn't have killed her.'

They came home, he and she, and she was the best wife there had ever been! There was nothing he asked her to do that she wouldn't do! But at the end of a year, when he was working in his carpenter's shop, whom did he see go past the door but his mother-in-law, with a load of canes on her back. He went after her to the door to hear what she would say. The old lady went in to the house, and turned to her daughter.

'Here,' she said, 'take these off me; I'm sure you've used up the ones you took with you on the back of that rascal long ago!'

'My goodness, mother, why did you bring them? Not one of those you gave me ever reached the house! If you only knew what he did to me!'

'What did he do to you?'

'We hadn't gone far before his dog went off after a hare, and as it had disobeyed him, he shot it when it did come back to him. Next he came to the river with the pony, and no beast could have got across at the place he was trying to put the pony across. When the pony wouldn't cross the river, he shot it, and I can tell you that I had to carry the saddle home myself on my back!'

'Oh, the devil!' said her mother, 'if only I had been there! He wouldn't have done that to me! Weren't you soft with him!'

When the farmer's youngest son heard that, he jumped in and caught the old woman and stripped her and slashed her backside with his knife and put salt in the wounds he had made, and then let her go. The mother-in-law went off lamenting. When she got home, the old man was sitting at the fire, having a rest; he hadn't had to be outside! She went up to him and put her arms around his neck.

'My darling husband,' she said, 'of all the men in the world! In spite of everything I ever did to you, you never treated me the way our son-in-law has; he's slashed me and injured me! I'll never say a cross word to you again!'

The young man had tamed the mother, and he had tamed the daughter! The daughter would do anything he asked her to do. One day when the three of them, he and his two elder brothers, were at home, he said to them:

'You've now got the daughters of big rich men; but I'll wager they won't do what you ask them as well as my wife will for me.'

'Yes they will, they'll do anything we ask them.'

'I'll bet a hundred pounds that they won't.'

'Right enough,' said the other brothers, 'we'll bet the same. How are you going to test them?'

'Well, there's a good fire in the room here. Ask your wife to come down and take off her dress and put it in the fire and see if she'll do it.'

The eldest brother called for his wife to come down. When she came she asked him, 'What do you want me for?'

'Nothing much. Take off that dress you have on and put it in the fire, so we can see if it'll burn.'

'Aye, aye! Haven't you anything better to do than that?' she said, leaving the room.

'Here,' he said to his second brother, 'you go and get your wife and ask her to do the same thing.'

The second brother's wife was sent for, and asked to do the same thing.

'Oh, you should have something better to do than this sort of thing,' she said, 'you don't know what you're thinking of.'

The youngest brother went and brought down his own wife.

'I want you' he said, 'to take off that dress you've got on and put it in the fire so we can see how well it burns.'

She looked at him. 'Indeed,' she said, 'it cost too much for me to go and burn it in front of you.'

'Won't you do it at all?' he said.

'Oh, of course, if it pleases you; I'll do anything to please you.'

She took off her dress and put it on the fire.

'Very good,' he said, 'you'll get a much better dress then that.' He turned to his brothers:

'Who's right now?' he said. 'Pay me the hundred pounds!' He took a hundred pounds from each of his brothers, neither of whose wives would do for them what the daughter of the bad mother did for him!

13

THE THREE QUESTIONS AND THE THREE BURDENS

ONCE THERE was a landowner who considered himself a very wise man. It happened there was a poor crofter on his estate (who had been caught poaching deer). The landowner sent for him and told him that he was going to put three questions to him, which he would have to answer (or be evicted for poaching). The landowner said that the crofter must come to him within three days, and tell him, first, What was the richest thing in the world? second, What was the poorest thing in the world? and third, What creature went first on four feet, then on two feet, and then on three feet? The poor man went home, not knowing what he should do. He lay down as if he were on his death-bed; he didn't know what he should do if the matter were to go any further.

He had a crop-headed, freckled daughter.[1] His daughter came and asked him what was wrong with him, saying that there must be something troubling him more than any sickness. He told her the questions the landowner had put to him, and how he had to go and answer them within three days (or they would be evicted).

'Tut,' she said, 'don't let that trouble you. You go. These questions are easy enough to answer. The richest thing on earth is the sea; though you were to take water out of it night and day, the sea will be as full as it ever was. The poorest thing on earth, is the fire; it makes no difference how big it is, it will fade away and only leave ashes.'

'What then,' her father said, 'is that creature that first goes on four legs?'

'That's man,' she said, 'he goes on his two arms and legs first before he learns to walk; when he learns to walk, he goes on two legs, and when he grows old, he goes on his two legs with a stick. That's his three legs. You go to the laird and answer his questions.'

The poor man got up and went to the laird. When he arrived, the laird said:

'Well, are you fit to answer the questions[2] I put to you, now?'

'I think I am.'

'What are the answers?'

He told the laird the answers that his daughter had told him.

'Oh, indeed,' said the laird, 'whoever put these answers in your mouth, it wasn't your head that thought of them. You must tell me who told you or I won't leave you alive.'

Frightened as he was, the crofter told the laird that it was his own daughter who had told him.

'Well,' said the laird, 'we'll go to see her.'

The laird went with the crofter to see the crop-headed, freckled daughter.

'Was it you who answered the questions I put to your father?'

'Yes; someone had to answer them for him, when you were being so hard on him.'

'Well, I can't say you didn't answer them very well; you have a good head. If you were the daughter of a laird, I would marry you. But I'll do this for you. I have a small estate over there, which I'll give to you.'

'Many thanks, but I can't make any use of an estate. If you'd assign it to my father, I'd be very pleased.'

'Well, I'll do that,' said the laird, and he assigned the small estate to her father, and gave her the title deeds.

'Now I'm a laird's daughter,' said she.

'Yes; and now I expect you'll marry me.'

'No, I won't marry you.'

'Why not?'

'If I were to marry you, you might send me away.'

'No I wouldn't.'

'Yes you would.'

'No I wouldn't unless you were to blame.'

'Well, I'll marry you on conditions,' she said.

'What conditions are you asking for?'

'That I can carry three burdens out of the castle the day you send me away, that I can do as I like with.'

'I'll agree to that,' he said.

'Well, if I can have that in writing, I'll marry you.'

'You can have it in writing,' said the laird.

He put it in writing, that if he were to send her away (after their marriage) she could carry three burdens out of his castle, whatever she chose, and do what she liked with them.

The laird and the crop-headed, freckled daughter got married, and they were very happy. They had not been long married, when they had an heir. The crop-headed, freckled daughter was better at running the estate than the laird himself. There were crofters near by, and when they began their ploughing, they used to put their animals out to the hill. There were two neighbouring crofters there, one of whom had a mare in foal, and the other an old white gelding. The neighbours were ploughing together;[3] and when they had finished their ploughing, they put the gelding and the mare out to the hill. The mare foaled out on the hill; and all three were out on the hill until the autumn, when it was time to bring the harvest home. When they went to fetch the horses to carry home the harvest, what did the foal do but follow the neighbour's gelding. The neighbour then claimed the foal because it was following his gelding. The two crofters fell out, and they had to go to the laird for a decision. They went to the laird, and told him the case.

'Come tomorrow to the castle with the foal and the mare and the gelding,' said the laird, 'and I'll give my decision.'

The next day the two crofts set out with the foal and the mare and the gelding. There was a field in front of the castle, with a gate at each end.

'Go and take the horses to the middle of the field,' said the laird, 'and then one of you stand at each gate; and the owner of the beast the foal follows shall be the owner of the foal.'

They took the horses to the middle of the field and then they went one to each gate. Alas, the foal followed the gelding. The crofter who owned the mare went home very much displeased that he had lost the foal. The other crofter was very glad that the foal had followed his gelding. The crofter who owned the mare didn't know what to do; but when he heard that the laird had left home, he thought he would go and see the crop-headed, freckled daughter and ask her advice. When he arrived he said:

'Oh, what a wrong the laird did me when he made me lose the foal!'

'It was a bad thing, indeed.'

'I've come to ask what advice you'd give me.'

'If I advised you, you'd give me away.'

'I'll never give you away.'

'Well,' she said, 'the laird is going fishing tomorrow in that loch over there. You make sure you're there first. Take some salt[4] in a sack, and when you see him coming, start sowing the salt beside the loch, and in all the ditches you see; and he'll come over and ask you what you're doing there. You tell him that you're sowing salt there because you think it will grow in a wet place; and he'll tell you then that you know salt won't grow there. You tell him that salt is as likely to grow there, as the foal is likely to have grown inside the gelding instead of inside its mother the mare. But promise me you'll die before you tell the laird that I advised you to say this!'

'I'll not tell him,' said the crofter.

The next day he went out, taking with him some salt in a sack, and went down to the loch. He hadn't been there long, when he saw the laird coming, with a fishing-rod on his shoulder. The crofter began to sow the salt beside the loch, in ditches, and in every low-lying spot. The laird stopped to watch him for a while, and then went over to him.

'What are you doing there, you wretched fool?'

'By the Book,' said the crofter, 'we are short of salt at

home, so I'm sowing some here, as I think it will grow in the wet places.'

'Oh, go home, don't you know perfectly well salt won't grow here (or anywhere else)?'

'I don't know,' said the crofter, 'that it isn't as likely to grow here as the foal was to have grown inside the gelding when it should have grown inside the mare.'

The laird stopped. 'It wasn't your head that thought that up,'[5] he said; 'tell me who put those words in your mouth, or you'll die.'

The crofter was so frightened that he told the laird that it was his lady who had told him to say this. The laird went straight home to his lady.

'Well, my dear wife,' he said, 'since you couldn't hold your tongue and are interfering with my decisions, you'll leave right now.'

'Indeed,' she said. 'I was sure it would come to this some day or other. But remember that if you send me away today, you must be so good as to keep your promise to me and let me carry away my three burdens and do as I like with them.'

'You can take them with you,' said the laird.

She went and the first thing she lifted and carried out was the cradle with the heir; then she came back into the house and took out the chest which held the title-deeds of her husband's estate, and put it beside the cradle; and then she came back in and said to him, 'Sit down on that chair so I can carry you out.' The laird sat down on the chair. When she had carried him out, she took back inside the cradle and the heir and the title-deeds and shut the door.

'Go away now,' she said, 'the heir is mine and the title-deeds are mine; you go your way!'

The laird could only agree to let the crop-headed, freckled lass have her own way thereafter!

LOCAL TRADITIONS

14

THE NORWEGIANS IN SOUTH UIST

MAOILEIN, son of the King of Norway, was living at Aird Mhaoile[1] in Bornish; this is why it was called Aird Mhaoile. Mór, daughter of the King of Norway, was drowned and found on the shore; she was the first woman buried at Togh-Mór (Howmore); this is why it was called Tó-Mór; *i.e.* Taigh Móire, 'Mór's House',[2] is its right name. The daughter of the King of Norway was the first woman buried there.

It was the Norwegians who made the submerged stepping stones to the islands in the lochs here; there is not an island in a loch throughout Uist that has not got submerged stepping stones going to it. That is what the Norwegians undertook, making these stepping stones in the lochs to protect themselves. It was they too who built the barps on the hill ground over there. I think there are graves under the barps, under the stones, because there is not one of them that hasn't got a place made under it like a culvert;[3] that is what the old men used to call *tung* where the Norwegians used to be buried. put in a *tung*, with stonework above them, put in without a coffin at all.

15

CLANRANALD AND GILLE PÀDRA' DUBH

THIS TIME, MacLeod of Dunvegan* had come to visit Clanranald from the Isle of Skye. There was a man at Gerinish in South Uist called Gille Pàdra Dubh, 'Dark Servant of Patrick'; he and his son Iain Dubh 'Dark John' were both very good archers. Clanranald was afraid that some day Gille Pàdra' Dubh and his son might fall out with him and take Ormaclate† from him. Clanranald and MacLeod plotted together to bring Gille Pàdra' Dubh and Iain Dubh to Ormaclate, and contrived a plan whereby one of them should kill the other; when Gille Pàdra' Dubh arrived, Clanranald was to say that he and MacLeod had been talking about archery, and that MacLeod had said that he had a man on the Isle of Skye who could break an egg on a man's head with an arrow at a distance of a hundred yards; and that Clanranald had wagered that he himself had a man who could do the same thing, 'and tell Gille Pàdra' Dubh' said MacLeod, 'that if there is anyone in Uist who can do it, it is himself or else his son Iain Dubh, and who knows but they won't try it, and one of them will kill the other, and it won't be difficult to deal with the survivor of them.'

So it happened. Clanranald sent a servant on horseback down[1] to Gerinish for Gille Pàdra' Dubh and Iain Dubh his

* The Clanranalds were connected with the MacLeods of Dunvegan by marriage in the sixteenth and seventeenth centuries.

† Clanranald's residence in South Uist. See note on the Clanranalds.

son, to tell them he had special business with them. They had never been particularly friendly with Clanranald at any time, but they went and prepared themselves, and left taking each of them a horse and bow and arrows. When they reached Ormaclate, Clanranald came out to meet them, and welcomed Gille Pàdraig:

'Oh, how are you, Gille Pàdraig? It's a long time since we've shaken hands.'

'I'm sure,' said Gille Pàdraig, 'we shook them too quickly.'

'Oh no, not at all,' said Clanranald. 'The two of us are getting old, and it won't do for us to be keeping up bad feeling. Come in!'

He took them both inside.

'What did you need us for in such a hurry?' said Gille Pàdraig.

'Well, I'll tell you. MacLeod and I were here, and when people get together they'll talk about all sorts of things. We were talking about archery, and he was telling me that there was a man on the Isle of Skye who could break an egg on a man's head with an arrow at a distance of a hundred yards; and I wagered him that I myself had a man who could do it. The wager is the estate. I believe if there's anyone in Uist who can do it, it's yourself or your son Iain Dubh.'

'Weren't you a fool,' said Gille Pàdraig, 'to make that wager with MacLeod, before you had seen the man do it?'

'Oh well, it's done anyway,' said Clanranald, 'and I believe that unless you or Iain Dubh can do it, I'll lose the estate.'

'Oh, you'll not lose the estate at all,' said Gille Pàdraig, 'but which of your men will stand a hundred yards away with an egg on his head while I try to hit it?'

They all remained silent.

'No,' said Gille Pàdraig, 'not one of you will. Will you do it for me?' he said, turning to his son Iain Dubh.

'I don't know,' said Iain, 'I'm afraid to.'

'Will you do it if I ask you?'

'Yes.'

'Well, we'll go out, then. Which of you now is going to measure the distance?'

'I'll measure it,' said MacLeod.

He went and measured a hundred paces right from the end of the house.

'Well,' said Gille Pàdraig, 'you must now do everything I ask.'

'We will,' said MacLeod.

'Get two men with two spades, then.'

Two men were got and made to dig a hole in the ground.

'Come here, now, Iain Dubh, and get into that hole there.'

Iain Dubh went into the pit, and when he was inside the top of his head was level with the ground. He had long hair.* The egg was got and tied in his hair on top of his head. Gille Pàdra' Dubh went to the end of the house and took out his bow, and stuck the first arrow he took from his quiver under his belt, and the second he put under his arm; he put six arrows on himself and the seventh in the bow, and he took a shot at the egg and put the arrow through the egg on top of his son's head. Then he went down to his son.

'Are you alive, Iain Dubh?' he said.

'Yes.'

'Come up, now.'

Clanranald came down to meet them.

'I could bet on you, Gille Pàdraig,' he said, 'but why did you take the other six arrows from your quiver?'

'I'll tell you why. If I had killed my son, this arrow was for you, and this one for your lady, and this one for your son, and this one for MacLeod, and the other two would have been for the two men who dug the pit for my son; if I had killed him, I would have left Ormaclate depopulated today.'

'Go, go, it's a good thing it didn't happen,' said Clanranald.

Gille Pàdra' Dubh went away, and Clanranald never troubled him again.

* Men usually wore their hair long in the Highlands in those times. This is often referred to in old songs.

16

HOW GILLE PÀDRA' DUBH PAID HIS RENT

CLANRANALD'S factor had his house at Loch Eynort and the place has been called Rubha Taigh a' Mhàil, 'The Rent House Point' ever since. That is where Clanranald had his rent collector's house.

Gille Pàdra' Dubh came down to pay his rent there; he was to pay it in grain. The grain used to be weighed by the peck. The last peck measure of his grain wasn't full, and the factor wouldn't accept it, as it was short.

What did Gille Pàdra' Dubh do but catch hold of the factor and stick his knife in the factor's throat and hold him above the peck measure until he had filled it with his blood. 'It'll be full now,' he said. That's as true as can be. That was the last rent ever collected there!

17

THE WIDOW'S SON'S REVENGE ON CLANRANALD

CLANRANALD was living at Ormaclate in his castle;* and MacLeod of Dunvegan came over from the Isle of Skye to see him. Clanranald had a ploughman at Ormaclate; and when he and MacLeod were out taking a walk,[1] what did the ploughman do but stoop down and pick up a blade of dulse[2] that he had seen amongst the seaweed (spread on the ground for manure) and start to eat it. MacLeod said:

'Dear me, it's a poor thing if your farm servants don't get better food to eat than seaweed!'

'Well,' said Clanranald, 'he won't do it again.'

He went over to the ploughman and asked him why he had let the horses stand still.

'I was bending down to pick up a piece of dulse which I saw in the seaweed.'

'Indeed! Wouldn't it be a fine thing if strangers happened to be passing at the moment! They would say that Clanranald's horses had given up, that there was no strength in them through lack of food. You won't do that again!'

Clanranald drew his dagger and stabbed the ploughman with it and killed him. He had an adviser along with him, and his adviser said:

'It's an evil thing you've done.'

* Presumably the 'hen-house' mentioned in Story No. 19. It cannot have been the new house built then, as bows and arrows are still the weapons used here.

'What's that?'

'Killing the ploughman. You have his brother Farquhar working for you at Ormaclate; he has a family of big strong sons, who may well seek revenge for their uncle's death.'

'Well,' said Clanranald, 'if that's how it is, they must be killed too, right away.'

They planned to put Farquhar and his family to death that night. They made the plan standing by a stone at a place called the Tràigh Bhàn, the 'White Strand', and ever since the stone has been called Clach na Mi-Chomhairle, 'The Stone of Ill-Counsel'. Farquhar and his family learnt about the plan, and fled. But Farquhar was caught behind the Tobhta Mhór, the 'Big Site',* he had got no farther than that, and he was killed there. Ever since then the site has been called Tobhta Fhearchair, 'Farquhar's Site'.

One of his sons tried to reach the boundary of Staoiligearraidh;† if he had taken sanctuary there, no one would have dared to have harmed him. Clanranald's estate officers went after him, and when he was near the boundary, there was a man coming down from the machair to get horses, with halters in his hand. The estate officers shouted to this man to stop him, and when he was running past, the man threw the ropes around his feet and the lad fell, and before he could get up the estate officers were on top of him and killed him. The place has been called Lag Raghnaill, 'Ranald's Dell', ever since.

Another of Farquhar's sons, called Neil, went out to Loch Eynort on the east side of Uist, and stayed hidden there in the banks of the shore; but the estate officers discovered him. When he saw them coming, he made for the hill; and they shot arrows at him and felled him. That place has been called Crùib Nìll, 'Neil's Bed', ever since.

Another of Farquhar's sons was killed in the glen at Kildonan, where the estate officers found him asleep; they just cut his throat with a dagger. The lad choked with his

* Ormaclate.

† Staoiligearraidh, the home of the MacVurichs, hereditary bards of the Clanranalds (see p. 206), was a sanctuary.

own blood; and ever since the place has been called Àirigh an t-Slugain, 'The Sheiling of the Gullet'.

Not one of Farquhar's family escaped except his widow and her little child. She made her way to Eriskay Sound (at the south end of Uist), and hid with her child in a cave above the shore. One day she went to the shore for shellfish. The estate officers were still searching for the child and its mother. If the child turned out to be a boy, they were to bring its heart and lungs to Clanranald, so that he could be sure that no one survived who might take vengeance on him. Two of the estate officers found the child in the cave, and the mother on the shore, and one of them said to the child:

'Come out, my little fellow, so we may kill you.'

The child was gnawing a bone, and he said:

'Wait till I've finished gnawing my bone.'

'Well, indeed,' said the estate officer, 'I'll wait for that and wait longer still after you've gnawed it, we've done enough killing.'[3]

'How can we let him live,' said the other estate officer, 'when we have to bring his heart and his lungs to Clanranald?'

'I'll tell you how. You've a dog here. I've heard that nothing looks more like the heart and lungs of a child than the heart and lungs of a dog. We'll kill the dog, and take its heart and lungs to Clanranald, and there's two who'll escape, you and I, if the child ever wants to take revenge.'

Then they saw the child's mother coming up from the shore with a lapful of shellfish. When she saw the estate officers, she threw them away[4] and began to cry. The estate officers told her to keep quiet; and to try to get clear away from Uist altogether,[5] and of their plan. They killed the dog, and took its heart and lungs to Clanranald. The widow got away with the child to Knoydart to MacDonell of Glengarry, who took pity on her when he heard what had been done to her, and supported her and the child, and brought the child up and had him educated.

When the lad was past eighteen years of age, he learnt from his mother all that had happened; then he wanted to get to Uist to avenge his father and his brothers. MacDonell of

Glengarry told him he would let him go, and send soldiers with him, if he would promise not to trouble anyone except his opponent,[6] Clanranald. The lad promised.

The lad and the soldiers reached Uist, and Clanranald learnt that the 'child' was alive, and he was very much afraid that he had come to avenge his father and his brothers. Clanranald had a boat taken over to a place on the west side of Uist called Cumhabhaig, near Stonybridge, and had a crew ready standing by it, so that if he were pursued, the boat would be ready for him to escape.

Clanranald's grieve had to go in to Clanranald's bedroom every morning to tell him the latest news. The lad and the soldiers had landed at Eriskay Sound during the night, and had moved northwards along the machair. At daybreak they were past Gearrabhailteas, at a place called Sìdhein Chill Donain, 'The Fairy Mound of Kildonan'. The grieve was outside keeping watch. He saw them and went in to report to Clanranald. Clanranald asked him what he had seen.

'Nothing but a party of women on Sìdhein Chill Donain. They must have been at a waulking* somewhere. They were going quickly,' he said.

'Go and look again,' said Clanranald, 'and make sure they aren't soldiers.'

The grieve went out, and was outside for a while. The sun was now rising above the hills,† and the party was now down beside Loch na h-Eaglais, 'The Loch of the Church', and the grieve could see the glitter of their arms. The grieve went in to report to Clanranald. 'Oh,' he said, 'they are soldiers; I can see the glitter of their arms. They are down beside the loch there.'

'Oh, you damned fool,' said Clanranald, 'why didn't you tell me in time!' He jumped out of bed and drew his sword and cut off the grieve's head. He then made for the galley he had at Cumhabhaig, which was ready for him to escape in.

Farquhar's son saw him leaving the house and make for the shore. Clanranald was making off for his life,[7] but Farquhar's son was gaining on him. When Clanranald got down to the

* *i.e.* a party held by women for fulling home-made cloth by hand.

† All the hills in Uist are on the east side of the island.

shore he shouted to the crew of the galley to come in for him as quickly as they could. They came in, and just when Clanranald was stepping aboard, Farquhar's son caught him from behind and dragged him back, and killed him on the shore.

That was that; it was all right, it was only a life for a life. Farquhar's son and his party went up to Ormaclate, and Clanranald's son was kind enough to them. A place was made in the barn for the soldiers who were along with Farquhar's son; but he would only sleep in the same room as young Clanranald. They went to sleep. Farquhar's son had put his own sword on the table, and young Clanranald on the far side of the bed. He wasn't long in bed before he began to snore[8] and pretend to be asleep. Then he felt young Clanranald getting up and stretching over him trying to reach the sword on the table. He jumped up and caught young Clanranald and pushed him back on to the bed, and caught hold of the sword and pinned him to the bolster on the bed. He went out and awakened the soldiers, and they made off; and he never returned to Uist again afterwards.

18

BLACK DONALD OF THE 'CUCKOO'

THIS BLACK DONALD of the 'Cuckoo', one of the Clanranalds, lived at Caisteal Tioram;* and I understand that he was not a very good man. He had a gun, which he himself called the 'Cuckoo'; and he would say to anyone who did anything to him, 'I'll put the "Cuckoo" to you.' That's how he was called 'Black Donald of the "Cuckoo".' He hanged an old woman at Caisteal Tioram for stealing a snuff-box; and the spot has been called Tom na Caillich, 'the Old Woman's Mound', ever since.

Once Black Donald heard that there was a priest on Canna who wanted to go to Uist. Black Donald went with his boat to Canna. It seems there was an animal† that followed the Clanranalds—it followed him, Black Donald, anyway—its picture is on the stone on their grave at Howmore. The animal was following the boat, and the day became very bad. The animal was on the top of each wave that followed the boat. One of the crew said it looked as if they wouldn't manage, that they would be lost. Black Donald himself was steering, and the animal came alongside the boat. At last Black Donald beckoned to it,[1] and it came on board. The sea improved then, and they got to Canna.

Black Donald made a plan[2] to remove a plank from every boat on Canna, so that the priest could not get away to Uist.

* In Moidart, on the mainland.

† i.e. a familiar spirit.

He kept the priest seven weeks on Canna. One day, when the priest was down on the shore, he saw a boat going past, and he began to beckon to it.[3] The boat kept in to the shore, and the priest got into it, and where was it going to but Loch Eynort! When the boat took off from the land, the priest turned and looked back and said:

'I am not asking torment for your soul, but that your body may be kept here unburied as long as you've kept me.'

When Black Donald was dying on Canna, he was in terrible distress. People were going in to see him. There was a widow's son there, a brave, strong fellow. A whistle was heard outside the house, and the man who was in his death-throes on the bed got up to go out. Everyone who was there cleared out[4] but the widow's son, who caught hold of Black Donald and put him back on the bed. There was someone standing on a knoll opposite the house, and he was so tall that they could see the island of Rum between his legs. This person went away, and they saw him walking on the surface of the sea over to Rum. This has been the worst piece of sea ever since, the sea between Rum and Canna.

As long as Black Donald was alive, he was thanking God and the widow's son that the widow's son had kept him in the house; and when he died, there came bad weather; and his body was seven weeks on Canna, before they got away with it to Howmore* and the day they went with it, there came such a gale that they had to land at Peterport in Benbecula, and take the body from there overland to Howmore. Black Donald is buried there along with the other Clanranalds, and I understand that he was not the best of them.

* The ancient burial place of the Clanranalds in South Uist, see Story No. 14.

19

HOW CLANRANALD BUILT ORMACLATE HOUSE

THIS CLANRANALD was in France. He fell in love with[1] the daughter of a duke who was in France, and married her.* When he brought his bride to Lochboisdale, there were no motors, nor any conveyance better than ponies; and it was two bare-backed horses without saddles that were awaiting them at Lochboisdale. When they reached Ormaclate, there was only an old house there, and she, Lady Clanranald, wasn't too pleased.

One day when they were out for a walk she said to her husband that Uist was a terrible place, there was nothing to be seen but the ocean on the one side and mountains on the other, 'and,' she said, 'I can't see anything here that pleases me.'

'Don't you like it here at all?' said Clanranald.

'No I don't; and as for the house we live in, I'd be ashamed to ask any of my relations to come and see it; my father's hen-house is better than it is.'

'Well,' Clanranald said, 'the mountains are over there, and the ocean is down here; that can't be helped. But as for the house, we can build a house that will be just as good as your father's. When I took you away with me, I believed I could keep you just as well as your father had. Anything you need you have only to tell me, and I'll get it for you.'

She was a little more pleased then. Clanranald then began

* See p 205.

to build the house at Ormaclate. He brought the workmen who built it from France, and it took seven years to build. It cost a great deal of money, and money was not very plentiful in those times. When the time came to pay for everything, Clanranald had not enough to meet the account. If he couldn't meet it, the estate would have to be sold. His creditors were going to impound every beast he had. Clanranald then sent for a wise old man whom he had at Ormaclate, and told him that there was a chance he would lose the estate.

'Well,' said the old man, 'if you do what I tell you, you won't lose the estate yet, but if you don't, you will lose it.'

'What is that?'

'You have some big strong lads on the estate?'

'Yes.'

'Well, get eight of them—how many can sit at your table at meals?'

'Fourteen.'

'How many visitors do you expect?'

'Four.'

'Well, get eight of the strongest lads you have on the estate, and dress them up, and give every one of them a *sgian dubh*, 'black knife'.* Kill an ox, and get a cask of whisky; and have the lads ready to sit at the table along with you when the visitors arrive. It won't make any difference for you and your lady to sit along with them for one day. Let the dinner be as Highland as can be—neither fork nor knife there, just the fingers. And see that the man who pours out the drinks for you uses quaichs† and not horn tumblers.'

Clanranald met his visitors outside the house; they told him they were going to look at every animal on the place.

'Oh, right enough,' said Clanranald, 'but come in and have something to eat first.'

They went in. The eight men I've mentioned were sitting at the table already. The visitors had eyes for nothing on or at the table but the frightful objects that confronted them. The man who was to pour out the drinks, Clanranald's

* A traditional Highland weapon.

† The quaichs would hold a bottleful, so Aonghus Beag tells me.

waiter, came in with a big tin jug.[3] Every one of eight men was given a quaichful, and it hardly moistened their lips! The visitors sat down to the meal, but all they could do was to watch these eight lads.

When the dinner was over, they got up and went out, and Clanranald got up and went out with them.

'Who were those lads along with you at the table?' asked one of the visitors.

'Ho!' said Clanranald, 'they're my bodyguard.[4] I have three hundred like them.'

'Three hundred?'

'Yes.'

'No wonder you're in debt if you have three hundred of them!'

'Yes, they're my bodyguard.'

'Strange that they sit at the same table as yourself.'

'Oh, they're always at the same table as myself.'

'Oh, well then, we needn't bother to go and look at your livestock today; we'll take your word for them.'

'Just as you like,' said Clanranald.

He told them he had so many deer, so many horses, and so many head of cattle.

'Well,' said one of the visitors, 'we'll be leaving today. When we get back (to Edinburgh) we'll try to do the best for you we can.'

'Very good,' said Clanranald.

When the visitors got back (to Edinburgh) they held a meeting, and told of what they had seen, and how it was no wonder Clanranald was in debt, considering the army he had raised, and that it would be a shameful thing to demand payment. They had been pleased enough to get away with their lives, when they saw what his men were like. 'An ox's bone in their mouths,' one said, 'was like a rabbit's leg in the mouth of a cat. And a big tin jug for filling the wine glasses! We think that the best thing that can be done is to cancel his debts and renew his credit.' So it turned out. All Clanranald's debts were cancelled, and his credit was as good as ever, and he finished the Big House at Ormaclate.

20

MACLEOD OF DUNVEGAN AND IAIN GARBH OF RAASAY

THERE WAS a man on the Isle of Skye called Iain Garbh mac 'Ille Chaluim Rathasaidh, 'Rough John, son of the servant of St Columba, of Raasay', who had the island of Raasay to himself and refused to pay a penny of rent for it to MacLeod of Dunvegan. Iain Garbh was a very strong man, and MacLeod was afraid to go and ask him for it.

One day a bully[1] came to Dunvegan Castle and threatened to impose cess on MacLeod if MacLeod didn't find a man who could take him on.*

'Well,' said MacLeod, 'I've a man who'll take you on, but he's not at home.'

'Will it be long before he comes?'

'Three days,' said MacLeod.

'Well, we'll wait till he comes.'

MacLeod went and sent a servant with a horse and a letter to Raasay to Iain Garbh, asking him to come as quickly as he could as he had some particular business with him. Iain Garbh did not know what business MacLeod could have to discuss with him. seeing that they were on such bad terms,

* 'It was the custom with the bullies in those days to demand a cess from the country, to which every gentleman and commoner was to contribute, unless the Laird could find a person who was able to defy them with the sword.' W. C. MacKenzie, *The Western Isles*, p. 130.

but he thought he would go anyway. He ate a quarter of an ox on Raasay before he went, and he walked from Raasay to Dunvegan.* When he arrived, MacLeod met him outside the house, and welcomed him, shaking his hand.

'I'm very pleased you've come, Iain. Come in.'

'All right, but before that I'll find out why you've sent for me in such a hurry.'

'You'll learn that yet. Come in.'

Iain Garbh suspected that MacLeod might have a plan to destroy him, seeing that they were on such bad terms; and he refused to go inside the castle until MacLeod told him what business he had to discuss with him.

Well, as MacLeod hadn't told him at first, he didn't care to speak of it, but 'come on in and I'll tell you'.

'If it can't be told outside I'll have to return where I came from,' said Iain Garbh.

He turned around to go back. MacLeod went back into the castle. The bully was awaiting him inside.

'Has the man come?' he said.

'No,' said MacLeod, 'but there is a blackguard of a Highlander down the road there, and if you'll go after him and give him a good slap on the backside,[2] I'll give you five pounds.'

'I'll give him that.'

The bully went off after Iain Garbh. When Iain Garbh heard his footsteps coming behind him, he thought it was MacLeod, and he slowed down. He was wearing his plaid.† The bully lifted the plaid and gave him a good slap on the backside. Iain Garbh jumped round and caught him and gave him one squeeze and let him go, and the bully was dead, with all his bones broken. Iain Garbh kept on. After he got home he discovered what business MacLeod had had for him. If he had known what it was, he would not have left the house though they had destroyed him! MacLeod got out of it neatly enough by trickery!

* About thirty miles.

† The old Highland dress worn before 1746.

21

MACVURICH ASKING FOR THE WIND

MACVURICH LIVED at Staoiligearraidh in South Uist. Once he and his son were away at Glasgow. They were preparing to return home to South Uist, and a merchant who belonged to Arisaig was going to come with them. When they left Canna (the last harbour on the way to Uist) MacVurich said that today each one of them would get his request. He would leave the first request to the merchant, and the second to his son, and would have the third himself. MacVurich then asked for the wind:

'A South wind from calm Gailbhinn,*
As the King of Elements ordained;
A breeze without rowing or clewing
That would do nothing faulty for us.'[1]

'What a soft supplication!' said the merchant. He wanted to get to Arisaig.

'Well, won't you ask for it yourself now?' said MacVurich. The merchant said:

'A North wind as hard as a rod
That would urge her above the gunwale,
Like a roedeer in her strength
Running down the hard peak of a hillock.'

* See p. 17.

There came a storm against them from the north, and they looked like being in Arisaig!*

'Well, my son,' said MacVurich, 'it's time for you to ask.'

His son got up and said:

'If in cold hell there's a wind
That turns the waves' sides to red,
O Conan! send it after me
In fiery flaming sparks!
Though to the bottom the merchant goes,
Let me and my father and my dog land!'

Then there came a storm behind them, and when they were coming in to Uishnish Point† in Uist, the boat broke in two pieces; and MacVurich came ashore on one of them, and his son and his son's dog came ashore on the other. The merchant was drowned; and MacVurich never allowed any man to make a request of this sort ever afterwards.

* Arisaig is about as far east of Canna as South Uist is west, *i.e.* about thirty miles.

† Uishnish Point is the big promontory on the east side of South Uist, north of Loch Eynort which was formerly the main harbour. It is now the site of a lighthouse.

22

MACVURICH AND THE CHANGELING

MACVURICH LIVED at Staoiligearraidh in South Uist; he had tenants there, who used to come to work for him, when he had work to be done; particularly at harvest time, the women used to come to reap for him.* Once there was a woman who had a small child, and word came to her from MacVurich that she must come to reap for him. The only thing she could do was to take the child with her when she went, which she did; and she left the child on a stook of corn when she began to reap. MacVurich himself was along with them. They hadn't been reaping very long, when the child began to cry on the stook. The woman started over to it to give it the breast, but MacVurich turned on her angrily and told her to go back to work and let the child be.

The child kept on crying unceasingly. The woman started over to it again, but MacVurich made her come back and stay at work, saying that this kind of thing wouldn't do. The child could not get its breath for crying, and the third time, the woman went, paying no heed to MacVurich; she lifted up the child and gave it the breast, and the child would have drunk twice as much milk as she had! She went home, and put on a pan to make porridge for the child; but the pan wouldn't do, she needed the biggest pot in the kitchen! The child ate all it could get, and never stopped crying. Then she understood very well that it wasn't her own child at all.

* With the sickle.

So she went to see MacVurich, to see what he could do for her.

'There's nothing,' he said, 'but for you to put up with him; you wouldn't pay heed to me before. You have him now, you must put up with him as best you can!'

She went to see him again, and said she would do anything in the world he asked of her, if he could help her at all.

'Well,' said MacVurich, 'I don't know who can help you, but there's a man in Lewis called Bowie; go and find him; he'll put the changeling away. When you arrive, he won't be in at all, there will be no one at home but his wife. And by all you've ever seen, don't sit at the far side of the fire, but stay at the near side. When Bowie comes home, he'll be wild enough at you, and he'll ask you to clear out. You come down a little from the fire, and say "Red pig".* When he tells you the second time to get out, come a little farther down and say "Red pig". The third time he tells you to get out, stand inside the door of the house, and say "Red pig".'

The woman went away with the child on her back, and kept on until she reached Lewis. She asked where 'Bowie's' house was, and was told, and when she reached it, she went in. Only his wife was at home. The wife asked her where she had come from, and she told her. She was as sorry for her as could be, and asked her to come up to the fire, and began to prepare a place for her, but the woman wouldn't go past the fire at all. She sat down at the near (door) side of the fire. She hadn't been there long when she heard Bowie coming. He came in and looked at her.

'Who's this straggler you have here today?' he said to his wife.

'Oh, she's only a poor woman who's come all the way from South Uist.'

'Poor or rich, put her out of the door, get her out of here!'

The woman drew a little towards him.

'Red pig,' she said, in a very small voice.

'What are you saying?' he said. 'Get outside the door or I'll kick you out!'

'Red pig,' she said, a little louder, and drawing a little closer.

* Aonghus Beag tells me that this was the coat of arms of the Bowries.

'Red or blue,' he said, 'clear out of here, or I'll take care I never see you again, even if I have to bury you alive if you won't go away.'

She stood in the doorway. 'Red pig,' she said, louder still.

Bowie turned and recited a verse. At the end of the verse he said:

'*Fàg uchd na mnatha bochd.* Leave the breast of the poor woman. Clear out of here!' At this the changeling leapt out of her bosom, and her own child was thrown into it through the door. Bowie* turned to her and said:

'Ho, MacVurich needn't have sent you all this way; he could have done this for you himself; it must be that you didn't do as he told you.'

'I'm sure that's what it was,' she said.

The woman returned to Uist with her own child; that's how she got clear of the changeling.

* *Mac 'Ille Bhuidhe* in Gaelic.

STORIES OF WITCHCRAFT

23

'KINTAIL AGAIN'

ONCE THERE was a crofter-fisherman in Kintail, who used to go to sea to fish every day with his sons. One day when they were out fishing, the weather became very bad. They had to clear a headland before they could get into harbour. The old man saw that the boat could not clear the headland, and that the only way they could save themselves was to let her run ashore. Some people saw them, and got together, and helped them to get ashore. But the boat's keel was broken.

After they had gone home and had a meal, the old man thought it would be just as necessary for them to go out fishing tomorrow as it had been today; so he went to the wood to see if he could find a tree that would make a new keel for the boat, taking an axe with him. He searched the wood, but he couldn't find a tree that satisfied him. Even if he had found one, he would still have had to get a carpenter to saw it, and he didn't know when it would have been ready. The tree he found that was of the right size, had a bend in it; he couldn't find one that suited him.

At last night fell. He was trying to get out of the wood, and some time during the night he succeeded. He didn't know where to go; but then he saw a light some way off, and he made straight for the light. When he reached it, he found a neat little house there, and he went in. There were three old women inside; one of them, who was sitting by the fire, was extremely old. Another was tidying the house. He asked them if he could stay until the morning. They looked at each other, and one of them said reluctantly that he could.

They asked where he had come from, and he told them. They told him how far he was from his home, and said he had gone a distance on the wrong way.

After a while, the one who was at the fireside got up and joined the others, and they were talking to each other on the other side of the room. The fisherman thought they were talking about him, but he didn't attach much importance to it. One of the old women turned to him and said that he had better go down* to the room at the other end of the house, where there was a bed in which he could sleep until the morning. He said that he didn't need a bed, he could manage at the fireside.

'Oh, you'd better go to bed, you'll feel better for walking tomorrow. Take the light, you can leave it burning,' she said.

He got up and went. In the room he found nothing but a bed and a table, and a big chest over beneath the window. He went to bed, but he didn't fall asleep; he was worried about his family at home, thinking they might be looking for him. He put out the light. Then he noticed one of the old women come to the door. He pretended to be asleep, and she came in, and went over to the chest, and took out a bonnet, and tied it on her head. 'London again!'[1] said the old woman. Away she went; he didn't get another glimpse of her! Then he heard another of the old women come to the door. She didn't wait so long at the door as the first; she went over and took a bonnet out of the chest and tied it on her head, and all she said was 'London again!' just like the first one. Then he noticed the third old woman at the door. She was afraid she was late; she went straight to the chest and took out another bonnet and put it on her head and said 'London again!' following the others, and he was left alone.

He thought he would not stay there any longer, but start on his way home. He got up and dressed. When he was ready to go, he thought he would look to see what was in the chest, since he had such a good chance. He opened the chest, but

* See p. 207.

all there was inside was one or two of the bonnets he had seen the old women put on. He tried one on his head, and it fitted him very well. 'London again!' he said. Out he went and in a twinkle he was standing in a whisky cellar in London. The three old women were there, stretched out dead drunk. He didn't bother about the old women, but he turned off the spigots—which were running as the old women hadn't closed them, being drunk. He then tried a mouthful of every kind of whisky there—he needed it all right!

He thought he would sit down, as the cellar was so close. He took off the bonnet, and put it in his pocket. His first awakening was someone in the cellar kicking him! There was no sign of the old women.

'You rascal, you've been coming here long enough! You've ruined me! But at last we've got you!'

The police were sent for, and the poor fisherman was taken away to prison. Then he was tried in court. He told the court what had happened to him, and how he came to be there. Who'd believe that? No one! He didn't need to be telling such lies. The loss had been going on a long time, and it wasn't what had been drunk by any means, but what had been spilt. All the policemen and all the detectives in London had been unable to catch the thief, until they caught the fisherman. He was sentenced to be hanged.

The day he was to be hanged, a large crowd collected near the gallows. The hangman brought the fisherman out and took him on to the scaffold and put the noose round his neck, and told him that he had now ten minutes in which to say anything he wanted to say.

'Oh, I haven't anything to say that I haven't said already,' said the fisherman. 'You are hanging an innocent man.'

'You're anything but that,' said the hangman.

The fisherman put his hand in his pocket, and what did he find but the bonnet.

'May I put this bonnet on my head before you hang me?' he said.

'Oh, you can put anything you like on your head,' said the hangman.

The fisherman tied the bonnet on his head. 'Kintail again!'[2]

he said. Away he went with the gallows through the sky! On the way he threw the hangman off the gallows into the sea, and the hangman was drowned. The fisherman with the gallows came to Kintail; and he had a fine straight plank that would make a keel for his boat!

24

THE WOMAN WHO WAS SHOD WITH HORSESHOES

ONCE THERE was a farmer who kept two farm-servants called Donald and James. They used to sleep in a bothy. Donald was getting very poorly, complaining every morning that his bones were so sore that he couldn't do a turn. He was steadily wasting away. James was wondering what was wrong with his companion, who wasn't complaining of any pain, or of anything except his bones. Donald used to sleep on the outside of the bed, and James on the inside, nearest the wall.

One night Donald said to James:

'Will you sleep in my place tonight? I'm not sleeping well there at all.'

'Yes, I can see that,' said James.

They changed places, and Donald slept on the inside of the bed instead of James. He was lying half asleep and half awake, when he heard the door being opened, and whom did he see come in but the farmer's wife, with a horse's bridle. She shook the bridle in the face of James, who was asleep on the outside of the bed, and said two or three words. James turned into a horse and jumped out of the bed, and she put the bridle on his head and went out with him.

'My word,' said Donald to himself, 'this is what must have been happening to me. No wonder I was miserable.'

Between then and daybreak the farmer's wife came back with him, and took the bridle off his head, and he became a man as he had been before, asleep on the bed. When it was time to get up in the morning, Donald called on him to rise. When James tried to move:

'My God, upon my soul, I won't get up, I can't do it. I'm done for.'

'What's wrong?'

'I don't know, I think every bone in my body is broken. If you've felt like this every night you've slept here, it's no wonder you were miserable.'

'Tut,' said Donald, 'that may be so, but one night wouldn't do it. There must be something accursed around here. But we must get up, all the same.'

They got up, and went out to work. The next night when they were going to sleep, Donald said:

'Will you sleep in my place tonight?'

'Indeed no, nor tomorrow night,' said James, 'and I don't envy you a bit going to sleep there.'

'Well, I'll have to sleep somewhere.'

They went to bed, and Donald put off going to sleep, and tried to stay awake. He was biting himself to keep himself awake. Then he heard the farmer's wife coming. She came in with the bridle, and shook the bridle in his face, saying the same two or three words. Donald turned into a horse and jumped out of the bed, this time awake. She went and rode over the sea on him, and they came to an island, where there was a big house, and a lot more accursed persons like herself engaged in every kind of unlawfulness[1] there. She took the bridle off Donald's head, and when this was done, he became a man as he had been before. There were plenty of others like him there, standing asleep like statues.

Donald looked to see where she had put the bridle, and went and got it, and when the coven was dispersing he stood at the door, and when the farmer's wife came out, he shook the bridle in her face and said the words that she had said to him, and she turned into a grey pony before him. He put the bridle on her and jumped on her back. When they were crossing the sea, she asked, hoping he'd say something blessed:

'What do you say when you shut the door?'

'Ride on, you devil!'

'What do you say when you get up in the morning?'

'Ride on, you devil!'

When they had reached dry land, and arrived at the farmer's farm, Donald rode her to the smithy that was there, where they always went. The blacksmith was asleep. Donald woke him, shouting to him to get up.

'What's wrong?' said the smith.

'Get up as quick as you ever did, and shoe this pony for my master; he has to go away today.'

'O son of the Evil One,' said the smith, 'you and your pony! This isn't the time to be coming here to shoe ponies!'

'My master didn't know he would have to leave until a very short time ago,' said Donald. 'Get up as quick as you ever did!'

The smith got up and began to make the smithy fire, and Donald brought in the pony. The smith looked at her and said:

'Where did you get this pony? I've never seen her before.'

'May the Devil fly off with you, shoe her, that's what I'm asking you to do, not to appraise her.'

The smith began to put the shoes on her. While he was shoeing her, the tears were streaming from her eyes.

'Well, well,' said the smith, 'I've never seen such a soft beast. Look at how the tears are streaming from her eyes!'

'May the Devil make tears stream from your own eyes if you don't get a move on!' said Donald.

'Go along with her now,' said the smith, 'and may you go to hell with her. I'm clear of her.'[3]

Donald went off with her, the shoes striking sparks from the high road. When they arrived, he took the bridle off her head, and she became a woman as she had been before, and went into the farmhouse. Donald went into the bothy.

In the morning when they had got up and gone out to the stables, who came in but the farmer, lamenting and crying that his wife was nearly dead.

'What's wrong with her?' said Donald.

'Oh, she's dying, she's done for.'

'Is she as bad as that?'

'Indeed she is,' said the farmer.

'Well, I'd like to see her myself while she's still alive.'

'You can come in, then.'

Donald went in with the farmer. The farmer's wife was lying with her face to the wall.

'You're looking very poorly,' said Donald.

'You keep away from me,' she said.

Donald went and put his hand under the bedclothes and caught hold of her arm and dragged it out. There was a horseshoe on her palm.

'Do you see that?' said Donald, turning to the farmer.

'Aye, aye!' the farmer said.

Her feet were caught and pulled out from under the covers. There was a horseshoe on each of her feet, as well as on each of her hands.

'There are the four horseshoes I had put on her last night,' said Donald. 'No wonder,' he said to her, 'that you made me miserable, riding me at a gallop every night, but that's what I've done to you in return.'

'Well,' said the farmer to his wife, 'you'll not do this kind of thing at all, you're not going to escape.'

There was nothing for it but to catch hold of her, make a fire, and put her on it. She was burnt. That is the way that witches were treated, whenever they were discovered. Burning was the final penalty inflicted on them.[4]

Donald was all right at night ever afterwards; and he worked for the farmer for a long time after the witch wife had been burnt.

25

THE LAIRD, THE PRIEST, AND THE EVIL ONE

THERE was once a laird, who grew old and died. He had a son who was to inherit his estate in his place. When his son went through the books, he found that the estate was heavily burdened with debts. He didn't know what to do. 'Everyone will say that I squandered it.' He went out one evening and sat on a seat that was in a plantation a little way from the castle, where his father used to rest when he was out for a walk. The young laird sat and thought what could be done; it looked as if the estate would have to be sold.

A stranger appeared beside him, and said:

'Your father's debts are worrying you.'

'Yes, they are,' said the young laird.

'What would you give anyone who gave you what would relieve you of the debts on the estate?'

'I don't know what I wouldn't give him.'

'Would you go with him?' asked the stranger.

'Upon my word, I think I would go with him anywhere.'

'Well, meet me here at ten o'clock tomorrow night,' said the stranger, 'and I'll give you every penny that's owing on the estate.'

The young laird went home. The matter worried him, and he began to wonder what kind of person it was he had to deal with. He was afraid that it might be someone uncanny.[1] He went to see the priest and told him about it.

'Take care you aren't being deceived,' said the priest. 'Mind that it isn't the Evil One. But all the same you must meet him, as you promised to do so.'

'I was thinking I wouldn't go on with it at all,' said the young laird.

'Oh, that won't do,' said the priest. 'Since you promised to meet him, you must do it. But see you get there early, before he does, and take this little book with you, and be reading it. If he approaches you, hold the book out to him. If he takes the book, you can go along with him.'

The young laird went back home. At the time he promised to meet him, the stranger appeared.

'Well, here you are,' he said.

'Yes.'

'Come here, then, so I can pay you what will meet the debts on the estate.'

'Oh, I think I'll put up with things as they are,' said the young laird.

'That won't do. You must take it now I've come with it.'

'No, I won't take it at all. I'd sooner remain as I am, even if I have to give up the estate.'

'Oh, that won't do, you promised you would go with me.' The stranger went over to catch him. The young laird held out the book. 'Take hold of that,' he said, 'and I'll go with you.'

'Aye, aye!' said the stranger. 'You've been with a man of learning today! Aren't you going to come at all?'

'No.'

The stranger then started to turn into the ugliest kind of shapes before him. The young laird kept on reading the book. At last, when the cock crew, the stranger disappeared in a ball of fire. The young laird heard a noise[2] where the stranger had been, a clinking like the sound of money. When the day lightened, he went over to it. There was a sack there, full of gold and silver.[3] He carried it home, and counted the money, and there was every penny owing on the estates in the sack!

But what did he hear next but that a bank had been robbed of exactly the same sum of money! He had never been in such a fix. 'It must be the bank's money that I've got. If I take it home, I'll be on the gallows! No one will believe me.'

He went to see the priest, and told him what had happened, and 'it's exactly the same amount that was taken from the bank that I've got in the sack,' he said.

'Well, if it is,' said the priest, 'it wasn't you who stole it, and they're only after the one who did steal it. Pay the debts on the estate with it. But I advise you never to spend a night at an inn, because the Evil One is always in such places.'

So the young laird went home and paid off every penny of debt on the estate with the Evil One's money, and had it clear of debt, and was very well off. He had a driver to drive him every time he went away from home. One time when he was being driven home at night, a blizzard started blowing in his face. The driver said:

'I'm afraid we won't be able to get home, but if we're lucky we'll reach a hotel.'

'Oh, we'll not stay at a hotel at all,' said the young laird. 'Keep ahead with the horses, and we'll manage on foot from where they give up.'

My word, this didn't please the driver. When they reached a hotel, he went into the close with the horses, and said:

'Well, if you're going to keep on, keep on; I'm not going to lose my life on your account or anyone else's.'

The driver went and unharnessed the horses and put them in the stable. The young laird went into the kitchen and sat down on a box of coal there. It wasn't long before there was a knocking at the front door. The hotelkeeper went to the door. The person at the door asked him to send such and such a man out to him as he had something he wanted to talk to him about. The hotelkeeper went back inside and asked if there was such a man staying in the hotel. He was told there was not. He returned to the front door. 'I haven't got that man here at all,' he said.

'Yes you have, he's in the kitchen sitting on a box of coal; sent him out here.'

The hotelkeeper went into the kitchen and told the young

laird that there was someone at the front door who wanted to see him, and that he must go out to see him.

'I won't go at all,' he said.

The hotelkeeper went back to the front door and told the stranger there that the young laird would not come out to see him.

'Unless he comes out I won't leave one stone of your building standing on another,'[4] said the stranger.

The hotelkeeper went back and took hold of the young laird by the shoulder.

'Tut, tut, won't you go to the door to speak to the man, whoever he is?'

'I won't go outside, but I'll go and stand inside the door.'

'Well, do that at least,' said the hotelkeeper.

The young laird went to the door. There was someone outside the door with a pony. 'Well,' said the person who was outside, 'I've some particular business to discuss with this man, so every one of you go to your rooms, as I don't want anyone to overhear it. Go to your rooms!'

Everyone went to his room. After they did so, they heard such a gunshot as they had never heard before. They all came out of their rooms. There was a man lying stretched out outside the front door. There was no sign of the pony. The man at the door had been killed by the young laird!

The dead man was lifted up and put in one of the taprooms. The young laird was put in prison, to be locked up there until he was tried,[5] for having killed the man. 'I didn't kill him at all,' he said. 'Can I get someone to take a letter to the priest?'

'Yes.'

He sent a letter to the priest, and the priest came to see him.

'Didn't I advise you never to spend a night at an inn?' said the priest.

'Well, you did, but it wasn't my fault. My driver wouldn't go any farther, and I didn't know what to do.'

The priest came out. He asked the hotelkeeper, 'Where is the man who was killed?'

'He's in one of the tap-rooms here.'

The priest went to look at him. Two young fellows came into the tap-room to have a dram, and called for drams. One of them kept looking at the dead man, and began to cry.

'What's making you cry, my lad?' asked the priest.

'Nothing in particular.'

'There must be some reason.'

'Well, the reason is, the day before yesterday I buried my father, and I never saw anyone more like him[6] than the man lying there.'

'I'm sure,' said the priest. 'Well, that is your father there, and you'll have to bury him again.'

'Oh no, my father's where I buried him.'

'Go and see if your father's where you buried him, then. When the Devil failed to get hold of that other Christian, the plan he made was to dig up your father's body, and make the gunshot himself, and leave your father's body outside the door. Go and see if your father's where you buried him.'

The young man went to the graveyard and opened his father's grave, and there was no sign of his father's body in it.

'Well, there he is, then, you must bury him again.'

The young laird was set free then; and he said to himself that he would never again spend a night in an inn. That's the story of his encounter with the Evil One!

GHOST STORIES

26

WILD ALASDAIR OF ROY BRIDGE

THIS WILD ALASDAIR lived at Roy Bridge. He was a very rough kind of man.[1] That's why he was called Wild Alasdair. It was a custom in the district to have dances at times, especially at Christmas. They used to collect money to buy the drinks. This year they collected a sum to buy drinks for their Christmas dance. There was no one more suitable to go to get the drink than Alasdair.

Alasdair went off with his pony. In those days men always used to carry a big stick or wooden staff. Alasdair arrived at the inn. There were people drinking there, and he spent a while along with them. Then he bought the whisky for the dance and tied it on the pony's back.

When Alasdair reached Roy Bridge on his way home, the pony stopped, and refused to go any farther, but began to back. Alasdair was cursing the pony, and beating it, but the pony would not go on. Alasdair then looked to see what was keeping the pony back. There was a man sitting at the far end of the bridge. Alasdair shouted to him to clear out or he would split him against the bridge. The man paid no heed. Alasdair went over and hit him across the back with his stick, and the stick flew into pieces off his back as if it had struck an iron bar.[2] The man got up and came to grips with Alasdair. Though Alasdair was big and brave, he could not stand up[3] to the man on the bridge, and he was beaten until he was unable to walk.

The pony went home. When it arrived, Alasdair's wife raised the alarm[4] that Alasdair was dead somewhere. A search was made for him. He met them on the road crawling home on his hands and knees; he couldn't stand. They took him home. They thought there was nothing wrong with him but the drink, something which had happened before often enough. Alasdair spent a fortnight in bed, and recovered. He didn't say a word about what had happened to him.

One night after he and his wife had gone to bed, they heard the cows lowing in the byre, which was behind the house.

'Goodness,' said his wife, 'one of the cows has got loose, you'd better get up in case she kills the others.' 'Oh'—Alasdair thought of something else—'they'll be all right.' The cows kept on lowing. At last his wife said, 'I'd better get up myself.'

When Alasdair saw she was going to get up, he said to himself that she mustn't go out, anyway. 'Stay where you are then, I'll go out.' He put on his clothes and went out, and when he got out, the man was before him in the door of the byre. What Alasdair had got at Roy Bridge, he got again that night, until he was left lying half dead there.

When his wife got tired of waiting for him, she went out herself. Alasdair was stretched out unable to move. She managed to drag him into the house and put him in bed. Afterwards he told her that this was what had happened to him at Roy Bridge the night he was bringing back the whisky. From that time he was always called 'Alasdair of the Ghost'. He was afraid to go outside the house after dark. He thought he would clear out of the place entirely, sell his belongings and go to America. So he did. He went to America, and when he got there he found it was but a wild place, nothing but forest. He managed to make a cabin in the forest, which was very thick. He began to cut a track through the forest to the cabin, so he could find his way there any time. He was only spending what little he had, there wasn't a penny coming in.

One night when he was coming home, what did he see but a man in front of him in this tunnel[5] who looked like the men who had met him at Roy Bridge. Alasdair didn't know whether to keep on or to turn back. Then the man spoke to him.

'Well, you think I'm the man who met you at Roy Bridge!'

'Yes,' said Alasdair.

'I'm he, right enough,' said the man, 'and it's just as easy for me to give you tonight what I gave you at Roy Bridge. You thought I wouldn't come to America at all, since you came over; but I came with you. But I'll not touch you tonight, as I think you've been through enough. The best thing you can do now is to return where you came from while you have enough to take you back. I shall not trouble you again. You were taking to do with a lot of things you had no business to. Neither will you learn who I am.'

Alasdair didn't want to return. He could barely afford the fare. When he got back to Roy Bridge there was nothing for him there. The people there had such pity on him, that everyone who had bought anything at his roup, gave it back to him to make him up as he was before. That's what happened to 'Alasdair of the Ghost'.

27

THE LITTLE OLD LADY OF ÀIRD MHÌCHEIL

ONCE THERE was a man who lived in Stonybridge here called Red Donald of Àird Mhìcheil; he had a house down on Àird Mhìcheil point, north of Stonybridge. He worked for a man called James MacLellan, who kept two or three farm-servants; Red Donald was his grieve.

They used to see the ghost of a woman down at Àird Mhìcheil at night, and no one dared to go there alone after dark. They called her Cailleach Bheag an Rubha, 'the little old lady of the point'. One time there was to be a ball at Ormaclate here, the harvest home ball, and the lads who were working under Red Donald were going to the ball, and Red Donald meant to go there too. But he didn't want to go to the ball until after the horses had been fed, which would be after eight o'clock. That wouldn't do for the lads, but 'we must go to the ball, likely we'll come back and feed and water the horses at eight o'clock'.

That was all right. They went off to the ball, but when eight o'clock came, not one of them would leave the ball along with Red Donald to feed the horses, for fear of meeting the 'little old lady of the point'. The ball was too good to leave. There was nothing for Red Donald but to go himself. The stable was down on the point. Red Donald went in. The first horse he untied after going inside the door, jumped into the stall on top of him. He looked and saw the little old lady sitting outside the stable door.

There was a window at the end of the stable; Donald turned to get out by the window, but when he got there, she was in the window before him. Then he went back and tried the door, but when he was rushing out of the door, he hit his head on the lintel and fell inside the door. When he lifted his head, the little old lady was sitting opposite him.

'God between you and me,' said Donald.

'Oh, I'll not harm you,' she said.

Something that she had left (in this world) without putting right, was troubling her; and she told it to Red Donald.

'Well,' said Donald, 'they won't believe me, even if I tell them.'

'Yes they will,' she said. 'A sign of it will stay with you. They'll believe you all right. You go to such and such a woman in South Uist and tell her never to do again what she was doing a week ago last Saturday.'

Well, Red Donald went to this woman and told her what the little old lady had asked him to tell her.

'Oh,' she said, 'I don't know what it was I was doing. I had a little cream in the house, and I didn't get time to churn it, and I began to churn it on Saturday night. I'm sure it was Sunday before I had finished, if that's what it is.'

The spot where Donald's head had hit the lintel of the door was as white as snow, while the rest of his hair was as red as live coals. The little old lady told him who she was; she had belonged to Bornish. She was never seen again. That's one of the ghosts that were seen in South Uist.

28

THE MERMAID

THERE WAS a man living at Lochboisdale called Donald MacLeod, whose people belonged to the Isle of Mull. He was at the East Coast fishing, and one morning when they were coming in from the sea, running before a strong wind with two reefs in their sail, they noticed a mermaid come to the surface aft of them, behind the boat. The boat was running before the wind with two reefs, and the mermaid was keeping up with them. The skipper threw out a herring, and the mermaid remained on the surface. The skipper then asked all the others to throw out a herring, and they all threw out a herring in turn, and she didn't submerge. Donald threw out a herring; as soon as he threw it, the mermaid went under. When the skipper got into port, he took Donald ashore with him and paid his wages and sent him home. He asked him to take care of himself, and said that no matter how long a time it would be, Donald would be drowned some day as sure as anyone ever was.

Donald stayed ashore a year. At the end of that time, a merchant in Loch Skipport came to Lochboisdale and bought a boat from the hotelkeeper there, and was going to take it to Loch Skipport.* He thought that Donald was the best man he could take with him. Donald went with him, and unfortunately the day changed and the weather became very bad from the north-east, and the boat was wrecked off Uishnish Point, and neither of them was ever found, Donald or the merchant.

* Loch Skipport is on the east side of South Uist, near the north end of the island. Uishnish Point is the large headland on the east side of Uist between Loch Eynort and Skipport. The whole coast is completely exposed to easterly winds.

Note

Major Finlay MacKenzie the present proprietor of the Lochboisdale Hotel, makes the following comment on this story:

'I was much interested in Angus MacLellan's story. I remember the incident perfectly. My father bought the boat concerned from a man called Duff who had something to do with the factory on Orosay in Castlebay harbour. She was known locally as the *Duffac*, and was about sixteen feet long. Mackechern, Loch Skipport, bought this boat from my father, and started to sail her for Loch Skipport with a Mull man called MacLeod, whose family were resident at Lochboisdale, on the croft lately owned by John MacLellan, carpenter.

'It was a lovely day and I saw them start off from below our garden, and watched them till they were half-way out of the loch. The Uishnish lightkeepers had her under observation for a considerable time. They were rather interested in her lines. She was rigged entirely different to anything here in those days. She had a round stern, a bowsprit, mainsail and jibsail, all of which could be handled from the stern sheets. The Head Keeper saw her last about a mile S.W. of Uishnish, laid down his glasses and went away to do something. He came back ten minutes later and the boat had completely disappeared. No trace was ever found of the boat or crew. I sometimes think that a basking shark or perhaps a small whale had surfaced underneath the boat and capsized her. Of course, the facts will never be known.'

My own guess is that the culprit was a killer whale, as I know from experience that killer whales are present in the Minch. They are very dangerous animals and quite capable of attacking small boats, and several unexplained accidents of this type may well have been caused by them.

J. L. C.

29

'SHIFT THREE POINTS TO THE STARBOARD'

ONCE A Uistman was sailing. One night the sailors were in the fo'c'sle talking about ghosts, as people often do when they get together. There was an Englishman there who didn't believe there were any such things as ghosts at all; he said they were something that only Highlanders believed in. But there was an old Lewisman there who said:

'Well, indeed, I don't know; I've been at sea since I was fourteen years old; I've only seen a ghost once, if it was one; I don't know if it was a ghost or an apparition. I'll tell you about it.

'When I first went to sea, it wasn't so easy to get a ship as it is today. Only a good hand could get one. This night, I was to take the wheel until midnight. The captain was going to turn in, and he said to the mate, "See you steer her well tonight; she wasn't steered well last night, as I could see for myself today. There's no use taking on someone who can't steer when there's many a good hand in Glasgow who'd be very glad to get the chance of the job."

'I took this to be meant for me; anyway, I took the wheel. The ship was very difficult to steer in a following wind. A man came up from the bow and told me to "shift three points to the starboard". I shifted. The mate was on the other side of the bridge, and he noticed I had changed course, and came over.

'"What course are you on now?" he said.

'I told him.

'"Is that the course you were given?"

'"No, but a man came up from the bow and told me to shift three points to the starboard."

'"Who was it?"

'"I don't know."

'"Are you trying to make a fool of me, or of yourself?" said the mate.

'"I'm not making a fool of anyone, I'm only telling the truth."

'"Keep the course you were given, then, and if you see the man again, give me a shout."

'The mate went back to the other side of the bridge. The man came up again from the bow. He was wearing a black oilskin and a collar and tie, and had yellow buttons on his clothing, and a round cap on. He told me the same thing, "shift three points to the starboard".

"I called to the mate 'there's the man in the door now!"

'The mate came over. Nobody was there. The mate went and reported it to the captain. When the captain came up to the bridge, he asked if this was what I was saying. I said it was; that the man had come to the door twice, and had asked me to "shift three points to the starboard", and that he had a black oilskin on, and a collar and tie, and yellow buttons on his clothes, and a round cap.

'"Well," said the captain, "I'll believe you because you're a Highlander; but you keep the course you were given."

'The captain went over to the mate. The man came to the door the third time, and asked me to do the same thing. I shouted to them "there's the man in the door again".

'The captain and the mate came over, and there was nobody there!

'"Well," said the captain, "it must be that something strange is going to happen."

'Anyway, in the morning, he got a message from a ship that had gone on fire; and we made for her on the same course as the one the man in the black oilskin had given me at the bridge. When we came in sight of her, her whole crew was on deck, and the man I had seen with the black oilskin on was there leaning against the rail. The captain asked me if I recognized anyone in that crowd. I said I recognized one man, "there he is, leaning against the rail, with a black oil-skin on".

'"That's the mate," said the captain.

'"Well, that's the man who was on the bridge last night," I told him.

'Later on the captain told him that the man who had been at the wheel the night before had seen him, giving him the course, on the bridge.

'"Well," said the mate of the other vessel, "no doubt I was worried enough about the ship and her crew, but I wasn't on your bridge, whoever was."

'That's the only ghost I ever saw,' said the Lewisman, 'and I don't know if it was a ghost or an apparition,[1] but I wasn't in the least afraid of it.'

30

THE COFFIN THAT CAME ABOARD

'I'LL TELL you another thing,' the Lewisman said, 'that happened to me just as sure as that, not very long ago. The ship I was on was going to Australia, heavily laden; at times her deck was awash. One day when the sea was coming over the rail, what came aboard with one wave but a new coffin, complete with lid and everything. The crew came around it and took off the lid; there was nothing inside. They made out that there had never been anyone in it. One of the crew said that it should be put overboard; another said that it was not right to put a coffin overboard.

'"Well," said the captain, "leave it there, since it's come aboard."

'It lay there on the deck, and the crew went back and forth looking at it. One day the men decided to get into it to see if it would fit. It didn't fit anyone who got into it, it was either too narrow or too short, until one man came up and tried it. He was the last man who had joined the ship at Liverpool, and he had to get into it. When he stretched himself out in the coffin, it fitted him as well as if it had been made for him. At that very moment a sea came over the rail and the lid swung shut on the coffin and the sea took it over the side, with the man in it. The crew shouted to the captain that there was a man overboard, and in a moment the captain put her about, but after he had put her about, they could see nothing.

'"Well," said the captain, "this is a terrible business. I

have to account for the crew when I arrive, and if I told the Australians about this, they wouldn't believe me, they'd think I was crazy."

'When we reached Australia, the captain reported that we had lost a member of the crew on the way over. When they found out who he was, we learnt that he was a man who had committed a murder the night before we left Liverpool; he had got the chance to join the ship that night, and he meant to escape when we reached Australia, but he didn't get the opportunity.

'It's only thirty-three years since that happened.'

HUMOROUS STORIES

31

DONALD'S WOOING

THERE WAS once a bachelor called Donald, who lived alone. One day he thought he would try to get a wife. He got up, and got his razor, and scraped off every single grey hair[1] he had, with it. He only wanted a young wife. He went and asked a neighbour to go along with him. The neighbour agreed, and they went off, neither saying much to the other. After a while his companion said:

'But where are we going, Donald?'

'I don't know where we had best go!'

'My word, then, I don't think we should pass up red Janet—she's a fine girl.'

'But she's very old,' said Donald.

'You're ill-advised,[2] Donald. You could go as far as your Gaelic would take you before you'd get anyone half your age.' Donald was over sixty.

'Well then,' said Donald, 'let's go straight there.'

They reached the house. Janet and her mother were the only people there; they were sitting down to a big plate of mashed potatoes for their supper. When the visitors arrived, they put the potatoes on one side, and Janet got up to put the kettle on and make tea. Donald's companion said to her:

'Well, we won't take tea or anything just now until you've first learned our errand.'

'What is it?' said the mother.

'Donald here has come to ask for Janet.'

The old lady let out a burst of laughter that could have split the stones in the wall of the house.

'I'm willing for him to have her, if she's willing; I think he deserves any girl he might ask; he's always been polite and respectable and tidy. What do you say, Janet?'

'I don't ask anything more,' said Janet, 'I couldn't get a better.'

This was fine. A toast was drunk on it. The old lady was given a dram, and it agreed with her very well. She stood up beside Donald and began to praise Janet.

'Janet's a good girl, Donald, a good girl. Out of doors and inside, fair weather or foul, there's nothing wrong with Janet, except she's a little quick tempered;[3] but it's as well to allow a good mare an occasional kick, Donald.'

That was fine too. Donald then asked when the wedding would be.

'A week from tonight,' said Janet.

'Well,' said Donald, 'that's very soon; I'd need a fortnight or three weeks.'

'Why waste time?' said the old lady, 'We're ready any time. There's nothing better, Donald, than to strike while the iron's hot,[4] and get the business over.'

Well, that was all right. Donald studied how the wedding could take place a week from tonight. He and his companion got up to go. When they had gone a little way from the house, Donald said:

'Let's go back to the window and see if we can overhear what they're saying.'

They went back, and eavesdropped at the window. Janet and her mother were sitting at the fire and talking about the wedding party, and about folk living at a distance whom they would have to ask to it.

'But don't you think, Janet,' said her mother, 'that Donald is pretty old?'

'Yes I do,' said Janet, 'but that will make it easier for me to keep him in order!'

When Donald heard this, nothing could make him go near Janet again,[5] and I'm sure his friend wouldn't, either!

32

THE FIRST GALVANIC BATTERY ON SKYE

THERE WAS once a big farmer on the Isle of Skye called Fear a' Choire, 'The Tacksman of Corrie'* who had a son called Hector. Hector was away at college on the mainland. He used to come home for his holidays. Every time he came home he used to bring some novelty or other that had never been seen on the Isle of Skye before.

This time he brought home with him a galvanic battery. It was considered a great wonder. There was an old woman called Mairi an Uillt, 'Mary of the Stream', who used to go cadging around the big houses to see what she could get. One day Hector was outside the house when whom did he see coming but Mary. He went indoors and brought out the apparatus[1] and put it on a table in front of the door. Mary met him and welcomed him:

'Oh, here you are, Hector dearie, welcome home!'

'Oh, thank you, Mary, I'm here, right enough.'

'Amn't I glad to see you looking so well, Hector! I needn't bother to ask if you're keeping your health, I can see it in your face.'

'Oh yes, thank you, Mary, I'm keeping perfectly well. How are you?'

'Only middling, I can just get around.'

* They were MacKinnons. They had a famous fold of Highland cattle. At one time they leased one of the farms in Canna in addition to their farm in Skye.

'You don't look very well, Mary. What are you complaining of?'

'It's the rheumatics. They're killing me. I can hardly walk.'

'That's not so good, Mary. Though I've never felt them, I know what they are.'

'Oh, you don't know what they're like, dearie, you nor your people. But what's this, Hector?'

'That's fishing-tackle, Mary; will you hold it while I put it in order?'

'I'll do that, dearie, I hope it will be the better for it.'

Mary took hold of the knobs with her hands, and began to sing a croon to Hector:

> 'Strike, with my love, on stream and boat
> Scales of fish on rudder and stone,
> Mesh tight round herring's head,
> For speckled salmon a sharp spear.'[2]

But Mary's croon was cut short with a resounding yell. The servants came out of the house, but before many of them had collected, Hector let Mary free, gathering up the apparatus and going off.

Mary turned on him and said:

'A corpse-band on your big scabby block-head and shame on all your ancestors and on your country!'[3]

'Oh, that'll do, Mary,' said one of the servants, 'come on in, it's good for the rheumatics!'

'Good for the rheumatics! There was nothing wrong with me except to be going around as I was, but now I feel as if I'd been swallowed by a whale and spat out again on the shore. I'll never be good for anything again! He and his fishing-tackle! That never caught anything but what had been poisoned!'

33

HECTOR AND THE BALLOON

ONE AUTUMN afternoon when there was a big squad reaping for his father, Hector saw nothing better to do than to start making a balloon of grey paper. His father had a married farm-servant on his farm, called Donald, who kept a cow. Hector shaped his balloon like a cow, and made it in every way like Donald's cow, as regards legs, tail, and horns. Then he went behind a knoll and let the balloon away so that it would go past over the reapers. One of them looked up and saw this lump coming, and shouted:

'Oh lads! lads! look at the cow!'

They all stood up to gaze at the wonder.

'God save me!' said Donald. 'Isn't it like my own cow?'

'Indeed,' said one of the reapers, 'if it isn't your cow, it's the image of it.'

'May Providence protect us! The Isle of Skye was always famous for witchcraft,[1] but we never heard of cows flying in the air before!'

Donald dropped his sickle and went off to see if his cow was in the field. When he reached the field, there was neither cow nor stirk to be seen, for Hector had put Donald's cow out to the hill. Donald went on home. When he got home he found his wife busy at her housework. She stopped and looked at him.

'Aren't you home early on such a fine evening?'

'Oh, I stopped working anyway, whatever the others did.'

'Is there anything wrong?'

'Indeed there is. Our cow's flown off in the sky tonight!'

'What nonsense is this you've thought up?'

'Anything I say you call nonsense. If I'm talking nonsense, so is everyone else who saw her along with me.'

'Isn't the cow in the field where you left her this morning?'

'The cow is *not* in the field where I left her this morning. At the speed I saw her going, she's in London by now.'

'I never heard of such a thing. You stay indoors with the children while I go out and see if I can find her.'

'Go and see if you can find her; you'll need to be speedy if you're to see her. I don't want to see any more of her. You never believe anything you don't see yourself, unless some lying baggage or other comes around,[2] when you'll believe every word she says. Go along, then.'

Donald's wife went off, paying no heed to him. She went walking to see if she could see the cow, and there wasn't cow nor stirk in the field. Then a heavy mist came down; and who arrived at Donald's house but Hector?

'Are you by yourself?' he said to Donald.

'Yes.'

'Where's your wife?'

'She's gone where she needn't have troubled to go, to see if she can find the cow. I'm sure you've heard about the cow already.'

'Indeed I have. It's a terrible business.'

'Well, I never heard of such a thing,' said Donald, 'and may it be long before I hear of the like of it again; as long as I keep my sight and hearing. It was bad enough to hear about, let alone to witness.'

'Indeed it was; the world is surely changing.'

'It certainly is, we never heard the like of this.'

'Well, a thick mist has come down,' said Hector, 'and you'd better go to look for your wife, or else if she starts flying off it will be worse for you than the cow was.'

'Providence protect me, I was never in such a fix. Will you stay in the house along with the children for a while?'

Donald went out and stood on the top of a mound, and began to shout for his wife; he shouted HO, ISABEL! ARE YOU

THERE, ISABEL? HO, ISABEL! The gloomy crags opposite him echoed HO, ISABEL! as loud as himself.

'God help me with my wife lost and my cow in the sky and the night falling,' said Donald.

He went back to see if he could find anyone to send to look for his wife. When he got back, his cow had come home by herself, and was standing at the door chewing her cud. Donald looked at her.

'Here you are, you witch,' he said, 'sniffing at the door, but by your nose you'll get no further inside.[3] God between me and you!' he said, going past her into the house. His wife had come home.

'The cow has come back,' she said.

'Let the cow come or go,' said Donald, 'you keep away from her; don't go near her.'

His wife did not dare to go near the cow.

As soon as day dawned, Donald went over to the farm to see his master. He went into the byre where the servants were milking the cows. He asked them if his master had got up, and they said he had, and that he was in the house.

'Hello,' said Corrie, 'is something wrong with you today that you've come here so early?'

'Yes, indeed there is,' said Donald.

'What's wrong?'

'Didn't my cow fly off in the sky last night? I'm sure you've heard about it by now. I've come over to ask you to shoot her, if she can be shot—I don't know—if she can't be shot we must think of some other way to destroy her.'

'Tut, tut,' said Corrie, 'you'd better put that nonsense out of your head. Go home and take care of the cow.'

'Take care of the cow! Not another drop of the creature's milk will go into my children's mouths. I'll put an end to her at once. If lead won't kill her, something else will. She's not going to be flying over the world like that!'

When Corrie saw that nothing could put this idea out of Donald's head, he said:

'Well, bring her over to the farm, and I'll give you another cow in exchange.'

'Well,' said Donald, 'that's very good of you; I don't know

what she'll do for you, unless you fatten her and send her to Glasgow around Hallowe'en; that's if she can be fattened. I'm told that the people of Glasgow will eat anything. Likely they'd eat the Evil One!'

Corrie gave Donald as good a cow as he had in his fold in exchange for Donald's cow; and Donald believed ever afterwards that his own cow had flown in the sky!

34

THE TINKERS' HOTEL

THERE WAS once a lawyer in Ireland called O'Connell. One time he stayed in an hotel for a week, and when he was leaving the hotel and got his account, he noticed that the hotelkeeper was overcharging him. He fell out with the hotelkeeper; but he had to pay the bill before he could get out of the door.

He went off, and on the road he met a tinker. He spoke to the tinker, and the tinker answered him politely. O'Connell asked the tinker where his home was, and the tinker answered that he had no other home than his tent.

'Are there many along with you?' asked O'Connell.

'There's eleven of us there altogether,' said the tinker.

'If you'll do what I tell you,' said O'Connell, 'I'll get you a very good home.'

'I'll do that,' said the tinker, 'if you'll get a home for me.'

'Well, come along with me.'

He took the tinker into a tailor's shop, and had him dressed there with as good a suit as could be got.

'Go along now,' said O'Connell, 'to such and such a hotel, and ask what the charge is for the best room in the hotel for a year; and whatever the hotelkeeper asks for it, take it; and then come back to me again.'

The tinker went off, looking like a gentleman now and not like a tinker at all. When he reached the hotel, the hotelkeeper came to meet him, very pleased that this gentleman had come his way. The tinker asked if the best room in the hotel was unoccupied. The hotelkeeper said it was.

'Well, I and my family are thinking of coming here,' said the tinker. 'What are you asking for the room for a year?'

'One hundred pounds.'

'All right,' said the tinker, 'keep it for me, don't let anyone else take it.'

'No, indeed I won't,' said the hotelkeeper.

The tinker returned to O'Connell.

'Well,' said O'Connell, 'did you take the room?'

'Yes.'

'What did he ask for it?'

'A hundred pounds.'

'He asked enough!'

O'Connell went and counted out the hundred pounds to the tinker. 'Go along now, and pay him, and come back to me again.'

The tinker went back to the hotel, and when he arrived he told the hotelkeeper he wanted to pay for the room.

'Oh, you needn't bother to pay for the room now, there's plenty of time yet to pay for it.'

'Well,' said the tinker, 'something that's paid doesn't need to be asked for again.'

'All right.' He paid the hotelkeeper the hundred pounds, and returned to O'Connell.

'Well,' said O'Connell, 'did you pay for the room?'

'Yes,' said the tinker.

'Now go and take off that suit you've got on (and put on your old clothes) and collect your party, and go and take the room. It'll make a good home for you for a year to come.'

The tinker went and collected his family, including his grandmother, and came back with them. When he reached the hotel, the hotelkeeper came out and told him to go to hell, himself and his party.

'Clear out or I'll put a gun to you.' The tinker shouldered him out of the way.

'Get out of my way, you shameless fellow, it's my room and it's paid for.'

The tinker moved into the room. It wasn't long before the

hotel began to smell of burning coal and horn spoons being moulded.[1] All the other guests got together and complained to the hotelkeeper that if these were the kind of people he was going to take, they were going to leave. The hotelkeeper went up to see the tinker, and asked him to clear out and he would give him fifty pounds over and above what he had paid already. The tinker wouldn't go. All the other guests left the hotel, and the tinkers had it to themselves. They were sometimes fighting and sometimes tinkering; the hotelkeeper couldn't get a moment's rest, and he was nearly going out of his mind. There was nothing for the waiters or the boots or for anyone else to do; the tinkers did everything for themselves. There wasn't a minute of the day the hotelkeeper wasn't going to see the tinkers to ask what they would take to clear out; he would give them as much again as they had paid, if they would go!

The tinker then went back to O'Connell.

'Well,' said O'Connell, 'how are you getting on?'

'Very well,' said the tinker, 'but that hotelkeeper gives us no peace, asking us to clear out. He's offering me twice as much as I've paid if we'll go, another hundred pounds.'

'Though he offers you a thousand pounds,' said O'Connell, don't move out of the place until you have spent a month there. If he offers you three hundred pounds then, go away.'

The tinker went back to the hotel. When he and his party had been a month in the hotel, he said to the hotelkeeper:

'Well, since I'm causing you so much trouble, if you'll give me three hundred pounds, I'll clear out of the place for you.'

'Oh, you son of the devil, I'd have given you that long ago if you and your tribe would have left us.'

Three hundred pounds were given to the tinker, and he went back to O'Connell.

'Well,' said O'Connell, 'have you cleared out of the hotel?'

'Yes,' said the tinker, 'and not empty-handed either. Here it is, it's your money.'

'Oh,' said O'Connell, 'I'm only taking back what I gave

you, you can keep the rest as you were so good as to do what I asked.'

No gentleman has entered that hotel since then, and ever afterwards it has been called 'The Tinkers' Hotel'. That's what happened to the hotelkeeper for overcharging O'Connell!

35

THE HOLIDAY OF DONALD AND MAGGIE

ONCE I had plenty of stories and anecdotes, and when I came back to Uist after being away from home, I would have plenty of tales to tell about what I had seen and heard. I would say 'I saw this, I heard that——' and at last it would only be 'I saw, I saw, I saw.' People used to make fun of me; and then I would talk about what I had heard. That was no better than what I had seen, and perhaps worse. I had to stop, and so I forgot a lot of things that I had seen and heard. But at any rate for fear of leaving the company tonight I am going to tell you a story, and I'm not going to say whether I saw it, or whether I heard it.

Once there was a Highlander called Donald. He had spent a great part of his life in Perthshire, and had married a woman who was every bit as Highland as himself, called Maggie. Donald and Maggie were both very good workers. They had a little croft to themselves, and were doing very well there too. They never left home. Other people used to go away for holidays and for sport, and they would have many stories to tell when they came back, as I used to myself. Donald and Maggie greatly envied these people on account of the wonders they were seeing, while they themselves never saw anything but the same things day after day.

This year Donald said to Maggie:

'By the Book, Maggie, I'm thinking that we should take a trip this year.'

'Indeed,' said Maggie, 'I'd be very willing to, just to see something we could talk about when we got back home to pass the time. I see people who go away just for a week and see things that keep them in stories for the rest of the year. We don't see anything except an occasional deer on the sky-line.'

'Well, you get ready and we'll go in a week,' said Donald. 'We'll take a week anyway, perhaps even a fortnight. Nothing can go wrong before we get back. People no better off than ourselves go away for holidays.'

'Where do you think we can go?'

'Well, I'm thinking we might go to Oban; a lot of people go there nowadays.'

'I was never there,' said Maggie.

'Nor was I. It's none the worse for that. There'll be boat races, and sports, and yachts, and steamers; there's lots of things to see we never saw.'

Maggie started to get her clothes ready, and packed two bags. Then they were ready. They locked up the house and went off. They arrived at Oban on the evening train, and when they got out at the station, the station was crowded with people. When they left the train, the porters were lined up on the platform; they were pointing at their bags and beckoning to them. Neither Donald nor Maggie had the slightest idea what sort of men they were at all. Maggie nudged Donald and said to him:

'What are those men standing over there? See what they're doing with their hands!'

'Well,' said Donald, 'likely they're the keelies* we've heard people talk about. You take care of your bags.'

'They don't need to be looking at the bags,' said Maggie. But one of them didn't stop pointing or beckoning to them. Maggie nudged Donald again:

'Look at that one, pointing his finger all the time!'

Over came the porter, and before Maggie could wink he had one of her bags in each hand and was away through the crowd like a rat! Maggie raised the cry that the keelie was away with her bags, and off Donald went after him. Maggie

* Scots for Teddy-boys.

was so stout that she was colliding with people right and left and making no progress. Before she had got out of the station, the 'keelie' was down the square, with a bag in each hand, looking over his shoulder to see if they were coming. Maggie was waddling after him like a duck, shouting, 'You needn't run away from us! We'll follow you wherever you go!'

The 'keelie' never stopped until he reached the Great Western Hotel. There he stopped at the door, where another man was waiting. Donald and Maggie were taken in, and shown up to a room, and treated ever so kindly. The 'keelie' went out and left them there.

'Goodness,' said Maggie, 'those weren't keelies at all, Donald!'

'No, they weren't,' said Donald, 'but it's little we have to do with this kind of place.'

'Providence alone can tell,' said Maggie, 'perhaps there isn't a more suitable place than this.'

'Don't let on how ragged we are at home,' said Donald. 'We'll stay here tonight anyway, we'll probably get to know the town better tomorrow.'

It wasn't long until a waiter came in and asked them if they wanted anything, did they want a bath?

'No, indeed,' said Maggie, 'we're clean enough.'

The waiter went away. Then they heard the dinner bell. 'What's that bell?' said Maggie.

'I don't know,' said Donald. 'There's that many bells here anyway.'

It wasn't long before the waiter came in again and asked them if they wanted dinner.

'Yes.'

'Didn't you hear the bell? Come this way, come this way.'

They were taken into the coffee-room. There were all kinds of people there. Among them was a big General with his sword hanging at his side. He was near to Donald, who had never seen anyone like him before, and was scared stiff, he looked so fierce. The General was taking his dinner and didn't notice them. When the first course was over, the waiters came back to serve them, very kindly, and then the next course came in, and it was better than the first.

'My word,' said Donald, 'there's food here, isn't there, Maggie?'

When the second course was finished, the dessert was brought in.

'Oh, Maggie,' said Donald, 'this'll be dear! This comes to three meals!'

When dinner was over, they got up and went out, and went up to their room, and stayed there until it was time to go to sleep. Donald hadn't been long in bed before he began to complain.

'Goodness,' said Maggie, 'are you ill?'

'Yes,' said Donald, 'very ill, too.'

'Oh dear!' said Maggie. 'What's wrong?'

'It's the colic.'

'Where do you feel it?'

'In my belly. I'm nearly done for.'

'Oh,' said Maggie, 'I'd better get up and get that mustard they had on the table when we had our dinner. I saw where they put it away. I'll put some on you so you won't get any worse; so we can get out of here when the day come, since we were so mistaken as to come here.'

'My God, go on then,' said Donald, 'I must have something.'

Maggie crept quietly down the stairs and found the mustard where she had seen it put away. She made a plaster downstairs carefully, and came back upstairs as quietly as she could in case she disturbed anyone. She opened the door, and went into the room. When she got in, Donald was asleep.

'Thank goodness you've got relief, anyway. I'll put this on you, as I've made it, in case the colic comes back.'

She lifted the bedclothes and put the plaster on the place where Donald had complained of the pain. She was waiting to take the plaster off him again before going to bed herself, when she heard soft groans from the room behind her.

'My God, Maggie, where are you, I'm nearly dead!'

Maggie ran out of the room. What had she done but put the plaster on the General! She was scarcely out of the room before the General jumped out of bed. He came out in the corridor in his nightgown with his drawn sword in his hand.

He shouted who were the blackguards who had come into his room to play jokes on him? and that he wouldn't leave the head on anyone in the hotel!

'Upon my soul, what's that, Maggie?' said Donald.

'Oh,' said Maggie, 'it's death for us, anyway. I went into the General's room in mistake for ours and put the plaster on him instead of you; if he comes in here, we're done for.'

'God save me,' said Donald, 'we only left home to find trouble! Where are my trousers?'

He began to get dressed. The General was running up and down the stairs, making the hotel resound. The manager and the waiters got up to see what was wrong. The General insisted he must find out who had done it. The manager was telling him that nobody could have done it; everyone was in bed. 'Someone did it and they needn't bother to deny it; blackguards had burnt his body with mustard; he *must* find out who had done it.'

In the rush that was going on, Donald and Maggie crept downstairs and got out of the hotel. Once they were outside, Donald ran down to the station as fast as a hare, with Maggie behind him. The first train that left Oban,[1] they took, and got away home on it; and they never went away on a holiday again. There was enough for them and their neighbours to talk about all night! That's what happened on the holiday of Donald and Maggie!

36

THE SHEPHERD WHO COULDN'T TELL A LIE

ONCE THERE were two farmers who were neighbours. One day they had been at a sale, and on their way home they were talking about how difficult farming was, rents were so high, and workmen such as carpenters and smiths and others had to be paid so much, there wasn't much left over for themselves.

'Well,' said one of them to his friend, who was called Robertson, 'that's true enough; but I think that when they are good servants, what they're paid is no loss. I have good servants myself, but if they were all like my shepherd, Donald, I could go to Spain all winter long. I never saw such a faithful servant and so truthful—he's never once told a lie.'

'Ho, ho!' said Robertson. 'I thought you had sense, but a man who never told a lie! Such a man doesn't exist!'

'Well, Donald's one, anyway.'

'Hunh! He's had no reason to tell one, I'm sure. That's why. No one tells a lie as long as the truth will do.'

'I'll bet you anything he won't tell a lie.'

'I'll bet twenty pounds he'll tell you a lie in front of me within a day,' said Robertson.

'All right, it's on. Now try him.'

'Well, leave him alone, and I'll come over one day next week and we'll try him to see if he'll tell you the truth.'

Robertson went home. He had a dairymaid[1] on his farm to

whom Donald had taken a great fancy, and whom he came to see quite often. Robertson knew she could be relied on. He said to the dairymaid:

'Well, Mary, I'd like you to do something for me.'

'I will if I can.'

'You can,' he said. 'I have some nice stockings here, knee stockings, which I've never worn, and I want you to take them to Donald the shepherd. I've got a big bet on with his master. There's a black sheep in his flock, and his master has a great notion for it, he thinks it's a terribly lucky beast to have in the flock. It's the first beast he'll ask Donald about when he gets home. I know Donald will be willing to give you anything in return for the stockings, but don't accept anything from him but the black sheep. If you get the black sheep from him, we'll win the bet and you'll get your share of it.'

'Oh, I'd be ashamed to go out there by myself.'

'Be quiet, you can make the excuse that you've come to see some of my beasts that are out on the hill there.'

Mary went off with the stockings, and made for the hill, watching to see if she could see Donald. She saw him on top of a knoll. Mary appeared herself; Donald saw her and went down to where she was.

'What in the world has sent you out here?' he said.

'Oh, I came to look for a cow of his on the hill that's in calf. I wanted to see you, I've got a little present here for you. I haven't had a chance to give it to you in private. I've brought it with me—look at it!'

'What is it?' said Donald.

'Just some stockings I've made for you.'

She went and gave him the stockings.

'Well, well!' said Donald. 'Aren't they lovely! Was it you who made them, Mary?'

'Yes,' said Mary. 'Many a night I was working at them late after the others had gone to sleep, in case anyone saw me knitting them; if they'd seen me they'd have been watching to see who'd be wearing them afterwards. That's the truth, Donald, that's their occupation, watching.'

'Well, I didn't know that you liked me as much as that.'

'Oh, I like you more than you like me, Donald.'

'That can't be, Mary. But what would you like to have in return?'

'Oh, I didn't expect anything in return, I didn't make them for that, Donald, I wanted to make them for you.'

'I know that, but you must take something.'

'Well, what I'd like to have would be no loss to you, if you'd give it to me.'

'What's that?'

'The black sheep.'

'Upon my word, if it were mine you'd get it, even if it were a flock. But it's the first beast himself will ask me about, when I go to the farm—have I got the black sheep? He thinks more of it than he does of the whole flock.'

'Tush, Donald, you can easily make an excuse. You know the black sheep won't live for ever. It's the first thing I've ever asked you for.'

'Well, no—seeing it's the first thing you've ever asked for, you'll get it, then.'

Donald went and gathered the sheep, and got hold of the black sheep, and gave it to Mary. She put a rope on it and went away with it. When she arrived, Robertson was very pleased.

'You've done very well, Mary. We'll see now if Donald always tells the truth as his master says he does.'

Robertson went over to see his neighbour.

'Has Donald been in since I saw you last?'

'No, I've had no reason to send for him.'

'Well, send for him now, and we'll see if he's as truthful as you were saying. Tell him you've something you want to see him about.'

'How are you going to test him?'

'You'll only need to ask him everything you usually do, and I'll ask the rest.'

The farmer sent for Donald, saying he had something he wanted to see him about. Donald didn't know what to do.

'I don't know what business he has to talk to me about today, unless he wants to gather the sheep. What will I do when I get there? He'll ask how the flock is; have you got the black sheep? Oh, I wish I had never seen Mary's present!'

He went and stuck his crook on a mound, and put his jacket on it. That's the farmer now! What am I going to tell him? I'll say I've lost her.

'Here you are, Donald!'

'Yes,' said Donald, answering the jacket.

'How did you leave the flock?'

'All right.'

'Have you got the black sheep?'

'No.'

'Aye, aye! So the black sheep's lost?'

'Yes.'

'Well, well! I'd sooner lose five others than her!'

'I'd sooner, too.'

'What do you think came over her?'

'The braxy.'[2]

'It didn't use to be very bad out there.'

'No, it wasn't, indeed. I haven't lost many since I went there.'

'Well, well! She was a pretty beast and a lucky beast in the flock.'

'Indeed, that she was, a lucky beast. I didn't lose many since she was out there.'

'Oh, it's certain that the beast you take a notion to will be the first one you'll lose.'

'Yes, I've always noticed that.'

'Yes, so have I, Donald. Did you bring the skin home?'

Look here! (said Donald to himself), 'No, nor hide nor hair!'[3] It's too difficult! I haven't got it. God help me! What'll I do now? That way won't do. I must try another. I'll say it has been stolen, and he'll never ask for the skin!

'Here you are, Donald!'

'Yes,' said Donald to the jacket.

'How did you leave the flock?'

'The flock's all right.'

'Have you got the black sheep?'

'No.'

'When did you see her last?'

'It's two days since I've seen her.'

'What's happened to her?'

'I don't know at all.'

'Did you cover the hill?'

'I've walked every inch of the hill, I've looked in every hole and stream, I've been everywhere. I couldn't find her alive or dead, not even a wisp of her wool.'

'Aye, aye! She must have been stolen.'

'Nothing surer.'

'Well, well! I've never heard the like. It seems there are thieves everywhere! Did you miss any others besides her?'

'No, I didn't.'

'Well, Donald, she can't have gone far.'

'Who knows?'

'No, Donald. Look, if it was a thief who meant to sell them, he would have taken as many as he could. She can't have gone far at all. We'll send for the police: even if the meat has been eaten, the wool won't have been.'

Look here! (said Donald to himself) the police will go out, and they'll find Mary has the sheep, and Mary will go to prison. I might as well go to prison myself, as to send her. What shall I do now? Lies won't do any good, only the truth will, be it soft or hard. If it can be paid for, I don't care if he keeps it off my wages; if that can't be done, he can do what he likes to me.

Donald went off, taking his jacket and his crook with him, and went straight to the farmhouse. When he arrived, he went into the kitchen. Robertson was waiting for him in the room along with the farmer. The farmer was told that Donald had come. Donald was sent for, and went down to the room mopping his brow.

'You've come, Donald.'

'Yes.'

'How you're perspiring! It's not hot.'

'No, it's cold right enough.'

'How did you leave the flock out there, Donald?'

'All right. Nothing wrong.'

'Have you got the black sheep?'

Donald didn't say a word. He hung his head.

'Have you not got the black sheep at all, Donald?'

'No, I have not.'

'What has happened to her?'

'I gave her away.'

'Have you *sold* her?'

'No, I wouldn't sell her.'

'Whom did you give her to?'

'I gave her to Mr Robertson's dairymaid. She came out about a week ago with some presents for me, and though I'd have given her my heart, she wouldn't take anything but the black sheep in return, though I'm sorry enough today for that. But what good will that do? If I can pay for it I'm willing enough to have it taken out of my wages. If that can't be done it seems you can do what you like with me.'

'Well, well, well, Donald, I never heard the like! I hear you've a great notion to that dairymaid. Were you giving her a dowry out of my goods, or what did you have in mind?'

'I probably was.'

'Well, I've never heard the like, Donald, I didn't think you'd do it.'

He turned to Robertson:

'What have you to say to him now? I've finished with him.'

'Well, nothing at all. It looks as if you can stand by what you were saying, all right.'

'Well, Donald,' said his master, 'though you gave away the black sheep, you'll be forgiven, as you've stood by the truth today as you've always done; if you hadn't done that, you wouldn't be with me another twenty-four hours. But the best thing for you to do is to marry that dairymaid, and you'll have both her and the black sheep as well, and you won't be a shepherd out on the hill any more, but my manager here.'

Donald raised his head when he heard this; nothing had ever fallen out so well for him as when he had given away the black sheep! He married Mary, and was the farmer's manager thereafter.

ADVENTURE STORIES

37

'PRIEST DONALD'

THERE WAS once a Uistman called Donald Mackintosh, who was distantly related to myself. He had a name for cleverness[1] when he was at school, and he was always called 'Priest Donald'. That was his nickname. At the time of the Napoleonic wars,[2] he was on the same ship as Lord Nelson. One night he was on the watch, and who came around but Lord Nelson. Nelson spoke to Donald, who thought it was someone else coming around to make fun of him; so he gave him a rude answer.

Next day, 'Priest Donald' was brought before a court. The ship's doctor was a Highlander who was very fond of Mackintosh. He went to see him and asked him 'what made you give such an answer to the Admiral last night?'

'Oh, the rascal, I thought it was someone else who had come to make fun of me.'

'Well,' said the doctor, 'I'm afraid you'll be severely flogged.' Flogging was the punishment in those days. If you did anything wrong, you were stripped and tied to the mast; and however many strokes were to be given you, unless you suffered them all at once, after you had been healed you had to get the rest later.

'Well,' said the doctor, 'it's likely you'll be severely flogged, Mackintosh.'

'It can't be helped,' said Donald.

The doctor gave him a florin. 'This is what you should do. Put this in your mouth when they start flogging you, and you won't feel the pain so badly.'

Well, the man giving the flogging had to make blood flow by the third lash, or else he himself was put in your place. Donald's flogging began. After a while the doctor called on them to stop, that Donald had had enough.

'Have I had them all?' asked Donald.

'No, only half of them,' said the doctor.

'If there are more strokes to come, I'd sooner have them now than be tied up here again.'

'No,' said the doctor, 'they don't dare to give you one more when I've asked them to stop.'

Donald was untied, and the doctor took him below, and he was bandaged and given treatment.

'Off with you now, Mackintosh, and don't do a hand's turn for them until you're healed. Maybe they'll overlook the rest of the flogging.'

Donald went off. The next day he went on deck. He was going around bent up pretending to be much worse than he was. There was an Englishman sitting there reading newspapers. He turned to Donald:

'Well, Mackintosh, I see here there's been a battle and the ladies won it.' That was casting up to Donald that Highlanders wore kilts.

'Ho, ho!' said Donald, 'if the ladies hadn't won it, the English wouldn't have.'

He and the Englishman began to fight on the deck, and at last Donald swung round with his fist and hit the Englishman and knocked him down, and before he got up he had parted with his dinner. Donald was brought before a court at once.

'What have you done now, Mackintosh?' asked the doctor. 'Why did you hit the Englishman?'

'Oh, I couldn't listen to him though I were hung for it.'

'Well, you'll do this when you go before the court: don't open your mouth even if they tell lies about you.'

'That'll be very difficult,' said Donald.

'Well, that's my advice. I'll put in a written statement on your behalf.'

Donald was brought before the court. The doctor put in a written statement on his behalf, saying that a Highlander never made excuses; that the Englishman had been trying to bait Donald, seeing that he was wounded; that Highland blood was so sincere and so fierce, that it could not put up with taunting, preferring death to humiliation. Donald was acquitted; and he was happy enough.

One day the crew was at food in the fo'c'sle. An Englishman sitting beside him began to bait Donald. Donald was giving him an occasional answer. 'Oh, shut your mouth, you dirty Highlander, or I'll do it for you with my spoon.' Donald paid no heed. The Englishman drew his knife and slashed Donald from his ear to his mouth cutting him to the bone. Donald ran up on deck and went to see the doctor, who staunched[3] his wound and put stitches in it. The Englishman was brought before a court and condemned to sixty lashes tied to the mast, naked.

'Well,' said Donald, 'if you'd give me five minutes of him, that'd be the best flogging he could get.'

'You can have him for that if you think you can do it.'

'I'll risk it, anyway,' said Donald.

Both of them were taken on deck, and Donald and the Englishman began on each other. Before five minutes were out, Donald was kicking the Englishman around the deck. The Englishman was taken away and put ashore, and Donald never saw him again alive or dead.

38

A WIFE FROM ENGLAND

WHEN SCOTLAND was an independent kingdom, no Scot dared to get a wife from England, nor did any Englishman dare to get a wife from Scotland. But when Scotland lost her independence,[1] every Scottish chieftain had to appear before the King.* There was one such called Lord MacDonald[2] who refused to appear; and the King put a price on his head. Lord MacDonald was afraid to remain in Scotland in case someone there betrayed him. He decided to go to England, thinking that he would not be looked for there at all, as people wouldn't think he would dare to go there.

He went dressed as a working man. It was the custom of the Highland chiefs at this time to have their children taught a trade after they had left school, carpentry or shoemaking or tailoring or whatever trade the children preferred, so that although they were chiefs, they could say they were craftsmen as well. Lord MacDonald had been taught fine carpentry,[3] but he had never worked much at the trade afterwards. (After he reached England) he was out one day in the street when a gentleman met him. The gentleman spoke to him, and Lord MacDonald answered him politely. 'I think you're a stranger here,' said the gentleman.

* It is certainly true that after the Union of the Crowns in 1603 many Highland and Hebridean chiefs were forced to make regular appearances before the Scottish Privy Council in Edinburgh, at great personal expense, and inconvenience. It is also the case that in the seventeenth century notable Scots at times took refuge in England from political and sectarian persecution at home. Sir James MacDonald of Islay was an example.

'Yes,' said Lord MacDonald, 'I'm only a poor fellow who's looking for work.'

'What can you do?'

'I can do several kinds of work, but I'm best at carpentry.'

'Are you a good carpenter?'

'Well, I haven't failed at any job I've taken on so far, anyway.'

'I'm looking for a carpenter. If you can do the job I have for you, I'll give you full pay for a year and for longer if we get on well.'

'I haven't been able to buy many tools yet for many different kinds of work.'

'Oh, you won't lack for tools. There's no tool a carpenter needs that I haven't got. If you need more tools you only have to tell me.'

'That's as good as can be,' said Lord MacDonald.

'Well, meet me here tomorrow at ten o'clock,' said the gentleman.

Lord MacDonald went out at ten o'clock the next morning. The gentleman arrived in a carriage[4] with a young woman. He asked Lord MacDonald to get in. They drove out of the town, and came to a big castle. This was his place. He asked Lord MacDonald to get out of the carriage. He was taken into the carpenters' quarters, and when he had had a meal, the gentleman came to see him.

'Come along now and see a carpentry job.' There were carpenters trying out tools there, who were looking at them.

'Well, the job I've got for you now,' said the gentleman, 'this sofa[5] here belonged to my father, and it's now old. I want to make another like it in every way—the same length and breadth. If you'll do that, I'll pay you full wages.'

'Well, I'll try, anyway,' said Lord MacDonald.

The carpenter began to work on the sofa; and when it was finished, the gentleman had a new sofa, and no one could tell the two sofas apart except that the one was old and the other new. The gentleman was very much pleased with the job, and he engaged 'MacDonald' for a year. 'MacDonald' was working every day, and at nights he used to go out to carpentry jobs to pass the time, or sit indoors reading papers. He didn't go out at any time.

His master used to tell him he didn't need to be so hard upon himself as that; he could visit the city on Saturdays.

'Oh,' said 'MacDonald', 'I don't care about that, I was never used to anything but work. When a man's working, the time passes; that's what I like.'

Things went on like that for a year; then the engagement was renewed for another year.

Then one day there was to be a big ball[6] held by the gentry in the town, and 'MacDonald's' employer and his daughter were to be there. The daughter said to her father:

'I'd like you to take the carpenter along with us, he's never gone out since he came to the place.'

'I'm glad you thought of it; we'll go and see him.'

They went to see the carpenter.

'Well, you needn't do any more today,' said the gentleman. 'Get ready, we're having a big ball in the town tonight and you must come along with us.'

When Lord MacDonald heard this, he didn't want to go in case somebody might be there who would give him away.

'Oh, I haven't anything to do with such society, I've never been accustomed to it, perhaps I would only embarrass you if I did go,' he said.

'I've no doubt you can conduct yourself in any society,' said the gentleman. 'You really must go.'

'Oh, of course you'll come,' said the daughter to 'MacDonald'. 'Haven't you been shut up here now for more than a year since you came? You've never gone out.'

Well, he didn't like to go against the two of them, so he began to get ready, and went with them.

The gentry were all gathered for the ball. They began to dance. The carpenter was sitting watching them. The M.C. got up and said:

'We think now it's right that the Scot who's in our company should get up and dance; he's seen how we dance in England, and we'd be very pleased if he'd show us how they dance in Scotland.'

'Well,' said Lord MacDonald, 'you must excuse me;

although I've come to the party, I'm no dancer, I was never taught to dance. I've no business here, I just came with my master.'

'It doesn't make any difference, you must be able to do some kind of a dance, you must get up,' said the M.C.

All right; Lord MacDonald got up and went over and paid his respects to[7] his master's daughter, and she took the floor with him as light as a feather. The reel began, and every eye in the room was watching the carpenter's feet. They had never seen such a dancer before. When the reel stopped, his master's daughter said:

'Well, I don't think you need to be ashamed to get up to dance. If they're as good as that in Scotland, you may well say there are dancers there.'

'As good as that!' he said. 'That was only something I picked up watching other people. I was never properly taught.'

He was taking his turn[8] after that, and every time 'MacDonald' got up to dance, his master's daughter was his partner. Then the ball ended and they came home.

The next day 'MacDonald' went to the carpenter's shop. In the evening his employer, with his daughter, came around and came in where he was working.

'Well,' said his master, 'I'm sure you're tired today after last night.'

'Oh, I don't notice it at all.'

'My word, I was pleased with you last night. I'd rather have what you did, than fifty pounds. Many a man there was ready to make fun of you, but instead you made fun of them. Nobody there knew how to dance but you.'

'Oh, I'm not a dancer at all amongst dancers. I'd be ashamed to get up with them.'

'Well, indeed, the next gathering we have, you'll be there.'

'I've no business being at these gatherings at all.'

'Indeed you have, while plenty who do go have not.'

When the gentleman had gone out, his daughter was following him through the door. She looked back at the carpenter. He was leaning against his carpenter's table, smiling. In a second[9] she came back inside.

'What's making you smile?' she said.

'Nothing at all.'

'You must have some reason.'

'Oh no, except I liked you so much.'

'Would you take me?' she said.

'That's not likely to happen to me,' he said. 'If I once thought you would take me—but you wouldn't like my sort.'

'What I'm asking is, would you take me?'

'Yes, I would, though I'm sure a humbler match would be more suitable for me.'

'Will you give me your hand on that?'

He stopped when he heard this.

'Well,' she said, 'now you're going back on your word!'[10]

'Oh no,' he said, 'I'm not going to go back on it. But though I'm willing to do it, there's one thing I can't do.'

'What's that?'

'Something that can't be helped.'

'What can there be that you can't tell me? I'll swear to you that no one else will ever hear it, if it would harm you.'[11]

'Well, I'll tell you. The King of England has put a price on my head. Even if I were richer than I am, a man in my position would suit you badly.'

'Whatever wrong did you do?'

'I didn't do anything wrong, but never mind that.'

'If I get a safe-conduct for you[12] from the King of England, will you keep your word?'

'Yes, indeed.'

'Well, my father is the King's brother,' she said, 'and I'm the King's only niece. He's never refused me anything I've asked him. I'd be surprised if he refuses me that. I go to see him every year, and it won't be long until it's time for me to see him now.'

The lady went off. Not long after, she went to see her uncle the King. She was given a great welcome.[13] After she had been there a while, she began getting ready to leave. The King asked her:

'I've never seen you come here but you wanted something. Do you want anything today?'

'Indeed, no—hardly anything.'

'What is it?'

'Oh, it's only a poor lad of a carpenter who's working for us at home, you've got a price on his head.[14] I'm only asking that you give him a safe-conduct so that he won't be pursued or troubled any more, but can go wherever he likes.'

'Oh, if that's all you want, you'll get that.'

The King sat down and wrote an order that the carpenter was not to be troubled any more, and gave her the paper. After she had said good-bye to him, it occurred to the King that the man might be Lord MacDonald. 'Stop,' he said, 'what did you say the carpenter's name was?'

She told him.

'Show me the paper again.'

'Indeed no, your majesty.'

'My word, I'm afraid you put one over on me just now.'

'If I did, it won't make much difference.'

'Good day to you,' said the King, 'I hope you'll be well when I see you again next year.'

My lady returned home. The next day she went to the carpenter's shop. (When she came in) she put her hand in her purse and took out the paper and held it out to the carpenter.

'Here's your safe-conduct from the King's hand,' she said. He took it and looked at it'

'Will you keep your word now?' she said.

'I'll keep my word all right, but it won't please your relations much, your marrying me, a poor lad who has nothing but what he can make with his two hands, you're a girl who could do better for herself.'

'I don't ask for better for myself.'

'Well, if you don't, I'll keep my word all right.'

But when the carpenter spoke to his master and asked for his daughter, oh, there was no chance in the world of it! How should he get the King's brother's daughter when he wasn't either of royal or of noble blood! But it made no difference to her even if he had tinkers' blood, she would never marry anyone but him. The upshot was[15] that the carpenter and his master's daughter got married. No wedding-feast or entertainment of any kind was made for them, nothing but 'be off and find a place for yourselves'. All they could do was to make for Scotland. At night they had to stay in poor places; they had no means to stay in hotels or castles. He kept asking her if she was getting tired, and she wouldn't admit that she was tired at all.

Then they reached Scotland. He managed to send word ahead to the nearest castle that he and his young lady wanted to stay there the night, but not to give any particular attention to them, and not to let on that they knew who they were.[16]

Then he asked her, 'Wouldn't you prefer to be with your parents now instead of accompanying me without knowing where I'll find work or a situation?'

'Don't let that trouble you,' she said, 'if I can put up with it, it's all right.'

'Well, it's all right, but it seems to me a poor thing for you.'

'What better could I get?' she said. 'But it seems we're in Scotland now.'

'Yes,' he said. 'I don't know where we'll stay tonight. We'll be at such and such a castle if we reach it.'

'Do you think they'll let us stay there?'

'I think so; they're not so unfriendly[17] in Scotland as they are in England, by any means.'

They reached the castle at dusk. They were welcomed, and stayed with the gentry of the castle all night, and were given a room as good as any in the castle. She was very much surprised how unassuming and kindly the people were.

They left the next day. At the next castle Lord MacDonald contrived for the same thing to happen. They were as well treated there as they had been the night before. They left there next day, and the owners of the castle saw them part of the way.

'Well,' she said, 'weren't they real gentry at the places where we spent the last two nights?'

'Oh yes,' he said, 'they're all like that in Scotland. There's a big difference between Scotland and England. Money is what they respect in England, but it's the man himself they respect in Scotland.'

'Yes, indeed, I can see that,' she said. 'and I can't but say they're right in a way.'

'They surely are,' he said.

'Where will we be tonight?' she said.

'My word, tonight we'll be in the castle of a kinsman of mine. Did you ever hear of Lord MacDonald's castle?'

'Do you know him?'

'I know him by sight.'

They reached the castle at dusk. The only people there were servants, staying there to look after it. They went in, and went round the rooms. There was no one there but themselves. In a short time food and drink was brought for them, and after they had eaten he said, 'I haven't seen Lord MacDonald himself since we arrived.'

'No.'

'You wait here and I'll go out to see if I can find him.'

He went off to his own room and put on his dress uniform, kilt, plaid, sword, and medals.[18] He came down with a heavy tread, and opened the door. She lifted her head; when she saw this resplendence in the door, she realized that this was Lord MacDonald. She bent her head. He stood in the door.

'Aye,' he said, 'what are you doing here.'

'I came here with my husband.'[19]

'With your husband?'

'Yes.'

'Where is your husband?'

'He went out to find yourself.'

'I haven't seen him yet. Is it long since you arrived?'

'No.'

'Does your husband look like me at all?' he said, standing in the door.

She lifted her head and looked at him. He burst into laughter.

'My God, what are you wearing now? You frightened the soul out of me!'

'Well, I'm now wearing my true clothes. And, as your parents didn't have enough respect for you to make a wedding-feast or any kind of entertainment for you because of the lowly contemptible marriage you made, write to them now and ask them to come to your wedding-feast, tell them you can now make just as good a wedding-feast as they could do in England, and that you are now the wife of Lord MacDonald.'

When she heard this, she was delighted;[20] she wrote to invite her father and mother to her wedding-feast and told them that it was Lord MacDonald whom she had married. No one knows how pleased they were when they got the invitation, and they came from England to her wedding-feast, and the King himself came to it, and she got untold presents and respect for her cleverness in getting a Lord. She was the first Englishwoman who made a Scottish marriage.

39

THE ADVENTURES OF THE DROVER BEFORE HE JOINED THE ARMY

ONCE THERE was a packman who was travelling through the Isle of Skye in the days when one could only go on foot. Night was coming on. He saw a house ahead of him and thought he would go there to see if he could get a night's lodging.[1] When he went in, he found an old couple there with their daughter. The packman asked if he could stay the night. The old man told him that it wasn't their custom to turn people away as late at night as this, and that he could stay till morning. 'Very well,' said the packman. They asked him where he had come from, and he told them the distance he had walked.

'I'm sure you're hungry,' said his host.

'I feel hungry, but I've felt hungrier.'

'I'd prefer the man who'd say that to the man who'd say he didn't need anything, when perhaps he needed it very much.'

'I'll not say that,' said the packman. 'A man who spent twenty years in the British Army, often felt hungry.'

'Aye, aye!' said his host. 'Were you twenty years in the British Army?'*

'Yes, I was,' said the packman.

'Well, I'm sure you were often hungry, and often in deadly danger[2] too.'

* The Napoleonic wars are referred to here.

'I often was. I had an arm broken in one battle, and my leg broken in another, and a bullet passed (across my forehead) above my two eyes (in a third). You can see its mark[3] yet.'

'You were in deadly danger then,' said his host.

'Yes, I was, but I was in deadlier danger once before I joined the army at all.'

'I don't know how you could have been in deadlier danger than that.'

'Well, my good fellow, I'll tell you, then. Before I ever joined the army, I was at the cattle droving, taking cattle to Falkirk;* and I used to herd the drove in the hills until near to market day; and in those days there used to be girls staying in the sheilings† with cattle on the hill. There was one sheiling where I always used to stay when I was herding the drove. The girls there were very kind to me, and I used to get plenty of milk there; and when I had sold the drove and was on my way home, I used to bring them little presents,[4] which was something they liked very much.

'But this year I was later in the year than usual, and when I had sold the drove at Falkirk and made a good profit on it (I started home). I was on my way back, and night was falling, and I said to myself that if I could reach that sheiling, I would be all right till morning. When I reached the sheiling, there was no one there; the girls had gone away. I thought I would stay there alone till morning. I went in, and lit a match, and what was there on the bed but a dead man, a young fellow. I said to myself I would stay there anyway. There was a gold watch with a gold chain on the dead man, and I thought I would take the watch and chain, and report it, thinking that the watch would identify him.

I went out behind the sheiling. While I was there, I heard the murmur of voices,[5] and I saw two young men come with a box; they went into the sheiling, and put the young man into the box, and went away with him. I followed them, keep-

* The great market to which cattle were driven every year from all over the Highlands.

† Huts or turf dwellings where women stayed to tend and milk the cattle while on the mountain grazings in the summertime.

ing them in sight. They came to a hole which they had dug, and they were about to let the box into the hole, when one of them said:

'Stop! He still has his watch on him!'

'They opened the box, and when they had looked:

'"God bless me!"[6] said one of them, "the watch isn't on him at all! Someone must have been at the sheiling since we were there. But he can't be far away yet. Hurry!"

'When I heard this, I made off as fast as I could. Frightened as I was, I lost my way,[7] and didn't know where I was going. Then I saw a light in the distance, and I made straight for it. When I arrived, I found a big, long black-house* there. The only people inside were an old wife and a big, red-headed young woman. I asked them if I could stay till morning. They said I could not, I had better clear off. I got up and went out to the end of the house. I didn't know where to turn. I thought I would get back into the far end, as it was dark, and stay there till daybreak.

'I did this, and I hadn't been long there until I heard a noise at the door, and who came in but the very pair of men I had seen at the sheiling! They asked the old wife:

'"Have you seen anyone here since night came?"

'"Well, we saw a man here who was asking to stay until morning, but we didn't let him, we sent him away."

'"It's a pity you didn't let him stay until we came. That's the very man who was at the sheiling. Have you food ready?"

'"Yes," said the daughter.

'"Well, then, let's have it quickly; we'll catch him yet with the horses before he can cross the river."

'When I heard this, I was for trying to get out by the door; and I took with me a stick which they had beneath a horse's tail, when it was carrying creels.[8] When I got out of the house, off I went, and I was as often stretching my length on the ground as I was standing up! But I reached the high road, and when I reached it, I ran for a spell until I got out of

* The old Highland black-house, with the people at one end around a fire in the middle of the floor, and the cattle at the other end, is meant. When the women put him out, the drover crept back in and hid in the end of the house where the cattle were.

breath, and then I walked for a while. Then I heard the sound of horses coming after me, and a dog ran past me and then turned back on me, with every one of its hairs[9] bristling. I hit it on the head with the piece of wood I had, and it fell stretched out stiff in the middle of the road.[10]

'I broke away from the road; and I heard one of them say, "He's here," as he jumped off his horse.

'"Oh," he said, "here's the dog killed by that devil, he can't be far away yet." He jumped on to his horse again and made off. I kept hearing the sound of a river, and I was making for it. The bank of the river was so rough[11] that I fell down it into the river, and the stream carried me away until I got hold of the branch of a tree that was growing on the bank, and clung on to it.

'I heard them coming back, and they began to walk along the bank of the river, throwing stones everywhere that was shaded by the trees. But they missed me. I was there until daybreak. The night was frosty. When I tried to get out of the river, it was difficult to manage. But I managed to drag myself out. When I got out, I found I could not stand up.[13] I was rolling myself out from the bank of the river, when I heard the creaking of a cart coming into the field with food for the cattle there. I tried to shout, but I could not shout or even utter a word. It was the horse that noticed me before the driver; then the driver came over to me and spoke to me, but I couldn't answer him. He then brought the cart over where I was, and lifted me into the cart. The cart belonged to the owner of the land, and the carter took me to the landowner's house. They lifted me out of the cart into the house, and when they were undressing me, they turned out my pockets, and what did they find in my pocket but the watch!

'When the landowner saw the watch he uttered a cry, and jumped forward with a revolver[14] in his hand. His wife came between us.

'"Look at my son's watch! I've lost my only son!"

'"If that's so, this won't bring him back," she said, "leave the man alone, don't do murder here."

'"What can I do but kill him on the spot?" he said. "What is he himself but a murderer?"

'Every time he looked at me he lifted his revolver to shoot me, but his wife stood between us. She remained on watch[15] all night, guarding me from the landowner. Next morning, I recovered my speech, and they asked me how I got the watch. I told them how, and what had happened to me, but they didn't believe me. I told him he could put me to death if he chose, but if he did, he would be killing an innocent man, and that I was telling the truth, though God was my only witness.

'"Well, if you're telling the truth," he said, "I'll send soldiers with you to that house."

'" I don't know if I can hit on the house, but I can find the sheiling anyway, I know it well enough. If you'll do that, I'll do what I can."

'The landowner sent six soldiers and a sergeant[16] with me. We set out, and when we had gone a bit of the way, one of the soldiers said:

'"Aren't we fools going with this murderer! No doubt he means to try to escape from us. We've gone far enough, let's go back!"

'They stopped, and I said to them:

'"Well, you can go back now, but if you do I'll tell the landowner you wouldn't go with me."

'"Well," said the sergeant, "he needn't think of trying to escape. He can't. We'll follow him; let him carry out his idea now."[17]

'I kept going until we had reached the sheiling; I told them this was the sheiling where I had found the landowner's son. I stopped to consider what way I had taken when I had left the sheiling. We kept on, and then I saw a light, which looked like the light I had seen the night I had been at the sheiling. When we reached it, I recognized the house well enough, and I said to the sergeant:

'"This is the house now, all right."

'"Well, if it is," said the sergeant, "you and I will go in, and my men will remain outside the door, three on each side of it, and don't let anyone in or out. If I call you, be inside as quick as you can."

'The sergeant and I went in. The old wife was sitting at

the fire;* no one else was up. We sat down, and the old wife got up and made for the up end of the house. The sergeant went to the door. The old wife woke the young men and said:

'"The man who was here last night is at the fireside, and another along with him!"

'"Very good," they said. They jumped out of bed, and shouted to the daughter, "Get up, red-head, you can wield a sword as well as any of us!"

'When the sergeant heard this, he shouted to the men at the door to come in. They appeared, and when the young men saw another six facing them with bared swords, they held up their arms, asking for quarter. They said they had only meant to frighten them.

'"That's all right," said the sergeant, "but you stay where you are and give up your arms."[18]

'They were all handcuffed, and the soldiers took them along with them and told them to go to the spot where the landowner's son had been buried. They reached the place where they had buried him, and they dug up the body, and made the young men carry it by turns until they reached the landowner's house. Then I was believed, and I was well rewarded[19] that night, so that I didn't need to be going with a pack[20] then, though I'm going with one tonight! Now I've told you how I was in greater danger before I ever joined the army, than I ever was after I joined it!'

* Which was presumably in the middle of the floor. See p. 207.

40

THE STORY OF NIALL BEAG AND MÀIRI BHÀN

THERE WAS once a rich farmer, called the Tacksman of Cornaig, in Tiree, who had a married farm servant called Niall Bàn, 'Fair Neil'. Niall Bàn had a young family growing up. It happened that Niall Bàn fell ill with a chill, and died. He left a widow and five or six children on the Tacksman of Cornaig's farm. The poor widow had nothing with which to feed the children but what she could earn. But Cornaig planted a rig of potatoes for her every year, and it was considered a great thing that he was doing this for the widow. But when we look into the matter, Cornaig was not doing so well by the widow as the widow was doing by him, for there was not a day from the time that the first sheaf was cut, until the last of the crop had been harvested, that Niall Bàn's widow was not the first woman in the field[1] with her sickle, so that Cornaig was not doing so well by her as she was by him.

Cornaig had two children, a boy and a girl. The boy, who was the elder, was called Alasdair. The girl, who was called Mary, was still going to school. The eldest child left by Niall Bàn was called Niall Beag mac Nìll Bhàin 'Little Neil, son of Fair Neil'. He was about the same age as Mary. They used to go to school together. The two children were very fond of each other. Neither of them would go anywhere without the other. They left school about the same time, and Niall Beag went to work for a crofter at the other end of the island. Mary had plenty to do at home. Niall Beag spent a year or two with the crofter, and then came home at the term.*[2] Cornaig heard he had come home and decided to engage him. He needed a lad for the cattle and to work outside along with his son Alasdair, so he engaged Niall Beag for Cornaig farm.

But after Niall Beag returned to Cornaig, the love between himself and Mary did not grow any less than it had been when they were at school. They used to work together outside, and they used to be together milking in the byres, and it was seen that there was a great bond between Mary and Niall Beag. Mary's relations were not pleased for that, but very much displeased with her. Cornaig did not want a widow's son for his daughter at all, but a rich farmer like himself. There was a farmer at the other end of the island, called the Tacksman of Cliat, a bachelor who was supposed to be rich;[3] this was the man Cornaig, and his wife particularly, wanted his daughter to marry.

Mary's parents were scolding her unceasingly; when they got tired of scolding her, Mary would give them no kind of an answer, good or bad,[4] so they knew as little when they finished as they did when they began. The affair went on like this. There was not a woman going to church who was prettier than Mary the daughter of the Tacksman of Cornaig. The Tacksman of Cliat used to call at Cornaig. But on the nights he called, Mary would pretend[5] to be so terribly busy that she had no time to stop and talk to him. But she had plenty of time to talk to Niall Beag.

One night, Cliat came to Cornaig, and he and Cornaig went out to the byre to look at Cornaig's cattle. Cornaig had a bull stirk to which Cliat took a fancy, and he asked Cornaig if he would sell it to him. Cornaig said he would, he would sell the stirk for five pounds as he didn't need it.

'Well, I won't take him away tonight. I didn't bring any money with me when I left home,' said Cliat. 'I wasn't thinking of such a thing. I'll leave him with you until I call again some evening, when I'll pay for him.'

* When his engagement ended. The Scottish custom was for farm workers to engage by the 'term' of six months, from Martinmas to Whitsuntide, or vice versa.

'Oh, you needn't leave him here because of that,' said Cornaig. 'I'd trust you with more than the stirk. Take the stirk with you, you can easily pay for him later.'

'All right,' said Cliat, 'I'll take him with me. The first time I see one of your men outside, I'll send you the money with him.'

'Don't worry about that,' said Cornaig.

Cliat went off with the stirk. It was harvest-time, and they were both very busy.[6] One wet day Alasdair, Cornaig's son, went out with his gun, and reached Cliat. Cliat met him out of doors.

'I'm glad to see you, Alasdair,' said Cliat, 'better come in with me, and I'll give you the money for your father.'

'What money?'

'The money for the stirk I bought from your father the night I called.'

'I never heard a word about it. I don't want to take it. Won't you bring it some night and give it to him yourself?'

'Well, that's all right, Alasdair, but I promised your father I'd send the money by the first one of you I met outside, and I don't want to break my word.'

'Oh, you mustn't make so much of it; bring it yourself when you next call.'

'All right. Alasdair, I'll bring it myself,' said Cliat. 'I hope you don't think I came out to ask for it.'

'Tut, certainly not. Easy now,' said Alasdair, 'why shouldn't we make a plan?'

'Well, Alasdair, what plan have you got now? You've often had good ones, though they don't always work.'

'Well,' said Alasdair, 'I've a key that will open Niall Beag's chest. I'll send him to the smithy with the white horse[7] tomorrow. You drop in at the smithy, and don't let on about anything. Then come and call some night between a week and a fortnight from today, and say you gave Niall Beag the money for the stirk to give to my father the day he was at the smithy. The money will be found in his chest, and we'll make him leave the island.'

'That seems a good plan to me, Alasdair. That's just what we'll do.'

Cliat went and got five one-pound notes, and wrote down the numbers on them and the name of the bank that issued them, in his pocket-book, and gave them to Alasdair, who went off. Next day Niall Beag was told to take the white horse to the smithy to be shod. Niall had not been long at the smithy when who came round but Cliat. I'm sure there wasn't much conversation between them, as neither cared much for the other. When Niall had finished, he went home.

A week later, when they were coming in for supper, Alasdair and his father were sitting at the table. Alasdair asked his father 'Did you get the money from Cliat, father? The money for the stirk?'

'I haven't seen Cliat since he took the stirk away with him.'

'I saw him yesterday,' said Alasdair, 'he was asking me if you got it. He said he sent it with Niall Beag the day he was at the smithy.'

'If he did, I didn't get it,' said Cornaig. 'It's a long time since he gave it to Niall Beag.'

Niall came in then, and sat down at the table.

'Who did you see at the smithy the day you were there, Niall?' said Cornaig.

'Hardly anyone.'

'Did you see Cliat there?'

'Yes.'

'Was he there for smithy work?'

'I didn't see him doing any there.'

'Did he give you anything to bring to me?'

'No, indeed, nothing.'

'Aye, aye!' said Alasdair. 'That's strange! I saw him yesterday, and he said he had sent the money for the stirk with you to my father, five pounds.'

'He didn't, nor one pound. If he had, I wouldn't have kept it until now without handing it over.'

'Aye, aye! It's very strange he should be telling lies, then.'

'If he was saying that, he was telling lies,' said Niall.

They heard a knocking at the door, and Mary went to open it. Who came in but the Tacksman of Cliat!

'Well,' said Cornaig, 'it's long since I heard "speak of the Devil, and he'll appear";[8] we were just talking about you.'

'Indeed,' said Cliat, 'I hope you weren't dispraising me.'

'No, no, not at all; but I don't know if we mightn't have come to it before we had stopped.'

'Is anything wrong?'

'No, but Niall Beag here—Alasdair says that when he saw you you told him you had sent me the money for the stirk by Niall Beag when you saw him in the smithy, and Niall Beag says you didn't. That's what we were talking about.'

'Does he say that?' said Cliat.

'I do,' said Niall. 'Where did you give me the money for Cornaig the day we were at the smithy?'

'Oh, you needn't deny it. I thought I didn't need witnesses that you took it for your master. I gave it to you behind the smithy.'

'You did not, you liar, nor in front of it,' said Niall, and he got up and hit Cliat on the ear with his fist and knocked him to the floor. Then the trouble really began.[9] Alasdair got up.

'Tut, tut, Niall, that won't do at all. That kind of thing won't do any good. You'd better hand over the money. I'll swear the man's not telling lies.'[10]

'He is telling lies, and you too. You needn't be thinking of making me out a thief. Here's the key of my chest; search it, you'll find no money there.'

The Tacksman of Cliat got up. He opened his pocket-book, and said, 'Well, I have the numbers of the notes here. If they are the same, they must be mine.'

'If they are,' said Niall, 'they won't be found with me, your notes.'

'Take it easy, Niall,' said Alasdair. 'I don't like this business. This isn't going to do any good at all.'

Alasdair got up, and opened Niall's chest, and wasn't long looking before he found the notes at the end of the tray, where he had put them himself. He turned them out.

'Well, there's money here,' he said, 'whatever it is.'

When it was turned out, there were the five one-pound notes of the Tacksman of Cliat.

'Well, Niall,' said Cornaig, 'I didn't think you were that kind of man at all. I knew your father well, and that was why

I engaged you; but you'll not be in my house another twenty-four hours.[11] You'll be clearing out at once, and you'll get what you've earned.'

There was nothing for poor Niall Beag to do but to take his chest with him out of the house. Alasdair went to help lift it on his back.

'Ah, well, Niall,' said Alasdair, 'since things are as they are, you'd better get away as quickly as you can, and we won't say a word about it. If the police found out about it, they'd put you in prison.'

Niall went home to his mother with his chest on his back. When he came in, his mother asked:

'What's this, Niall?'

Niall told his mother what had happened.

'Oh, indeed,' she said. 'This wouldn't have happened to you if you hadn't been so fond of Cornaig's daughter Mary.'

'Well, it can't be helped, mother. Please get my clothes ready so I can leave tomorrow.'

His mother started to wash his clothes, and the tears she wept would have washed his clothes all night.[12] She washed what he would take going away. Niall went to bed, but he couldn't go to sleep; too many thoughts were coming to him, and he was greatly troubled that he hadn't said good-bye to Mary, before he had left. But it happened that next day was Hallowe'en, and Niall Beag said to himself that he wouldn't go away that day as he might see Mary at Hallowe'en. When he got up in the morning, he said to his mother:

'Well, mother, I don't think I'll go away today, as it's Hallowe'en tonight; I'll be with you for this Hallowe'en anyway, though I don't know if I'll ever be with you for another one.'

'I'd sooner you put going away out of your head altogether.'

'Oh, that can't be done, mother, but even one night is something.'

Niall stayed indoors all day until night fell. When it was dark, he went to see a friend[13] of his called Alasdair Beag. When he came in, Alasdair Beag said:

'Is that you, Niall?'

'Yes.'

'I hear you've left Cornaig.'

'Yes, I have. It's not leaving Cornaig that's hurting me, but being sent away as a thief.'

'O ho!' said Alasdair Beag, 'I was sure they'd play some sort of trick on you.'

'I'd like it if you would come over to Cornaig with me to see if I can see Mary; with all the rush[15] there was I didn't get a chance to say good-bye to her,' said Niall.

'I certainly will,' said Alasdair.

They went off over to Cornaig. When they got there, it was no use for them to go into the house; they were looking in at the windows. There was a crowd inside celebrating Hallowe'en with *fuarag** and presents, all looking very happy. Cliat was in their midst. They could see Mary going back and forth past the window, but there was no way they could get a word to her. But then they began a game called *Cleas a' Chaorain*, at which one player had to go out to the peat stack and bring in a single peat from it. Eventually it was Mary's turn to go out and bring in a peat from the stack. When Alasdair Beag saw she was about to come out, he went to the end of the house, and caught her from behind as soon as she came out of the door.

'Who's that?' said Mary.

'It's me,' said Alasdair Beag. 'Niall Beag is behind the house and wants to see you.'

It was not to the peat stack that Mary went; with three steps she was behind the house.

'My God, are you here, Niall?'

'Yes,' said Niall.

'I thought you'd gone away today!'

'I would have, if I'd said good-bye to you last night, but I didn't manage to do that. Do you believe I did that, Mary?'

Mary was silent for a little.

'No, I don't believe it at all.'

'No, my dear, you needn't think I did it. But whoever did it, God will requite him for the distress he has caused my mother and myself, and for getting me sent away as a thief

* A mixture of oatmeal, sugar and cream.

when I'm innocent. But I'm sure you'll be married to Cliat before I ever see you again.'

'No, by the Book,[16] not to him nor to anyone else.'

'I don't ask that of you at all, but I'd be very pleased if you'd do what I do ask.'

'I'll do anything I can.'

'If you'll wait seven years for me. If you don't hear from me before seven years are out, I want you to marry, I don't want you to lose the chance. God knows what will become of me, but if I live you'll hear from me sometimes before that time is up.'

'Yes, I'll promise you that, and for longer.'

'Well, there isn't time for you to stay long outside tonight. I'd better say good-bye.'

They said good-bye to each other behind the house, and then Niall went home and Mary went back indoors. The next day Niall left for Glasgow, and he wasn't there long before he got the chance of a job on a sailing ship that was going to America. When he returned to Liverpool from that voyage, he wrote to Mary. But Mary's mother took good care that there was not one letter that came for Mary that she didn't herself see first; and she got Niall's letter and burnt it. Niall never got a reply.

Niall left on the next voyage, and when he returned from it he wrote to Mary again; but the same thing happened to that letter as had happened to the first one; Mary never got it. But Niall understood very well that Mary was not getting his letters; if she had been, he would have had a reply. So he didn't write again. He was sailing on one voyage after another. Time was passing; the Tacksman of Cliat was calling at Cornaig every other night, but for all his wooing Mary would not promise to marry him at all. Mary was never scolded as she was now; losing her chance of marriage for a thieving blackguard of a widow's son! For better or worse Mary would take no other man.

Then Mary's brother Alasdair got ill, and took to his bed. It turned out to be consumption; he was unable to do any work. Mary's father grew ill with rheumatism, and could only walk with two sticks. Cornaig farm was going down; the stock was being sold off. It looked as if they would have to give the place up.

Mary's mother was giving her no peace, scolding her every day; if she would marry Cliat, he would come and live there with them and keep the place up. 'You'll have nothing but what you can earn by your labours,[17] you wretched creature; you've no consideration for your own folk or for anyone who cares for you, when you won't take the advice I've given you.'

Poor Mary had to listen to her. But one day, when they were planting potatoes above the shore, Mary was thinking about Niall, and how she had never heard from him since he had left, and how the seven years were up now, and that it would surely be better for her to take her parents' advice and marry the Tacksman of Cliat, as if he lived at Cornaig he could keep the place going; however bad that would be, it would be better than going out to work. She thought this over, and when she came back home, she told her mother so.

'Providence must have looked on you since you went out, my dear; if you had decided this long ago our home would not have gone as it has; but better late than never.'

Mary's mother told her husband, who at once sent for the Tacksman of Cliat, telling him that Mary was now willing to marry him. Cliat came; they held a big betrothal ceremony.* Mary asked for a delay, she didn't want to get married until the harvest was in. That was all right, Cliat would come himself and help them gather it. Harvest-time came, and Cliat was going back and forth. They got the harvest in, and when it was in they began to prepare for the wedding. Everything went ahead until it came to 'the day of the cocks and hens'.† The Tacksman of Cliat came on his way to the wedding. The day turned very stormy, with squalls. The party started out; they had a fair way to go to the church. When the squalls came they had to hold on to each other so as not to be blown away by the wind.

* *Réiteach,* formal betrothal ceremony, considered binding and nearly as important as the wedding itself.

† The day of the wedding. Large numbers of hens were killed for wedding feasts.

Then they saw cloud gathering, and a big lump in the cloud, and they were very much frightened, they thought it was a fire or something. One of them said:

'Well, we'd better shelter under the bank of the river until this squall passes, it looks like being a bad one.'

They sat down in the shelter of the river-bank, and when the squall came, the sand of the machair flew like smoke.

'Well,' said a man called Lachlann Mór, 'we never saw such a day since that ship was wrecked down there; this day must be causing shipwrecks too, it's a day for drowning.'[18]

When the squall was over, they got up to go on. What did they see coming towards the shore but a ship without a shred of canvas.

'Didn't I know it was a day for shipwreck,' said Lachlann Mór, 'she'll go on the Bodha Mór* out there and not a soul on board will be saved.'

'I don't know,' said another man, 'that she won't come in on the strand the way she's running.'

'Oh, keep quiet. She won't. The big current will take her towards the Bodha Mór. She won't be the first one.'

As Lachlann Mór said, so it happened. The ship ran on the Bodha Mór. The first time she hit her three masts went over the side.

'Well, well,' said Lachlann Mór, 'isn't that sad! All those people aboard and no way to save them.'

She was so close they could see the men on her deck. They saw them gathering together by a small boat they were going to launch.

'Wait,' said Lachlann, 'they still have a small boat; maybe they'll manage.'

But when they launched the small boat, a sea came and swept it from their hands. It came in on the strand broken into matchwood.

'Alas there's no saving them!'

Then they saw a man on the deck in white, he was stripped to his semmet[19] and his drawers. They saw him make two jumps on the deck as nimble as if he were at a sports meeting, and the third jump he made he was into the foam.

* 'Big submerged rock.' *Bodha* in Gaelic derives from Old Norse *bodhi*.

'Upon my soul,' said Lachlann Mór, 'did you see that, fellows?'

'Yes, we did.'

'Well, indeed, whoever he is, he's a Highlander.'

'No matter whether he's a Highlander or a Lowlander,' said another, 'he won't get far.'

Then they saw him swimming strongly on the crest of a wave.[20]

'God bless me,' said Lachlann Mór, 'he's coming.'

'Yes,' said someone else, 'but his brains will be knocked out when he strikes the rocks there.'

'I think he knows the place better than you do. Look how he's avoiding the rock. Come on down and we'll go out as far as we can to meet him, so he can see us; it may encourage him. It would be worth saving even one soul of them.'

They went down to the shore. Lachlann Mór went out into the waves, with another man after him holding on to his jacket. When the seas came in, they had to retreat; when the seas ran out, they rushed forward. Mary remained standing at the top of the shore.

'My God,' said Cliat, 'where are you going, Mary? Have you forgotten what you left home for?' Mary didn't say a word. She stood above the shore. The sailor was coming. As he drew near to them, he began to weaken, and the seas were covering him. As he was coming towards them, there came a sea that broke beneath him and spread in on the beach and nearly took the men on the shore out with it. As the wave was receding, Lachlann Mór saw the man going out with it on his back in the foam; he grabbed at him and caught him by the shoulders with his big forearms that never let go of anything of which they had taken hold. He shouted that he had got him, and that they should catch hold of himself. They caught hold of the sailor, and carried him up. There was a thin line tied around his middle. His cheek and eyebrow were black where he had hit the bottom; he couldn't utter a word. They untied the line, and Lachlann said to them:

'Pull on the line, lads, and you'll see that a heavier rope will follow.'

They carried the sailor up to the shelter of the bank, and

spread clothing around to cover him. They pulled on the line, and it was not long until there came a hawser[21] with a loop on the end of it.

'Now put that loop on a standing stone that won't move,'[22] said Lachlann, 'and you'll see that a strain will be put on it.'

They did so, and made signs to the men on the ship. It wasn't long until drops of water were being wrung out of the dry part of the rope (as it stretched). Then they saw the crew gathering together, and they came off by the hawser, one man after another. The men ashore went out to meet them and to help them to land, until every man had got off. Not a man was drowned.

Then they went up and gathered around the sailor who had come ashore with the line. Some of them were rubbing his feet; Mary was down on her knees rubbing his hands.

'Is he alive?' asked Lachlann Mór.

'Yes,' said one of them, 'he's alive, but he got a bad blow.'

'Indeed he did,' said another, 'and it's a pity. He's an able fellow and a hero.[23] His own folk will miss him. He deserves it.'

'My word,' said Alasdair Beag, who was there, 'isn't the back part of his head more like that of Niall Beag the son of Niall Bàn's than anything I ever saw!'

'Won't you keep quiet? It isn't Niall or anyone like him.'

'I don't know,' said Alasdair Beag, 'it's a long time since Niall Beag went away.'

At that moment, the sailor lifted his head and opened his eyes. Mary was kneeling beside him.

'My God, aren't you Mary Bhàn, daughter of the Tacksman of Cornaig?'

Mary looked at him. 'Niall, darling, is it you?'

'Yes,' he said.

Everyone jumped up to help him to his feet. Alasdair Beag supported him on one side, and Mary on the other, and back they went to Cornaig. Cornaig himself was looking out to see if he could see the wedding party coming; when he saw them he went to meet them, walking with a stick. When he got near them he didn't know who in the world was the man in white between Mary and Alasdair Beag, while the bridegroom was following three hundred yards behind! Cornaig stopped and stood. 'Upon my soul, what's this?' he said.

'It's a brave lad who's saved his own life and the lives of the men who were along with him,' said Lachlann Mór. 'A ship was wrecked over there, and this is the man who saved all the crew by swimming ashore with a line.'

'My, my, wasn't it lucky they were saved!'

'They were saved, and this is the man they can thank for it. Do you recognize him?'

'No, I don't, how can I, I never saw the man before.'

'Indeed you did,' said Lachlann Mór, 'this lad once worked for you.'

'For me?'

'Yes, certainly. Don't you remember Niall Beag, the son of Niall Bàn?'

'Upon my soul, this isn't Little Niall but Big Niall!'

'Well, here he is, then.'

Niall Beag was taken in, and given dry clothes. Alasdair, Cornaig's son, was coughing in bed listening to the news. He called them to come up and lift him into a sitting position in the bed. They went and lifted him.

'Well, men,' he said, 'listen to me. Many a day and night the departure of Niall Beag was on my conscience. But thanks to God I am in the world yet. It was Cliat and myself that were responsible for sending Niall Beag away.' He told them of the plan they had made to put the money in Niall's chest.

When the Tiree men[24] heard this, they all jumped up. 'Where's that devil Cliat? Let's tear him to pieces! Sending away the poor widow's son as a thief! He and his wooing that he didn't know how to do!' The Tacksman of Cliat took to the door and fled as fast as he could; they were looking for him in corners[25] and sheds to catch him and kill him. He was glad enough to get home!

Niall only stayed at Cornaig that night; his mother had left there after he had left home, she didn't care to stay there. She had got a little house at the other end of the island. Next day Niall went to see her and his sisters and brothers. You can imagine how they welcomed him. When he got his affairs in order,—every penny he had earned while he was away was in a bank in England—he got the money from England and married Mary Bhàn and they had Cornaig farm afterwards. That's how Niall Beag's wooing turned out.

41

THE STORY OF ST CLAIR CASTLE

THE DUKE of Monteith had a daughter, who was his only child. A commander in the army[1] was paying court to her. This commander was to go over to France and when he came back they were to get married. It happened that she was secretly with child[2] by the commander. When the time came for her to be delivered, she left the Duke's castle for fear that this would be found out, and she went to the house of a crofter called MacRae on her father's estate, who was married but had no family. The child, a boy, was born there.

When the Duke's daughter recovered she left the child with MacRae and his wife, and 'you rear him yourselves, go away from here altogether in case it's discovered that this has happened. Wherever you go I'll support you.'

So it happened. She returned to the castle, and MacRae went away over to Harris (in the Outer Hebrides). He got a house there, and was out at the fishing every day. The Duke's daughter kept writing to him. When the commander returned from France, they got married. They were not long married when she had another boy.

But now the Duke's health broke down, and his doctors advised him to go to the Western Isles to get fresh air and fresh fish, which they said would be the best things for him. He went to Harris, and whom did he meet in Harris but MacRae. He recognized MacRae, who had been a long time on his estate, and went to stay in his house. The boy was well grown by this time. The Duke took such a fancy for the lad, and thought he would be very useful for doing errands.[3] The Duke was going out fishing with MacRae, and recovering his health very well. He spoke to MacRae and asked him if he would let the boy go away with him for a while.

MacRae did not want to let the boy go away; he knew very well[4] what was waiting for him if he did. 'Well,' said the Duke, 'you needn't worry at all about him; I'll see you get him back just as safe as I'm taking him with me. I'd like to have him with me for a while anyway. He's a nice lad and eager and polite in every way.'

However it was, MacRae let the boy go away with the Duke. When he arrived, his daughter heard that he had come home, and she and her husband went to see him and took the other boy with them. He came dressed up in long trousers;[5] 'MacRae's son' had only a kilt on. The Duke's daughter asked her father where he had brought this boy from.

'I brought him from Harris, from a man called MacRae who used to be here on the estate. I stayed in his house most of the time while I was away. I thought I would bring the boy back with me for a while; he is very good for doing errands.'

His daughter understood at once who the boy was.

'What had you got to do with that sort of man?' she said.

'Tut, there's nothing wrong with the lad; though he isn't as dressed up as your son, he can be dressed.'

'You shouldn't have had anything to do with him.' She was very much displeased with her father for having had anything to do with the lad.

The two lads went out into the garden. The 'commander's son' started to make a horse of 'MacRae's son'. 'MacRae's son' asked him to behave, but he only acted worse! He went and got a briar for a whip, and pulled the briar up between 'MacRae's son's' legs and scratched his thighs with it. The other lad lost his temper[6] and caught him and squeezed him.[7] The 'commander's son' went into the house crying, to his mother. Oh, my dear, then she was wild. 'I was sure you brought him here to be an affliction,' she said to her father, 'my boy has been nearly killed by that bastard.'

The Duke sent for 'MacRae's son'. He came in. 'Well, my

lad, I hoped when I took you from your father that your visit[8] wouldn't be so short; now get ready, you must go away. I promised your father that I would see you got back safely to him.'

The lad gave a sob[9] when he heard this. 'I never heard a man would be condemned without first knowing the reason.'

'What are you saying?' said the Duke.

'Nothing.'

The Duke looked and saw blood on the lad's legs. 'What's that blood on your legs?' he said.

'He was making a horse of me, and he cut me with briars, and I couldn't let him do that.'

The Duke lifted the lad's kilt, and saw his thighs were both torn by briars. He turned to his daughter furiously:

'Oh, you and your wretched son. If he had any manners, he wouldn't have done that. You should have taught him to behave. See how he's treated that child! You're not going home to your father like that, my lad,' he said, 'go and get undressed and into bed.'

When the Duke's daughter heard this, she and her husband left the Duke in a rage,[10] and weren't going to go near him again. He and 'MacRae's son' could have the place to themselves.

When the lad's legs were healed, she wrote to MacRae to come and get the lad at once, that he had promised her when she left the boy with him that he would not let him away. The Duke also wrote to MacRae and told him to come for the lad, and that he himself would pay for his keep. MacRae went off in a quandary. When he arrived, the Duke said to him:

'When I took the boy away with me, I really didn't expect his stay would be so short; but my daughter and her husband came to visit me here, and they brought their boy, and he and your lad went out into the garden to play, and I understand they had a set-to there. Your lad gave their boy a squeezing that hurt him;[11] their boy was to blame as he had cut him with briars. They went off in a rage, and I haven't seen them since. That's why I'm ready to part with your lad so soon.'

'Oh, I knew it would be like that when you took him with you,' said MacRae. 'On the other hand I can't take him from you, knowing you have a better right to him than I have.'

'What right have I got to him?' said the Duke.

'Oh, he's hers as sure as the other one is,' said MacRae.

'What's this slander you're saying about me and my family?' said the Duke. 'Clear out, you and your blackguard of a son.'

'I'm not slandering you at all. I'm telling the truth. Here's the napkin your daughter left with the child when she left him in my house. See if it doesn't belong to you, there's a coat of arms[12] on it.'

'This is ours, right enough; but have you any better proof?'

MacRae put his hand in his pocket and took out the Duke's daughter's letter and handed it to the Duke. 'If you need a proof, read that.'

The Duke looked at it.

'Oh, well, well! If this is the way it is, this is the way it will be! You can go when it suits you, but the lad won't go.'

MacRae went home. The Duke sent for his daughter and her husband. When they arrived, the Duke asked her what had made her turn against her son.

'Has MacRae been telling you lies? Did he dare to accuse her of that?'[13]

'Wasn't my daughter pregnant by you when you went to France?' the Duke said, turning to the commander.

'Well, yes, she was.'

'It was born dead,' she said.

'It's not dead yet either,' said the Duke, 'but since you've been as bad as that, I'll rear the lad now, and see he gets schooling and education, and he'll inherit my estate when I die.'

Well, my dear, when she heard this, she went away and refused to go near her father again. It was then that the lad was baptized and called St Clair Monteith.

When the lad had grown up into a strong and able young man, his grandfather bought him a commission[14] in the army, of equal rank to his father's; and when the Duke died, he bequeathed his estate to St Clair, and he was then in his grandfather's place, and a commander in the army. But his mother began to petition the King that St Clair had no right to the estate, that her (legitimate) son was the rightful heir, and that St Clair was only a fisherman's son whom her father had grown foolish about in his old age, and that St Clair had talked the Duke into bequeathing him the estate, and that he had no right to it. Eventually the matter came to St Clair's being put out of the castle. He took this as such a disgrace that he deserted from the army. An Italian and a Frenchman followed him. He came to Barra, and it was there that he built the castle on the loch.*

There was a price on St Clair's head for anyone who would betray him, because he had deserted from the army. Then it was found out that he was on Barra, and a warship was sent there with soldiers to capture him. St Clair saw it coming, and collected every man on Barra—he was a sort of king there—on top of the mountain behind Castlebay.† There was no pier then, and the ship had to anchor out in the bay. The captain came ashore with a commander in the army to see if they could find out where St Clair was. St Clair came down to meet them, asking his men to remain on the top of the hill and to show themselves. He met the captain and the commander. They recognized him at once, and told him that they had come for him and he must go along with them.

'Which do you prefer,' said St Clair, 'to go back as you come, or to have your heads taken off where you are?'

'Oh, we won't trouble you at all, you needn't come with us unless you want to,' said the captain.

'Do you see my army up on top of the hill there? I have only to whistle for them, and even if you had three men-o'-wars[15] here, not one of you would leave the spot.'

'Oh, we aren't going to trouble you,' said the captain.

'Well, then, return as you came.'

They returned and related what they had seen; there was no knowing what army St Clair had raised on Barra. 'Oh

* On an island in Loch Tangusdale. The ruins are still standing.

† Heaval, 1,200 feet, the highest hill in Barra.

well,' said the King, 'it doesn't matter much; we'll let him alone until we find out what he means to do.'

St Clair used to go over to the mainland and come back to Barra. One time when he was on the mainland they were holding sports, with competitions in swordsmanship. When St Clair arrived, who was standing in the ring but his brother? His brother had the first prize.[16] He didn't know that St Clair was his brother, but St Clair knew their relationship, well enough. The Queen and Lady Ambleton were sitting side by side, and the Queen said to Lady Ambleton, 'There's a man who would suit you (pointing to St Clair's brother); I'll order him to marry you.'

'I wouldn't care to get him that way,' said Lady Ambleton, 'unless he came of his own free will.'

The Queen was insulted at the way Lady Ambleton turned down her offer. St Clair overheard this, and went over to his brother. 'You won't get the first prize until you've taken me on.'

'All right.'

The contest started, and in two minutes St Clair's brother was cut out of the ring by St Clair. St Clair went over to Lady Ambleton. 'Well, it's for your sake I fought today.'

She got up and paid her respects to him, and thanked him very much, for what he had done.

St Clair returned to Barra. Then he learned that his brother was going to marry Lady Ambleton; and he said to himself that if it could be done, he would keep her from him out of spite. He went over to the mainland, taking the Frenchman and the Italian with him, and they went to Lady Ambleton's castle. The Frenchman and the Italian were very good musicians at the violin and the harp. They played outside the castle, and the servants came out, and made them come in to the hall[17] and play for a dance. They all went in. St Clair had a ring which he wanted to give to Lady Ambleton, and he didn't know how in the world he could manage to do it. 'Give it to me,' said the Italian, 'I'll find a way to get it to her.' The Italian got hold of Lady Ambleton's tablemaid, and said to her:

'Well, I don't know what to do!'

'What's that?'

'I met a female saint[18] who gave me a gold ring and made me promise to give it to a woman who had had nothing to do with man. I don't know where such a one is.'

'I know one like that.'

'Who?'

'My mistress.'

'Are you sure?'

'Yes, indeed, I can swear on it.'

'Well, if you're sure of it, I'll give you the ring to give to her.'

He gave the ring to the tablemaid, who took it to Lady Ambleton.

'My word, those men outside——'

'What men are they, my girl?'

'Hasn't one of them given me a gold ring he got from a female saint, which he's obliged to give to a woman who's never had anything to do with a man; I told him I knew one like that, yourself.'

'What, my girl, how do you know that?'

'I know, all right. Look at the ring!'

The maid handed Lady Ambleton the ring. Lady Ambleton looked at it, and saw St Clair's name inside it. She understood who it was.

'Many thanks, my girl, for bringing me this. Go and tell them they can stay where they are tonight.'

The girl came out. 'Well,' said the Italian, 'did she accept it?'

'Yes, and she was pleased.'

'Good enough. I'm clear.'

'And she said you may stay here tonight.'

'Very good,' said the Italian.

When everyone had gone to sleep, Lady Ambleton came out, and St Clair got a chance to talk with her. She told him that his brother was coming to marry her, and that her relations were very willing that she should marry him. 'But if I look like having to do it, I'll find a way to let you know.'

'Well, remember that,' he said.

St Clair and the Italian and the Frenchman returned to

Barra. Then he found out that his brother was getting ready to marry Lady Ambleton; and he returned to the mainland by himself. He reached the castle the day the marriage was to take place, in a little chapel opening off the castle. His brother had arrived and was getting dressed in one room, and Lady Ambleton was getting ready in another. St Clair found out the room she was in, and went in and caught her by the hand, and took her out through the chapel. The cry was raised that the bride had been stolen, and St Clair's brother went after him. When St Clair was going through the chapel, his brother appeared in the door behind him. St Clair stopped.

'Are you going to take her from me? As sure as I stripped you in that field, I'll strip the head off you before the altar,[19] unless you go back at once.'

His brother retreated, overcome by fear. St Clair went off with the lady and took her to Ireland. When they landed there, she said:

'My God, what a fate it is for me to go off like an outlaw[20] like this, when I didn't need to.'

'Do you regret it?' he said.

'No wonder if I do.'

'Well, this is a fine time to say that. Good-bye to you,' he said, holding out his hand.

When he held out his hand to say good-bye, she began to weep. When he saw she was crying, he caught her by the hand.

'Well, well, you won't be going like an outlaw any longer.'

They went up to a church above the shore. They were then in Carrickfergus in Ireland. They got married there; then they returned to the castle on Barra. There was not a man on Barra who didn't run to them with everything he had! She was never so happy in any castle as in his castle on Barra.

His brother then went and married a woman St Clair had been making up to when he was in the castle on the mainland. 'If he has got that one, I'll have this one.' His brother's wife was then hearing how happy Lady Ambleton was with St Clair, and she envied her greatly; she much preferred St Clair to the one she had got. She didn't know how she could get hold of St Clair, or what revenge she could inflict on him, for not having married herself. She had a factor called MacLellan, whom she bribed to go to Barra with a ship to see if he could get hold of St Clair. By now St Clair had been a good time on Barra and his family had grown up, his eldest son was eighteen years old.

The factor went off on this errand, and when he appeared off Barra he lowered every sail that was over him[21] and put up a flag[22] to signal that he was in distress. St Clair saw it, and went out to the ship in a boat to see what was on board, or if there was anything in her that might be of use to poor people. When he reached her, they put a ladder against her side, and St. Clair climbed up. When he had got on board, he was taken below deck[23] and locked up in a room. The men in his boat were told to make for the land. When they got back to land they told how St Clair had been taken from them. His wife began to lament and weep for her orphaned children. She didn't know what to do.

The Frenchman and the Italian and St. Clair's son left for the mainland to see if they could find out what had become of him. When they reached the mainland, they separated. They arranged where to meet; they were going in disguise[24] to see what they could discover. St Clair's son went to the castle of the Duke of Monteith, which now was his uncle's. His uncle's wife saw him and took such a fancy to him, he was a fine, strong lad, that she asked him if he would be willing to stay as a soldier in the castle guard. He said he would. That was all right. He was parading every day along with the others. He became friendly with one of the maidservants. His uncle's wife often talked to him, and asked him if he wouldn't marry one of the pretty maidservants there.

'I don't see any prettier than yourself.'

'Am I the prettiest?'

'Indeed you are. I'd willingly adore you, you're so pretty.'

Oh, this pleased her very much. But the lad wasn't finding out anything. One night he went to see MacLellan, and he recognized his father's gloves[25] hanging in MacLellan's house. He said to himself that it was certainly here that his father had met his end. He used to see four men go out of the castle every night and come in again in the morning. He didn't know where in the world they were going. He asked the girl one night, 'Where do those four men go, who go out every night?'

'I don't know,' she said.

'Do you know if they have a man imprisoned here?'

'I don't know.'

'Surely you know,'[26] he said. 'Why are you hiding it from me?'

'They have a poor man who was on Barra in prison. I believe that tonight's his last night,' she said. 'Death's no worse for him than the treatment he's been getting.'

'Oh, yes.' He didn't let on at all.

St Clair's son went out that evening to see what he could see or hear, reflecting on what he should do. Whom did he meet but the Frenchman and the Italian! They asked him if he had heard anything about his father. 'Yes; they have him imprisoned here. I understand that tonight's his last night on earth. Go and steal four horses from some stable or other. Have them ready at ten o'clock, and I'll come out to see what we can do about it.'

The Frenchman and the Italian went off, and St Clair's son returned into the castle. When it was ten o'clock in the evening, the guard used to be posted at the gate; no one could get in after ten o'clock. St Clair's son went to go out; when he reached the gate, the guard was there before him.

'Where are you going?'

'Never mind where I'm going.'

'I do mind where you're going. Haven't you grown bold[27] since you came here! Thinking you can go in and out as you please! Go back at once!'

'Not for you,' he said, and he caught hold of his dagger and stabbed the guard and killed him, and went out. The Frenchman and the Italian were there before him with the horses.

They went to the prison. The door was locked, and there were four of the guard inside. When St Clair heard them coming to the door, he cried 'Oh, you've come, you devils! This looks like being my last night.'

When the lad heard his father speaking, he backed and came at the door with his heel, and broke it into pieces. In they went, and the fight began; the room was only eight feet long, and there were eight men fighting in it! They took our St Clair, and kicked and killed the guard. The horses were ready there, and they only had to jump on them and be off. St Clair and his son and the Frenchman and the Italian then returned to Barra; and there was never such a feast[28] as they had that night, so glad was his wife to get St Clair back again.

His son then went to the mainland and enlisted[29] in the army. One day they were having sports and horse races and the King was competing himself. There was a river beside the park where the sports were, and the King's horse got so excited[30] that the King lost control of it, and it went out into the river with him, and in the middle of the river the King lost his seat. He seemed likely to be drowned.[31]

'Upon my soul,' said St Clair's son, 'is there anyone who'll save the King?'

'Will you save him yourself?' said the commander.

'I don't know,' he said.

St Clair's son rushed out and just when the King was going down, he caught him and swam ashore with him. The King was taken away, unable to speak a word. When he recovered, he had to find out who had saved him. He was told that a soldier had done it. He ordered the soldier to be brought before him. The commander told St Clair's son that he had to go before the King. 'All right.' The commander took him with him, and when they arrived the King asked that he be sent in to him.

St Clair's son went in and went down on his knee before the King. 'Get up, get up,' said the King, 'don't kneel to me at all; it is I who should kneel to you. You saved my life for me, but I haven't saved your life at all. It's not for that that I've sent for you, but to give you a reward for saving my life. You can now have from me whatever you ask.'

'Well, your majesty,' said St Clair's son, 'I won't ask for much. What I ask of you is to give back to the man on Barra whom you've outlawed, St Clair Monteith, his own place, of which he was deprived by trickery and lies. I'm his son.'

'Well, for your sake,' said the King, 'he'll get his place back.' So St Clair got back to his castle on the mainland, and his brother was put out of it. He and his brother lived at peace with each other ever afterwards; they used to visit each other; it was their mother who had been to blame for everything. There I left them well enough off.

42

WHY EVERYONE SHOULD BE ABLE TO TELL A STORY

ONCE THERE was an Uistman who was travelling home, at the time when the passage wasn't as easy as it is today. In those days travellers used to come by the Isle of Skye, crossing the sea from Dunvegan to Lochmaddy.[1] This man had been away working at the harvest on the mainland.[2] He was walking through Skye on his way home, and at nightfall he came to a house, and thought he would stay there till morning, as he had a long way to go. He went in, and I'm sure he was made welcome by the man of the house, who asked him if he had any tales or stories. He replied that he had never known any.

'It's very strange you can't tell a story,' said his host. 'I'm sure you've heard plenty.'

'I can't remember one,' said the Uistman.

His host himself was telling stories all night, to pass the night, until it was time to go to bed. When they went to bed, the Uistman was given the closet[3] inside the front door to sleep in. What was there hanging in the closet but the carcass of a sheep! The Uistman hadn't been long in bed when he heard the door being opened, and two men came in and took away the sheep.

The Uistman said to himself that it would be very unfortunate for him to let those fellows take the sheep away, for the people of the house would think that he had taken it himself. He went after the thieves, and he had gone some way after them when one of them noticed him, and said to the other:

'Look at that fellow coming after us to betray us; let's go back and catch him and do away with him.'

They turned back, and the Uistman made off as fast as he could to try to get back to the house. But they got between him and the house. The Uistman kept going, until he heard the sound of a big river; then he made for the river. In his panic he went into the river, and the stream took him away. He was likely to be drowned. But he got ahold of a branch of a tree that was growing on the bank of the river, and clung on to it.[4] He was too frightened to move; he heard the two men going back and forth along the banks of the river, throwing stones wherever the trees cast their shade; and the stones were going past him.

He remained there until dawn. It was a frosty night, and when he tried to get out of the river, he couldn't do it. He tried to shout, but he couldn't shout either. At last he managed to utter one shout, and made a leap; and he woke up, and found himself on the floor beside the bed, holding on to the bedclothes with both hands. His host had been casting spells on him during the night! In the morning when they were at breakfast, his host said:

'Well, I'm sure that wherever you are tonight, you'll have a story to tell, though you hadn't one last night.'

That's what happened to the man who couldn't tell a story; everyone should be able to tell a tale or a story to help pass the night!

NOTES

THE CHIEFS OF CLANRANALD AND THE MACVURICHS OF STAOILIGEARRAIDH

The Clanranalds

The chiefs of Clanranald, who were descended from Somerled, Lord of the Isles, possessed the territories of South Uist, Benbecula, Canna, Eigg, Arisaig, and Moidart. Their residences were at Caisteal Tioram, in Moidart, Ormaclate in South Uist, and latterly at Nunton in Benbecula.

The Clanranalds who were chiefs during the period of the stories on Local Tradition translated here were as follows:

Allan MacDonald, chief 1584 to 1593. He was married to a daughter of Alasdair Crotach MacLeod of Dunvegan.

Sir Donald MacDonald, his eldest surviving son, chief from 1593 to 1619. He was married to Mary, daughter of Angus MacDonald of Islay.

John MacDonald, his eldest son, chief from 1619 to 1670. He married Marion (Mór) daughter of Sir Roderick MacLeod, Ruairi Mór of Dunvegan, in 1613. He received the Irish Franciscans at Caisteal Tioram in Moidart in 1624 and was reconciled by them to the Catholic Church, thereafter giving them much encouragement. In 1626 he wrote a letter to Pope Urban VIII appealing for help for the Catholic chiefs in the Highlands and Islands. He was a staunch Royalist throughout the Civil Wars and fought under Montrose against the Covenanters.

Donald (Dòmhnall Dubh), his eldest son, was chief from 1670 to 1686. He was married to his cousin, Marion, daughter of John MacLeod of Dunvegan, and sister of Roderick of Dunvegan and John of Dunvegan, three brothers who were chiefs of the MacLeods of Harris in succession. Donald, who also fought in the Civil Wars under Montrose, has not a good reputation in the Highlands, and his marriage turned out unhappily. He is the subject of Story No. 18.

Allan MacDonald, his eldest surviving son, was chief from 1686 until his death at the Battle of Sheriffmuir in 1715. He took part in the Battle of Killiecrankie on the Jacobite side in 1689 and was thereafter in exile in France, where he met and married Penelope, daughter of Colonel MacKenzie, who had been governor of Tangier. He is the subject of Story No. 19.

He was succeeded by his brother Ranald MacDonald, who died unmarried in France in 1725.

He was succeeded by his cousin Donald, grandson of Ranald (Raghnall mac Ailein 'ic Iain), younger brother of Sir Donald above-mentioned. He married his cousin Margaret, daughter of Dòmhnall Dubh and sister of his two predecessors in the chiefship. He died in 1730.

Ranald MacDonald, his son, was chief from 1730 until 1753, when he renounced the life-rent of his estates in favour of his heir, owing to infirmity. He was married to Margaret, daughter of William MacLeod of Bernera. He took no part in the Rising of 1745, but his heir, Ranald was a devoted follower of Prince Charles.

Ranald was succeeded by his eldest son, John, by his second wife, Flora, daughter of MacKinnon of Strath. John died in 1794 at the age of twenty-nine. He was married to Katherine, daughter of the Rt. Hon. Robert MacQueen of Braxfield, Lord Chief Justice of Scotland. He was succeeded by his eldest son Reginald George, born in 1788, who, in the words of Charles Fraser-Mackintosh, 'succeeded to his great estates when a child (and) was brought up with an exaggerated idea of his importance and wealth. Bad management, inefficient supervision, and above all the fall in the value of kelp, proved fatal, and one after another of his great estates had to be sold, until nothing remained but Caisteal Tioram and a few acres in Moidart.'*

The Macvurichs of Staoiligearraidh

The MacVurichs, now called Curries, were the hereditary bards and historians of the Clanranalds. They kept commonplace books in which clan history, genealogical information, panegyrics and elegies for their own and for other chiefs were entered. These were written in the classical Gaelic which was the common literary language of Ireland and the Scottish Highlands and Islands down to the beginning of the eighteenth century; in fact, the MacVurichs were the last practitioners of Gaelic bardic verse anywhere. The composition of this poetry demanded a careful study of metres and a thorough knowledge of Gaelic genealogy and tradition back to Old Irish times. It is probable that the MacVurichs once possessed a considerable library of Gaelic MSS. Their Red Book of Clanranald has been published, with a translation, which is not always accurate, in the second volume of Reliquiae Celticae.

* *Antiquarian Notes*, p. 320. Cp. also A. Mackenzie, *History of the MacDonalds*.

Many of the Clanranalds mentioned here are eulogized in that book, one of the latest poems being to Ranald who was in exile after the Rising of 1715.

It is to be hoped that some day the poetry of the MacVurichs will be collected and translated; this would be the most fitting memorial that could be made for them.

THE OLD ISLAND HOUSES

The nomenclature of the old Island houses, both black houses and three-roomed thatched cottages, differs from that of English in a way that makes literal translation impossible; for example, in English, to 'come down' in a house means to come downstairs; but Island houses had no upper story, and to 'come down' in such a house means to go from the kitchen into the parlour end. Here a literal translation of the Gaelic into English would be quite misleading.

I am obliged to Miss Annie Johnston, of Castlebay, Isle of Barra, whose name is well known to students of Gaelic folklore, for the following description of the two kinds of old-fashioned houses that existed in the islands:

'The earliest thatched houses that I can remember had the fire in the middle of the floor in the middle of the house, with the ends of the house partitioned off for sleeping quarters. The *ceann-shuas* ("up end") was usually the women's quarters, while the *cùlaiste* on the left-hand side of the front door was the men's sleeping accommodation. The middle portion, where the fire was, was the kitchen part where all the work was done. There was a door in each partition, of course. The last of these houses I saw here, about fifty years ago, was Taigh Màiri a' Bhealaich, "The House of Mary of the Pass", in Bealach Bhreubhaig. I was at a wedding there in 1908. The supper was served on trestle tables on each side of the fireplace, which was going full blast to keep the kettles and teapots hot. The place was so hazy with peat smoke that I got the shock of my life when I saw a door opening in the partition at the *ceann-shuas*, "up end", and a woman coming out. I had not noticed the partition, as it was black with the smoke, and I thought it was the house-end.

'The next type of house was such as you describe (a three-roomed thatched house with the kitchen at one end and the parlour at the other, with a small room called a *clòsaid* between them).* It had

* A picture of one of these houses can be seen in *Folksongs and Folklore of South Uist* by Margaret Fay Shaw, Illustration No. 3a.

chimneys, but the names *ceann-shuas* and *ceann-shìos*, "up-end" and "down end", were retained for the kitchen and room end. The term *rùm* was not used;* the *ceann-shìos* was termed the *cùlaiste* as in the old pre-chimney house already described. The *cùlaiste* and the *clòsaid* were just the sleeping-quarters. In a family of boys, some of them at least would have bunks in the *sobhal* or outhouse.

'The "reception-room" was the kitchen, and *thig a nuas*, "come up", was an invitation to come and join the company. *Chaidh e sìos*, "he went down", would be "he went down" to the *cùlaiste* or room.

'I have seen the *clòsaid* door in some houses opposite the outer door,† but that made the *clòsaid*, which was a small bedroom, very cold, and latterly in most thatched houses, the *clòsaid* door opened off the kitchen.

'If there was any private business to be transacted between the man of the house and a visitor, they went *sìos do'n chùlaiste*, down to the *cùlaiste*, sometimes also referred to as *ìochdar an taighe*, "the lower part of the house", while the kitchen was *uachdar an taighe*, "the upper part of the house". Food was always served in the kitchen.

'The *ceann-shìos*, "down end", had two large box-beds, a couple of chairs, a table and some clothes-chests, a blanket-chest and a large cupboard in most houses. Of course different places had different ways, but that is how I remember them in Barra.'

It is important that the reader should realize that when houses are referred to in these tales, they are nearly always of the types described. There is really nothing in the older stories, but such houses and the castles of the rich and powerful, the interiors of which I have never heard described by storytellers.

AONGHUS BEAG'S INFORMANTS

The stories translated in this book were learnt by Aonghus Beag from the following persons:

Angus MacLellan (*Aonghus mac Eachainn 'ic Dhòmhnaill*), his father, No. 27.

John Beaton, Milton (whose father came from Skye), 13.

Archie Cameron, Rannoch, 36.

John MacAlister, a pedlar settled in Uist, 34.

Allan MacDonald, Peninerine (*Ailein Mór mac Ruairidh 'ic*

* The word *rùm* occurs frequently in Aonghus Beag's tales, *cùlaiste* never as far as I can remember.

† Cp. pp. xxi, 201.

Ailein), Nos. 4, 8, 12, 22, 24, 26, 32, 33, 39, 40. He was unable to read English or Gaelic.

Donald MacDonald, Peninerine (*Dòmhnall mac Dhunnchaidh 'ic an Tàilleir*, father of Duncan MacDonald the late famous storyteller), 1, 2, 3. He could read English and a little Gaelic.

Donald MacDonald, Stonybridge (*Dòmhnall mac Alasdair 'ic Dhunnchaidh*), 5.

James MacDonald, Locheynort, 31, 35.

Alasdair MacIntyre, Beinn Mhór (*Alasdair Mór mac Iain Dheirg*), 6, 14–22, 25, 37, 42. Could read Gaelic but not English.

Neil MacIntyre, postmaster, Howmore, 7, 38, 41. Could read English.

Rev. Fr John Mackintosh, Bornish, 27.

Angus Morrison, Locheynort (still living), 29, 30.

Neil Smith, postmaster at Howmore after Neil MacIntyre, 11. Could read English.

John Wilson, Howmore, 10.

'A man from Tiree', 9.

Notes on the Stories

THE STORYTELLER'S OWN STORY

[1] MacLellan. This is *Mac 'ill' Fhialain* in South Uist, not *Mac 'ill' Fhaolain.*

[2] There wasn't a sign of any of them, *cha robh sgial air càch.*

[3] a noise, *brag*. Usual word for a short sharp noise.

[4] fourpence ha'penny an hour. These words in English.

FINGALIAN AND OTHER OLD STORIES

Fingalian stories and ballads used to be tremendously popular in the Scottish Highlands and Islands, as they were in Ireland. In 1567 the Calvinist Bishop Carswell of the Isles denounced the Highlanders' fondness for them as an obstruction to the spreading of the principles of the Reformation in the Highlands, in the introduction to his translation of John Knox's Liturgy, the first book to be printed in Gaelic.

See *passim* Neil Ross, *Heroic Poems from the Book of the Dean of Lismore;* Eóin Mac Néill, *Duanaire Finn;* J. F. Campbell of Islay, *West Highland Tales* and *Leabhar na Féinne;* J. G. Campbell, *The Fians* (Waifs and Strays of Celtic Tradition, Vol. IV); James

MacDougall, *Folk and Hero Tales* (*idem* Vol. III); George Henderson, *The Fionn Saga* (Celtic Review, Vols. II and III); Reidar Christiansen, *The Vikings in Gaelic Tradition*; Calum I. MacLean, *The Birth and Youthful Exploits of Fionn* (Scottish Studies, Vol. I, p. 205).

I. HOW THE FINGALIANS WERE FOUNDED

Mar a thogadh na Fiantaichean

Learned by Aonghus Beag from Donald MacDonald, Peninerine. Recorded on tape at Frobost on 12th January 1960.

A version of this story and the next one, running consecutively, was taken down by Fr Allan McDonald from Alasdair Ruadh, Alexander Johnston, on Eriskay in 1892. A good deal of the Gaelic text was printed by Dr George Henderson in the Celtic Review, II 263–272, 351–359, and III 56–61. It breaks off with the incident of the death of Aodh, and though marked 'to be continued' was never completed. No translation was printed. No. 2 here is actually complete in Fr Allan's notebook; part of it is written in by another hand, perhaps Dr Henderson's from Fr Allan McDonald's rough notes.

Aonghus Beag did not actually recite Duan na Ceardaich, 'The Ballad of the Smithy', while telling the story; he simply said 'it was then that the Ballad of the Smithy was made, which you have heard before'. He had recorded the Ballad for me at Lochboisdale on 23rd November 1949, the first time we met. His sister sings this ballad, as well as others, and recorded it for Fr John MacLean on my machine in November 1957. It was an extremely popular ballad in the islands. See *Duanaire Finn*, II, 2; Margaret Fay Shaw, *Folksong and Folklore of South Uist*, p. 31; Reidar Christiansen, *The Vikings in Gaelic Tradition*, p. 197, 345; J. F. Campbell, *Leabhar na Féinne*, p. 65; *West Highland Tales*, III 396; J. G. Campbell, *The Fians* (Waifs and Strays IV 64, 149. A version of the air to which the ballad is sung was printed by Miss Amy Murray in *Fr Allan's Island*, p. 100. Fr Allan McDonald took down a version around 1891 from a boy called Kenneth MacLeod at Dalabrog who recited it on Hogmanay night. He had learned it from his grand uncle.

[1] they would go to rack and ruin, *gun rachadh iad gu dràibh.*

[2] if I didn't get her by consent, I'd take her by force, *mura faighinn a dheòin i, gu faighinn a dh'aindeòin i.*

[3] what the child was, *dé 'n urra bha 'n siod.*

[4] she had twins, *bha dithist aice.* The Gaelic for one of two twins is *leth-leanabh.*

[5] watching them, *a' gabhail ealla riutha.*

[6] Who is the crop-headed, white-haired, tough-eyelashed boy, *Có e an gille maol, fionn, agus rasg ruighinn 'na cheann.* The bishop is an anachronism. In the *Duanaire Finn* the name is said to have been thus bestowed by the High King Conn (p. 134).

[7] a mark of burning, *ball-losgaidh.*

[8] a blister, *poca-losgaidh.*

[9] power of divination, *fiosachd.*

[10] tooth of knowledge, *deud-fios.*

[11] 'He squealed like a pig'. The Gaelic is:

> '*Sgiamhadh e mar gum biodh muc,*
> *Agus rànadh e mar gum biodh torc,*
> *Agus bhramadh e mar gum biodh gearran,*
> *Agus a shleagh fhéin 'na bhreaman.*'

[12] 'Aye, aye!' This Scots expression is used fairly often in Aonghus Beag's stories, with the sense 'Is that so?'

[13] a mop, *mapaid.* See *mabaid* in Fr Allan McDonald's Gaelic *Words from South Uist.*

[14] Bran's colour. The Gaelic is:

> '*Casan buidhe bh'aig Bran,*
> *Dà thaobh dubh agus tàrr geal,*
> *'S druim uaine chon na seilge,*
> *Dà chluais chorracha chrò-dhearg.*'

[15] The Hammer of the Fingalians, *an t-Òrd Fiantaich.* This is a corruption for *An Dòrd Fiantaich,* which must have been some kind of musical instrument. The pronunciation is the same. See Professor Angus Matheson, *Éigse* VII 257.

[16] They let out their belts, *lig iad a mach am bronnaichean.* Literally 'they let out their stomachs'; but see the beginning of the next story, where they were holding in their bellies with oaken pins, when suffering great hunger.

2. HOW THE FINGALIANS LOST THEIR HUNTING AND RECOVERED IT

Mar a chaill na Fiantaichean an t-sealg aca 's a fhuair iad air ais i

Learned by Aonghus Beag from Donald MacDonald, Peninerine.

Recorded on wire (No. 497) at Lochboisdale Hotel on the 1st November 1950, and again on tape at Frobost on 3rd June 1958.

The translation is based on the recording made in 1950, with the addition of a few sentences from the 1958 recording omitted from the 1950 one.

See notes to No. 1.

[1] to keep a watch on the women, *a waitseadh nam boireannach.* English word used, here and elsewhere.

[2] a lapful, *sgiùrd.*

[3] could not make an uncompleted blow, *cha n-fhàgadh e fuidheall beum.*

[4] seven oaken beams, etc. *Seachd sailghean daraich, agus seachd seichdeannan do sheann-leathair, agus seachd pluic réisg.*

[5] a paddle, *sluasaid.* Also means 'shovel'. Compare Middle Irish *râma*, meaning both 'oar' and 'spade'. T. F. O'Rahilly, *Celtica* I 363. From which 'we infer that the primitive paddle or oar served also as a spade or a shovel.' My own impression is that it is easier to row with a spade than to dig with an oar!

[6] weak, *slac.* English word.

[7] lump of a carle, *lùireach do bhodach.*

[8] you can have what you can carry, *gheobh thu t'eallach.* Cp. *eallach do dhroma* in Fr Allan McDonald's *Gaelic Words* from South Uist.

[9] you've made a hopeless blunder, *rinn thu do mhiapadh.* See *miapadh* in Gaelic Words from South Uist.

[10] 'I impose tabus on you.' The formula as used by Aonghus Beag is, *Tha mi cur mar chrosaibh agus mar gheasaibh ort, agus mar naoi buaraichean mnatha sìdheadh siùbhla seacharain, gach laochan beag as miotaiche 's as mi-threòiriche na thu fhéin a thoir do chinn 's do chluas 's do chaitheamh-beatha dhiot, mura . . .* He uses *thoir* for *thoirt.*

No one knows what conferred the power of putting another person under *gheasa* or tabus.

[11] you wretched apparition, *a thamhaisg na truaighe.*

[12] a little currach, *currachan beag do bhàta.*

[13] far end of the cave, *ìochdar na h-uamha*, cp. *ìochdar an taighe*, p. 208.

[14] the poker, English word used here and elsewhere. Cp. *Sia Sgialachdan*, p. 45.

[15] an iron bar, *gàd iarainn.*

[16] two pieces of silver, *dà airgiod.* Quite distinct.

[17] he jumped, *gheàrr e cruinn-leum;* means he jumped from a standing position.

[18] it fitted as well as if it had grown on my foot, *bha i fiod cho math dhomh 's ged a dh'fhàsadh i air mo chois.*

[19] They took me below deck *thug iad sìos fo rùm mi.*

[20] I tried to catch her and she turned into a mouse, *thug mi tàradh oirre agus leum i 'na luch.*

[21] the scaffold of the gallows, *sgafal na croiche.*

3. THE FINGALIANS IN THE ROWAN MANSION

Na Fiantaichean anns a' Bhruidhean Caorthainn

Learned by Aonghus Beag from Donald MacDonald, Peninerine. Recorded on tape at Frobost on 13th January 1960.

Cp. *Waifs and Strays*, III 56, 'How Finn was in the House of Blar-Buie (Yellow-Field), without the power of rising up or lying down'. See also *Leabhar na Féinne* p. 86. I recorded a version of this story from Duncan MacDonald, Peninerine, on 21st July 1950.

The version told by Aonghus Beag here is only a précis of the traditional story. The name of 'Rowan Mansion' is not mentioned, but when it occurred in the ballad on the Death of Diarmaid, Aonghus Beag remarked that it referred to this story.

[1] generous, *bronnach.* Cp. Irish *bronnmhar.*

[2] a big, plump female, *boireannach mór tula-reamhar.* Diarmaid had a weakness for women, and they for him.

4. THE DEATH OF DIARMAID

Bàs Dhiarmaid

Learned by Aonghus Beag from Allan MacDonald, Peninerine. Recorded on tape at Frobost on 12th January 1960. The story of the elopement of Diarmaid with Grainne, and his subsequent death through his encounter with the venomous boar and Fionn's refusal to bring him a drink of water, is one of the most popular of all the Fingalian ballads. Fortunately in this case was a version taken down by the Dean of Lismore in Perthshire over 450 years ago and this, although incomplete, enables us to see what lies behind the contemporary versions of the same ballad, which have suffered some corruption in transmission.

See Neil Ross, *Heroic Poems from the Book of the Dean of Lismore*, p. 70. Extensive references are given in the notes to this, p. 221, and need not be repeated here, except for *Leabhar na Féinne*, p. 158, and *West Highland Tales*, III 49. A version of the story and ballad was taken down by Fr Allan McDonald from Angus MacInnes, aged 84, of Smercleit, on 15th October 1896. Other versions of the ballad were taken down by Dr George Henderson from Donald MacInnes 'Dòmhnall Chailein', Parks, Eriskay, aged 60, and from John Smith, South Boisdale, both probably in 1892. Duncan MacDonald recorded a good version for me on wire on 10th January 1950 and 21st July the same year (Nos. 207, 347).

[1] a wild boar, *torc nimh.*

[2] a mole, *ball-dòbhrain.*

[3] the boss of the shield (?), *an sgian-ubhail.*

For other Uist versions, Angus MacInnes, Smercleit, had *sgian-urla* (Fr Allan McDonald); Duncan MacInnes had *sgian-ubhla;* John Smith, *sgiath-umhla* (Henderson). In the version printed in *West Highland Tales*, III 75, which appears to be a collation of several versions taken down from reciters in Barra and South Uist, the word is given as *an sgiath urla* and translated 'The well Skilled Shield'; a note by Hector MacLean says '*Sgiath urla* or *urlaimh.* Expert shield, a name for Diarmid, from his adroitness in the use of the shield'. I doubt this. Unfortunately the Book of the Dean of Lismore version does not help here, though it does show that what happened was that Diarmaid threw three spears at the boar, one after the other, and each broke; then he took his sword.

[4] The son of Duibhne, i.e. Diarmaid.

[5] Ideal son, *A dhealbh-mhic;* not *dhearbh-mhic.*

In another context a reciter quoted in *West Highland Tales* had *A(n) dealbh-chuilean* (III 85 and note 24).

[6] Cheerfully, *le meobhail.*

[7] 'Wooing has not raised her eye.' I translate here the line as it occurs in the version of the Dean of Lismore, p. 76, *An t-suirghe char thog a súil*, not as it occurs in Aonghus Beag's version, *Suirghich' nach togadh a shùil.* The entire point of the line has been lost through corruption in transmission, cp. Hector MacLean's speculations in *West Highland Tales*, III 89.

5. THE BYZANTINE BRIGAND

An Gadaiche Greugach

Learned by Aonghus Beag from Donald MacDonald, Stonybridge.

Recorded on wire (No. 194) in the Chapel House at Bornish on 9th January 1950, and on tape at Frobost on 13th January 1960.

Aarne-Thompson Type 953, The Old Robber Relates Three Adventures to Free His Sons, in a Gaelic setting. See Stith Thompson, *The Folktale*, p. 172.

[1] a high summer-palace with a single tree, *grianan àrd an aona-chruinn.*

[2] The Queen's crown fell from her head, *thuit an còmhdach rìoghail far a cinn.*

[3] wouldn't be as good a mother to him, *nach deanadh tu gnìomh màthar dha.*

[4] I impose tabus on you, see p. 212, note 10.

[5] palfrey, *fàlairidh.*

[6] it's enough for me to have to go without your coming *cha diuc mi fhìn a' falbh ged nach biodh sibhse a' falbh.*

[7] to a great feast, *gu banais mór.* See *banais* in Fr Allan McDonald's 'Gaelic Words from South Uist'. Not necessarily a wedding-feast.

[8] the highest stone of your palace would be the lowest (*cha n-eil fhios agam*) *nach e clach a b'àirde clach a b'isle agad.* A frequent threat in old stories.

[9] a block of wood, *cnag.*

[10] he pulled a standing-stone into the door, *tharraing e carra-creige as an dorus.*

[11] The second time the story was recorded, Aonghus Beag said that it was more like a hoop than a ring.

[12] danger, *crois.*

[13] I'll . . . let you go free, *gheobh thu do cheumannan saor.*

6. BOBBAN THE CARPENTER

Boban Saor

Learned by Aonghus Beag from Alasdair MacIntyre, Beinn Mhór. Recorded on tape at Frobost on 30th April 1958.

Another version recorded from Duncan MacDonald, Peninerine, on Canna on 11th August 1951.

Fr Allan McDonald took down a version from John MacKinnon, Iain mac an Tàilleir, Dalabrog, in January or February 1898. See *Records of Argyll*, p. 282–283, 'Caisteal na h-Inghinne Ruaidh, *i.e.* the Castle of the Red-Haired Girl. From the Gaelic of Donald MacVicar, Oban'. The hero's name is given as 'a housebuilder' who 'lived in Edinburgh' (!) and the location of the castle as Lochavich in Argyll.

Boban Saor is called Gobán Saor in Ireland, where he was well known. See Larminie, *West Irish Folk Tales*, pp. 1 and 241 'The Glass Gavlen'; *Irisleabhar na Gaedhilge*, VIII 191–193.

[1] a wink of sleep, *dùnadh cadail.*

[2] secret, *seugrad.* Cp. Irish *séicréideach,* MacCathmhaoil, *Scathán Sacramuinte na hAithridhe,* l. 5769.

[3] the apprentice, *am preantas.*

[4] a turn with a turn, etc., *car mu char agus car an aghaidh cuir, agus an acfhuinn bheag.*

[5] my father-in-law, *mo chliamhainn.*

7. THE WEDDING-FEAST AT HACKLETT

A' Bhanais a bha ann an Hà-cleit

Learned by Aonghus Beag from Neil MacIntyre, Howmore.

Recorded on wire (No. 493) at Lochboisdale Hotel on the 1st November, 1950.

A typical story of the literal-minded numskull, so popular in folklore; also of 'the fool in the next parish'.

8. GEORGE BUCHANAN AND THE DOGS

Seòras Bochanan agus na Coin

Learned by Aonghus Beag from Allan MacDonald, Peninerine.

Recorded on tape at Frobost on 12th January 1960.

[1] George Buchanan, the sixteenth-century Scottish historian, Latinist, and traducer of Mary Queen of Scots, has passed into Scottish and Gaelic folk tradition as a type of the smart trickster, who, like the literal-minded numskull, is a popular subject of folk anecdotes.

[2] Isn't he a smarty! it wouldn't take much to send him scurrying! *Nach ann a tha an Donas! Bu bheag a ghabhainn a chur 'na chabhaig!*

9. THE REASON WHY THE SEA IS SALT AND NOT FRESH

An Reusan a tha am Muir saillte seach an Uisge

Learned by Aonghus Beag from a man from Tiree.

Recorded on wire (No. 63) at Lochboisdale Hotel on 23rd November 1949, and on tape during the winter of 1958–59.

Aarne-Thompson Type No. 565 'The Magic Mill'. Explanatory legend regarding nature of sea. See Stith Thompson, *The Folktale,* p. 240.

[1] ham. English word used.

[2] A crofter. No name given him in the Gaelic.

[3] you have brought fortune and happiness, *bu tusa ceann an fhortain 's an àigh.*

[4] millionaire. English word used, provides a pun in translation!

[5] granary. English word used.

10. THREE MORE FOOLISH

An Triùir Gòrach

Learned by Aonghus Beag from John Wilson, Howmore.

Recorded on tape at Frobost on 12th January 1960.

Aarne-Thompson Type 1450 'Clever Elsie'. See Stith Thompson, *The Folktale*, p. 193; West Highland Tales, II 28 and 393; Fionn, *Leabhar na Céilidh*, p. 78, 'Sgire ma-Cheallaig'. I recorded a version from Patrick MacCormick on Benbecula on 22nd November 1949 (wire No. 48).

[1] without gossip or shame or scandal, *gun ghuth gun nàire gun sgannal.*

11. THE PRIEST, THE MINISTER, AND THE TWO HENS

An Sagart, am Ministeir, agus an dà Chirc

Learned by Aonghus Beag from Neil Smith, Howmore.

Recorded on tape at Frobost on 30th April 1958.

Another version recorded on wire (No. 142) from James MacKinnon, Seumas Iain Ghunnairigh, on 2nd January 1950, 'An Tuathanach, am Ministeir, agus an dà Thunnaig'.

Aarne-Thompson Type No. 1741 'The priest's guest and the eaten chickens'. See Stith Thompson, *The Folktale*, p. 208, 'False Accusations'.

[1] a certain date, *là ainmichte.*

[2] a young man, *lad, i.e.* an admirer.

[3] a bit of chicken meat, *bìdeag do shitheann.*

[4] he left nothing but the bones, *cha do dh'fhàg e caiteag ach na cnamhan.*

[5] steel sharpener, *staoil.* Cp. O.E.D., under 'Steel', 8b. 'A rod of steel, fluted or plain, fitted with a handle, used for sharpening table or butcher's knives.'

[6] to crop his ears. This is the expression used in the story as described by Stith Thompson; but I suspect that it is not a literal translation of what is actually said in a number of languages, including the Gaelic, which is *spothadh.*

[7] Hey, hey! Actual words used.

12. HOW A BAD DAUGHTER WAS MADE A GOOD WIFE

An Tuathanach 's a Thriùir Mhac

Learned by Aonghus Beag from Allan MacDonald, Peninerine.

Recorded on wire (No. 199) at the Chapel House, Bornish, on 9th January 1950. Another version was recorded from Patrick MacCormick on Benbecula on 22nd November 1949, wire No. 51, 'Am Fear a rinn dà deagh-bhean de Dhithist droch-mhnathan'.

This is the Gaelic version of the 'Taming of the Shrew'. Aarne-Thompson Type No. 901. See Stith Thompson, *The Folktale*, p. 104.

[1] just as well-born, *cho àrd fuil.*

[2] If her mother is bad, my daughter is seven times worse, *Ma tha an truaighe air a' mhàthair, tha seachd air an nighinn.*

[3] her mother will never let you have her at all, *cha n-fhaigh thu cnàimh dhi o màthair.*

[4] revolver, English word used.

[5] a worthless creature, *preasan.* Fr Allan McDonald says *preasan* is the Uist form of *peasan*, a scamp. But Peigi MacRae distinguishes *peasan* 'pàisde mi-mhodhail', a bad-mannered child, from *preasan* 'duine nach gabh comhairle', a man who won't pay heed.

13. THE THREE QUESTIONS AND THE THREE BURDENS

Na Trì Ceistean agus na Trì Eallaich

Learned by Aonghus Beag from Jonathan Beaton, Milton, whose father came from the Isle of Skye.

Recorded on tape at Frobost in November 1957.

Aarne-Thompson Type No. 875, 'The Clever Peasant Girl'. See Stith Thompson, *The Folktale*, p. 158. See also *Records of Argyll*, pp. 274–281, 'The King and the Labourer' translated from the Gaelic of Archibald M'Tavish, Oban. In this version only two questions are asked, and the girl (Queen) advises the crofter to sow boiled peas. Also Larminie, West Irish Folk Tales, p. 174, 'The Little Girl who got the Better of the Gentleman', told by P. M'Grale, Achill, County Mayo.

I recorded a very similar version of this story from Duncan MacDonald, Peninerine, on wire (No. 257) at Lochboisdale on 16th February 1950. In this version, the crofter is to be evicted for poaching if he cannot answer the three questions. The recording is at present unfortunately lost.

[1] crop-headed freckled daughter, *nighean mhaol charrach.*

[2] are you fit to answer the questions, *bheil thu fiod air son na ceistean a fhreagairt.*

[3] the neighbours were ploughing together, *bha na nàbuinnean a' treobhadh am pàirt.* This implies runrig. See *pàirt* in Fr Allan McDonald's *Gaelic Words from South Uist.*

[4] some salt, *deannan salainn.*

[5] It wasn't your head that thought that up, *cha b'ann ad cheann fhéin a sgeumaich sin.*

14. THE NORWEGIANS IN SOUTH UIST

Na Lochlannaich ann an Uibhist

Learned by Aonghus Beag from Alasdair MacIntyre, Beinn Mhór, who was his source for all these stories of local traditions.

Recorded on tape at Frobost on 13th January 1960.

[1] Aird Mhaoile is a grassy headland on the west coast of South Uist, about half-way down the island, with a magnificent view north and south. It contains a loch which at one place is only separated from the sea by a few feet of shingle. I am told by the Rev. John MacLean that old people told him that once a tremendous storm removed this shingle and revealed a channel lined with dry stone masonry by which boats could have been taken in and out of the loch. This may well have been of Norse construction. Used in this way, the headland would have provided one of the very few safe anchorages on the west coast of South Uist.

Near the inland end of the loch are a number of ruins of very old stone dwellings, some of which have been used as sheilings by lobster fishermen until quite recently. Aird Mhaoile is an isolated spot of great beauty and a favourite haunt of wild birds.

[2] Popular etymology, but Howmore probably contains Old Norse *haugr*, a burial site.

[3] a culvert, *saibhirean.*

15. CLANRANALD AND GILLE PÀDRA' DUBH

Mac 'ic Ailein agus Gille Pàdra' Dubh

Learned by Aonghus Beag from Alasdair MacIntyre, Beinn Mhór.

Recorded on wire (No. 192) at the Chapel House, Bornish, on 9th January 1950.

See note on the Clanranalds, p. 205.

This is clearly a localized version of the 'William Tell' folktale. Fr Allan McDonald noted a short précis of it in English from Neil Johnston on Eriskay on 4th February 1896.

[1] down, *sìos, i.e.*, northwards. In Uist *sìos* is northwards and *suas* is southwards; on the mainland, these words are used for 'east' and 'west' depending on the direction in which the rivers flow, that is, on the west coast, 'west' is *sìos*, on the east coast, sìos means 'east'.

16. HOW GILLE PÀDRA' DUBH PAID HIS RENT

Mar a phàigh Gille Pàdra' Dubh am Màl

Learned by Aonghus Beag from Alasdair MacIntyre, Beinn Mhór.

Recorded on wire (No. 193) at Chapel House, Bornish, on 9th January 1950.

Fr Allan McDonald took down in 1897 a story of this kind in which Gille Pàdra' Dubh was the victim. MacNeil of Barra's bard 'Bàrd Dubh Mhic Nìll' has been killed in a brawl in Benbecula by one of Clanranald's men.

'Gille Pàdra' Dubh was the collector of *eirig*, or fines for Clanranald, and each great crime had its corresponding penalty. A human life cannot have been of much value when the fine for the murder of Bàrd Dubh Mhic Nìll was only seven pecks of grain. . . .

'As Gille Pàdra' Dubh was speeding to Nunton with the *eirig* of grain from the murderer of the Bard, he passed by a *Brugh* or a house dug out of the sand on his way, in which *brugh* there dwelt a man distinguished by the name of Mac 'Ille Chusbaig. His forebears, paternal or maternal, hailed from Barra. On seeing the chieftains' collector of *eirigs* pass he called out to him to come to him tomorrow to receive another *eirig*. Gille Pàdra' Dubh who doubted not but that the underground man had been convicted of some crime, came duly on the morrow. Mac 'Ille Chusbaig was busy cleaning grain in a tub with a spade or some similar weapon. He asked Gille Pàdra' Dubh to examine it to see if it were clean enough from chaff. The *eirig* collector stooped, and Mac 'Ille Chusbaig avenged himself on Clanranald by having his *eirig* collector thrown into the balance with the seven pecks of grain as a meet and a suitable retaliation for the rather low estimate set on a Barraman's life and poetic talents. It is said that there is in Benbecula a place called Cnoc 'ic 'Ille Chusbaig where dwelt the slayer of the collector of fines.'

Fr Allan McDonald does not state the source of the story.

17. THE WIDOW'S SON'S REVENGE ON CLANRANALD

Tòrachd Mac na Banntraich air Mac 'ic Ailein

Learned by Aonghus Beag from Alasdair MacIntyre, Beinn Mhór.

Recorded on wire (No. 62) at Lochboisdale Hotel on 23rd November 1949.

This story must be well known in South Uist. Fr Allan McDonald took down a version from Angus MacInnes, Smercleit, on 20th October 1896, running to thirteen pages in a quarto notebook. The story is well told in good Gaelic, but direct speech is hardly used at all, hence it is not so vivid as Aonghus Beag's version.

In Angus MacInnes's version, Clanranald saw his grieve stop and pick up and eat some silverweed (*brisgein*) while ploughing. He went on to spend the day hunting and then decided that the grieve's sons must be disposed of. These were named Angus, Tormod and Raghnall. Clanranald pursued them himself, armed with a dagger (this seems unlikely, compared with Aonghus Beag's version, in which he sent estate officers, *na maoir*, after them to kill them for him). Angus was killed near Loch Eynort; Tormod at a place in Bòirnis Shiarach, called after him Creag Thormoid; Raghnall was killed at Lag Raghnaill when trying to gain the sanctuary at Staoiligearraidh.

The rest of the story closely resembles Aonghus Beag's version, except that the youngest son was still unborn at this time, and that the story ends with his killing young Clanranald with his knife, after young Clanranald had tried to kill him in bed.

On 4th February 1896 Neil Johnston, Eriskay, told Fr Allan McDonald that the spots where two of the grieve's sons had been killed were Lag Raghnaill and Lag an t-Slugain, 'Throat Hollow'.

[1] out taking a walk, *a' gabhail wàg a mach.*

[2] a blade of dulse, *bileag do dhuileasg.*

[3] we've done enough killing, *cha diuc na rinneadh,* literally 'what has been done is not insufficient'.

[4] she threw them away, *sheòl i bhuaich' iad.*

[5] to get clear away from Uist altogether, *faighinn air falbh clìor is an t-eilein air fad.*

[6] his opponent, *fear adhbhair,* literally 'the man of his cause'.

[7] making for his life, *a' deanamh mar a bheatha.*

[8] to snore, *tarraing strannd.*

18. BLACK DONALD OF THE CUCKOO

Dòmhnall Dubh na Cuthaige

Learned by Aonghus Beag from Alasdair MacIntyre, Beinn Mhór.

Recorded on wire (No. 495) at Lochboisdale Hotel on 1st November 1950.

This story is well known. The house on Canna in which Black Donald died in 1686 is within a hundred yards of the writer's. See Rev. Charles MacDonald, *Moidart or among the Clanranalds*, pp. 80 to 100 for various stories about Black Donald, including this one. See also 'Morar', *Three Clanranalds*, p. 53.

[1] Black Donald beckoned to it, *smìd Dòmhnall Dubh oirre.*

[2] plan, *plàn.* Assimilated loanword, frequently used.

[3] began to beckon to it, *thòisich e air smìdeadh oirre.*

[4] cleared out, *chlìor iad a mach.* Frequently used.

19. HOW CLANRANALD BUILT ORMACLATE CASTLE

Mar a thog Mac 'ic Ailein Caisteal Ormaclait

Learned by Aonghus Beag from Alasdair MacIntyre, Beinn Mhór.

Recorded on wire (No. 190) at Chapel House, Bornish, on 9th January 1950.

[1] fell in love with, *ghabh e nòisean do.* Assimilated loanword.

[2] cask, *buideal.*

[3] a big tin jug, *cuach mhór thun.*

[4] they're my bodyguard, *siod an fheadhainn a tha gleidheadh mo chinn dhomhsa.*

20. MACLEOD OF DUNVEGAN AND IAIN GARBH OF RAASAY

MacLeòid Dhun Bheagain agus Iain Garbh Rathasaidh

Learned by Aonghus Beag from Alasdair MacIntyre, Beinn Mhór.

Recorded on tape at Frobost on 30th April 1958.

Iain Garbh MacLeod of Raasay was a well-known strong man in the Highlands in the seventeenth century. He was drowned in 1671, supposedly through witchcraft. The MacLeods of Lewis were the chiefs to whom Raasay owed allegiance, and the landlord of Raasay was actually the Bishop of the Isles, but they got a charter of the island from King James VI in 1596. See I. F. Grant, *The Clan MacLeod*.

[1] bully. English word used. See footnote to story.

[2] a good slap on the backside, *deillseag*.

21. MACVURICH ASKING FOR THE WIND

Mac Mhuirich ag iarraidh na Gaoithe

Learned by Aonghus Beag from Alasdair MacIntyre, Beinn Mhór.

Recorded on tape at Frobost on 3rd June 1958.

The MacVurichs were the hereditary poet-historians of the Clanranalds. The ruins of their house, a comparatively large one, may still be seen at Staoiligearraidh. There is more than one hint in the stories current about them that they possessed preternatural powers.

Versions of this story were taken down by Fr Allan McDonald around 1888 from Oighrig an t-Soighdeir of North Lochboisdale, and from the widow of Neil Morrison, South Boisdale. See also *Carmina Gadelica* V 306, where several versions are given, also references to others in print.

[1] The verses in Aonghus Beag's version are as follows:

MacVurich:

'*Gaoth a deas o'n Ghailbhinn chiùin,*
Mar a dh'òrdaich Rìgh nan Dùl,
Le soirbheas gun iomaireadh gun abhsadh
Nach dianadh gnìomh fhabhtach dhuinn.'

Merchant:

'*Gaoth a tuath cho cruaidh ri slait*
A dh'fhuraileadh os cionn stuic,
Mar earba 's i 'na tailc
'S i ruith le ceann cruaidh cnoic.'

MacVurich's son:

'*Ma tha gaoth an ifhrinn fuar*
Na thionndas na tonnan taobh ruadh,
A Chonain, cuir as mo dheoghaidh i!
'Na strada teine teinntein;
Ged bhiodh am marsanta 'sa ghrùnnd,
Ach mis' is m'athair 's mo chù dhol gu tìr.'

The place-name Gailbhinn occurs in the Ballad of the Smithy, see p. 17. *Cnoic* is regularly the genitive of *cnoc* in South Uist. Conan was one of the Fingalians, see pp. 20, 27.

Hell is cold in Gaelic folklore, cp. *Duanaire Finn*, Vol. II, p. 172.

> '*Uch tri fichid bliadhain búan*
> *Ro bhí misi a n-ifreann fhúar.*'

Fionn's soul was there for sixty years.

22. MACVURICH AND THE CHANGELING

Mac Mhuirich agus am Bodach

Learned by Aonghus Beag from Alasdair MacIntyre, Beinn Mhór.

Recorded on tape on 3rd June 1958.

Fr Allan McDonald took down a fragment of a version of this story around 1888 from Donald MacCormick.

'MacVurich of Stilligarry when going through his fields one day, found a child lying out at the end of a rig, and wondering whose it could be, asked *Có as a thàinig thusa?* "Where did you come from?"

'"*Muc Dhearg*" "Red Pig," answered the phantom or fairy child (*bodach*). "*Muc Dhearg*," said MacVurich. "*Muc Dhearg*," said the *bodach*. "*Muc Dhearg*," said MacVurich. "*Muc Dhearg*," said the *bodach* again. "*Muc leathchluasach leth-dhearg! Gabh, a mhic cocaire nan ceann, air falbh as a seo 's nach fhaicear air an fhonn chianda tuilleadh thu*," "One-eared part-red pig! Go, son of the cooker of heads, away from here and don't be seen on the same ground again."' There seems hardly much point in this, compared with Aonghus Beag's story.

23. 'KINTAIL AGAIN'

Learned by Aonghus Beag from Allan MacDonald, Peninerine. Recorded on tape at Frobost in November 1957.

[1] 'London again.' In English.

[2] 'Kintail again.' In English likewise.

24. THE WOMAN WHO WAS SHOD WITH HORSESHOES

Té nan Cruidhean

Learned by Aonghus Beag from Allan MacDonald, Peninerine. Recorded on tape at Frobost on 30th April 1958.

Compare 'The Unlucky Horseshoes' in *Folk Tales of the Borders,* published by Winifred Petrie in 1950. Pp. 166–168, source not stated; all in oratio obliqua.

I have called the two farm servants 'Donald' and 'James'. They have no names in the original.

[1] engaged in every kind of unlawfulness, *ris a h-uile mi-riaghailt.*

[2] 'Ride on, you devil!' '*Marcraich romhad, a dheomhain*'. If he had given a blessing, it would have freed her from the spell.

[3] I'm clear of her, *tha mise clìor is i.*

[4] Burning was the final penalty inflicted on them, *sin an lagh a rinneadh dhaibh mu dheireadh.* It is interesting that the last witch to die in Scotland was burned in 1722 for having 'transformed her daughter into a horse, and having had her shod by no less a person than the Fiend Incarnate himself'. Calum MacLean, *Scottish Studies* III 189, where this story is referred to.

25. THE LAIRD, THE PRIEST, AND THE EVIL ONE

An t-Uachdaran, an Sagart, agus an Donas

Learned by Aonghus Beag from Allan MacDonald, Peninerine.

[1] It might be someone uncanny, *nach e duine ceart a bh'ann.*

[2] A noise, *tustar.*

[3] Full of gold and silver, *agus taosg do dh'òr 's do dh'airgiod innte.*

[4] I won't leave one stone of your building standing on another, *'s e clach as àirde clach as ìsle agad* (Cp. 5[9]).

[5] Until he was tried, *gus an rachadh cùirt a dheanamh dha.*

[6] I never saw anyone more like him, *cha n-fhaca mi dùradh riamh as collaiche ris.*

26. WILD ALASDAIR OF ROY BRIDGE

Alasdair Fiadhaich a Drochaid Ruaidh

Learned by Aonghus Beag from Allan MacDonald, Peninerine.

Recorded on wire (No. 494) at Lochboisdale Hotel, on 1st November 1950.

Inquiries made at Roy Bridge have failed to identify Alasdair. There was once a well-known man there called Dòmhnall Bàn a' Bhòcain, who was haunted by a poltergeist, but not for any shortcomings of his own. See MacLean Sinclair, *Glenbard Collection of Gaelic Poetry*, p. 297; K. N. MacDonald, *The MacDonald Bards*, p. 24.

[1] a very rough kind of man, *duine uabhasach curs dheth fhéin a bh'ann.*

[2] an iron bar, *gàd iarainn.*
[3] he could not stand up to the man, *cha seasadh e cas dha'n fhear.*
[4] she raised the alarm, *lig i na creachan.*
[5] tunnel. English word used.

27. THE LITTLE OLD LADY OF AIRD MHICHEIL

Cailleach Bheag Àird Mhìcheil

Learned by Aonghus Beag from his father.
Recorded on tape at Frobost on 3rd June 1958.

28. THE MERMAID

A' Mhoighdean-Mhara

Learned by Aonghus Beag from the Rev. Fr John Mackintosh, parish priest of Bornish.
Recorded on tape at Frobost on the 12th January 1960.
See Note following story.

29. 'SHIFT THREE POINTS TO THE STARBOARD'

Learned by Aonghus Beag from Angus Morrison, Locheynort.
Recorded on tape at Frobost in November 1957, and again on 30th April 1958.
The words of the title occur in the story in English. I am informed by a naval friend that the order correctly given would have been 'Alter course three points to the starboard'.
[1] an apparition, *sealladh, i.e.* an instance of second sight.

30. THE COFFIN THAT CAME ABOARD

Learned by Aonghus Beag from Angus Morrison, Locheynort.
Recorded on tape at Frobost in November 1957.
Told consecutively with preceding story and has no separate title in Gaelic.

31. DONALD'S WOOING

Am Baidsealair ag iarraidh Mnatha

Learned by Aonghus Beag from James MacDonald, Loch Eynort.
Recorded on tape at Frobost on 30th April 1958.

[1] He scraped off every single grey hair, *cha robh fiasag no ciabhag no peallag bh'air liathadh nach do sgrìob e sìos leis a' ràsar.*

[2] You're ill advised, *tha droch-comhairl' ort.*

[3] a little quick-tempered, *car bras 'na nàdur.*

[4] to strike while the iron is hot, *an teanga thoirt as a' ghlag* The Gaelic means literally 'to take the tongue out of the bell'.

[5] nothing could make him go near Janet again, *cha chuireadh an Gearmailteach an còir Seònaid tuilleadh e.* Literally, 'the German (? Kaiser) would not send him near Janet any more'.

32. THE FIRST GALVANIC BATTERY ON THE ISLE OF SKYE

Eachann mac Fear a' Choire agus Màiri an Uillt

Learned by Aonghus Beag from Allan MacDonald, Peninerine. Recorded on tape at Frobost on 30th April 1958. A version of this and the next story was printed by John MacFadyen in *An t-Eilean-ach*, a book which was first published in 1890, in a section headed *Sgeòil-Aithris*, 'Traditional Stories'. In this version the stories are placed on one of the Argyllshire islands, not on Skye.

[1] the apparatus, *na cnagan.*

[2] Mary's croon was:

> '*Buail le m' cheist air eas 's air eathair*
> *Lannan éisg air stiùir 's air lic;*
> *Mogal teann mu cheann an sgadain,*
> *'S morghaich geur a' bhradain bhric.*'

[3] A corpse-band on your big scabby block-head, *Spriolag air do sporra-cheann mór carrach gun tuigse, agus inisg air a h-uile duine o'n tàna tu agus air an dùthaich as do rugadh tu.*

33. HECTOR AND THE BALLOON

Eachann agus am Ba-lùn

Learned by Aonghus Beag from Allan MacDonald, Peninerine. Recorded on tape at Frobost on 30th April 1958.

Told consecutively with preceding story.

[1] The Isle of Skye was always famous for witchcraft. This, anyway, is the opinion of the Outer Hebrides. See, for instance, the witch stories in *Tales of Barra, Told by the Coddy.*

[2] unless some lying baggage or other comes around, *o nach tigeadh pacaid bhriagach eile.*

[3] sniffing at the door, but by your nose you'll get no further inside,

a' snòmhainich ri dorus, ach do shròn-sa cha n-fhaigh thu staigh ach na fhuair.

34. THE TINKERS' HOTEL

O'Connell agus na Ceàird

Learned by Aonghus Beag from John MacAlister.

Recorded on wire (No. 1066) at Lochboisdale Hotel on 31st October 1951.

[1] began to smell of burning coal and horn spoons being moulded, *thòisich fàileadh a' ghuail agus nan adhraicean.* Tinkers used to make horn spoons with moulds. See *laghaid, laghainn* in Fr Allan McDonald's 'Gaelic Words from South Uist'.

36. THE HOLIDAY OF DONALD AND MAGGIE

Holiday Dhòmhnaill is Magaidh

Learned by Aonghus Beag from James MacDonald, Locheynort.

Recorded on wire (No. 1067) at Lochboisdale Hotel on 31st October 1951, and again on tape at Frobost in November 1957.

36. THE SHEPHERD WHO COULDN'T TELL A LIE

An Cìobair nach innseadh Briag

Learned by Aonghus Beag from Archie Cameron, from Rannoch.

Recorded on tape at Frobost during the winter of 1958–1959, and again on 12th January 1960. The translation is based on the second recording.

[1] dairymaid, *banchag.* Dairymaids were important people on Highland farms in the old days, when cattle were the main stock kept. See Alexander MacDonald, *Song and Story from Lochness-side,* p. 245.

[2] The bracsy, *am brags.*

[3] nor hide nor hair, *cha tug, no 'm boiceann.*

37. 'PRIEST DONALD'

Dòmhnall Sagart

Learned by Aonghus Beag from Alasdair MacIntyre, Locheynort.

Recorded on tape at Frobost during the winter of 1958–1959.

[1] He had a name for cleverness, *fhuair e ainm cleabhar.*
[2] Napoleonic wars, *cogadh Bhònaidh.*
[3] staunched, *stail.*

38. A WIFE FROM ENGLAND

Bean a Sasann

Learned by Aonghus Beag from Neil MacIntyre, Howmore. Recorded on tape at Frobost during the winter of 1958–1959.

[1] when Scotland lost her independence, *nuair a chaidh Alba fo lagh Shasainn.*

[2] Lord MacDonald. Here and elsewhere in English, except at times when he is in disguise, when he is called *An Dòmhnallach.*

[3] Lord MacDonald had been taught fine carpentry, *dé chiùird a dh'ionnsaich e ach a bhith 'na shaor geal.* Fr Allan McDonald says in a note to the version of the story of Boban Saor he took down from John MacKinnon, Dalabrog, in 1898, that a *saor geal* was 'a superior joiner who could do fine work'.

[4] The gentleman arrived in a carriage, *thànaig an duin' uasal is ma-sìn aige.* 'Machine', O.E.D. 'a vehicle of any kind, usually wheeled'. Obsolete except Scots. 1687.

[5] Sofa, *sòfa* (sɔ:və). English loanword, assimilated.

[6] a big ball, *so-rì mór* (*sö-ri*:). From 'soirée', a word used in English since 1820 (O.E.D.).

[7] paid his respects to, *rinn e modh ri.* See *modh* in 'Gaelic Words from South Uist'.

[8] He was taking his turn, *bha e gleidheadh a thùrn.*

[9] in a second, *as a' mhionaid.* 'Minute' is the minimum space of time in these stories, where 'second' would be the word used in English.

[10] now you're going back on your word, *tha thu nist a' dol an cois t'fhacail.*

[11] if it would harm you, *ma tha e chum deifir dhut.*

[12] a safe-conduct for you, *do phas dhut.*

[13] she was given a great welcome, *rinneadh othail mhór rithe-se.*

[14] you've put a price on his head, *airgead-ceann agaibh péin air.*

[15] The upshot was, *'S e bun a bh'ann.*

[16] not to let on that they knew who they were, *gun iad a ghabhail sian orra.*

[17] unfriendly, *coimheach.*

[18] medals, *stars.*

[19] with my husband, *comhla ri m' chompanach.*

[20] she was delighted, *bha i air bàrr an uisg' fhuair.*

39. THE ADVENTURES OF THE DROVER

Am Pacman a bha 'san Eilean Sgitheanach

Learned by Aonghus Beag from Allan MacDonald, Peninerine. Recorded on wire (No. 496) at Lochboisdale Hotel on 1st November 1950.

Compare *Records of Argyll*, pp. 245–246, 'Big John Clerk'. This is a mere précis of a version of this story, and the names of reciter and collector are not given. In this version the article belonging to the murdered man is a gun, not a watch.

Many tales are told in the Isles of the old droving days, when cattle were driven from all over the Highlands and Islands to the annual fair at Falkirk (An Eaglais Bhreac). See Eric Cregeen, *Scottish Studies*, III 143.

[1] a night's lodging, *cuid na h-oidhche.*

[2] often in deadly danger, *'s iomadh sian-bàis a chaidh oirbh.*

[3] its mark, *an draft aige.* Borrowing of English 'draught' in obsolete sense of a stroke or line.

[4] presents, *preusants.*

[5] the murmur of voices, *monbar bruidhne.*

[6] 'God bless me', '*God bless mise*'.

[7] I lost my way, *chaill mise mo chùrs.*

[8] when it was carrying creels, *'nuair a bha acfhuinn chliabh air.* Creels or panniers were used for carrying home peats, etc.

[9] every one of its hairs, *a h-uile gas cuilg air.*

[10] it fell stretched out stiff in the middle of the road, *stioff e air miadhain an rathaid.* Borrowing of Scots verb 'stiff' = to stiffen.

[11] rough, *cùrs.*

[12] throwing stones, *a' seòladh chlach.*

[13] I could not stand up, *cha b'urrainn mi cas a chur fodham.*

[14] revolver. English word.

[15] on watch, *'na caithris.*

[16] seargeant, *séirdsein.*

[17] let him carry out his idea now, *dianadh e mach a phuing a nist.*

[18] give up your arms, *libhrig ur lamhan.*

[19] I was well rewarded, *fhuair mi deagh-shìneadas.*

[20] so that I didn't need to be going with a pack, *nach robh mi 'n taing a bhith falbh le pac.*

40. THE STORY OF NIALL BEAG AND MÀIRI BHÀN

Fear Chòrnaig agus Fear Chliait

Learned by Aonghus Beag from Allan MacDonald, Peninerine. Recorded on wire (No. 500) at Lochboisdale Hotel on 1st November 1950.

Aonghus Beag called this the story of the Tacksman of Cornaig and the Tacksman of Cliat, but in translating it I have preferred to call the story after its hero and heroine. The scene is Tiree.

[1] field, *achadh*. Usually *pàirc* in Uist. Niall Bàn's widow would have been the first woman in the field with the sickle, which was used for reaping in the Highlands and Islands in old days, as many visitors who wrote accounts of their journeys attest.

[2] term, *terms*.

[3] supposed to be rich, *agus amharas airgid air*.

[4] Mary would give them no kind of an answer, good or bad, *cha toireadh Màiri 'n t-olc no 'm math do fhreagairt dhaibh*.

[5] Mary used to pretend, *bha Màiri a' gabhail oirre fhéin*.

[6] they were both very busy, *bha iad trang taobh air thaobh*, i.e. *bha iad cho trang le chéile* (Peggy MacRae).

[7] with the white horse, *leis a' chapall bhàn*.

[8] 'speak of the Devil, and he'll appear', *thig an Donas ri iomradh*.

[9] the trouble really began, *bha an ceòl air feadh na fìdhle*.

[10] 'I'll swear the man's not telling lies, *mo làmh-sa nach eil an duine sin ag innse na briagan*.

[11] but you'll not be in my house another twenty-four hours, *ach oidhche no latha cha bhi thusa 'nam thaigh-sa ach na bha*.

[12] the tears she wept would have washed his clothes all night, *chaoin i na nigheadh aodach fad na h-oidhche*.

[13] a friend, *companach*.

[14] that's hurting me, *a tha 'gam ruighinn*.

[15] rush, English word used, *ruis*.

[16] by the Book, *a leabhara*. See *leabhar* in 'Gaelic Words from South Uist'.

[17] but what you can earn by your labour, *ach do chosnadh. Cosnadh* in Uist implies earning a living by labouring work. See 'Gaelic Words from South Uist'.

[18] a day for drowning, *là millidh. Mill* is a euphemism for 'drown'.

[19] semmet. English word used.

[20] on the crest of a wave, *air bàrr stuaigheadh*.

[21] a hawser, *hasair*. Assimilated loanword, short *a*.

[22] a standing-stone that won't move, *carragh nach tréig*.

[23] a hero, *diumlaoch.*
[24] the Tiree men, *na Tiridhich.* Not *Tirisdich.*
[25] in corners, *anns na clobhsaichean.*

41. THE STORY OF ST CLAIR CASTLE

Caisteal St Clair ann am Barraidh

Learned by Aonghus Beag from Neil MacIntyre, Howmore. Recorded on tape at Frobost on 12th January 1960.

This story is a précis of the romantic novel *St Clair of the Isles, or the Outlaws of Barra, a Scottish Tradition,* by Elizabeth Helme, editions of which (384 pages) appeared in 1803, 1861 and 1867. The period of the novel is the first half of the fifteenth century, and it appears to have no foundation in local tradition whatever, but to be purely a work of imagination. In spite of its prolix style and inherent improbability, it is not without dramatic excitement. As an example of the style of the original I quote the passage describing the emotions of the hero on discovering his father's dirk—in the Gaelic version it has become a glove—in the castle of the lady who has imprisoned his father:

> 'As he reflected, his eyes were fixed upon the dagger, when suddenly a universal trembling shook his whole frame, he breathed with difficulty, his eyes projected beyond their sockets, and every function of life seemed suspended: somewhat recovered from his emotion, he rushed upon the dagger, and clasping it in his clenched hand, he sunk upon a seat, and gave a loose to all the bitterness of grief' (p. 143).

In the original story, the villainess is the Duke of Monteith's sister Mariam, not his daughter; her husband is the Earl of Roskelyn, not 'a commander in the army'; St Clair's wife is Ambrosine, not 'Lady Ambleton' (her rejection of the Queen of Scotland's offer of a husband, who is not St Clair's brother but the brother of a lady who has rejected St Clair, involves a speech of twenty-three lines of print in the original!); the 'Frenchman' is De Bourg, one of St Clair's fellow exiles; there is no 'Italian'. MacRae's home is in Lewis, not in Harris. With all these inaccuracies, inevitable when a long novel in English passed into oral Gaelic tradition as a short story, the dimensions of the prison at the castle, eight feet square, is accurately remembered, also St Clair's son's words to the lady of the castle, 'methinks I could worship you' (p. 154), has become in Gaelic 'bhithinn deònach adhradh a thoirt dhut'.

I have been unable to discover anything about the authoress of this novel, Elizabeth Helme, or whether she had any first-hand local knowledge, though the novel gives the impression that this was not the case. In her second chapter, which is a résumé of preceding events, she writes of St Clair, the hero of the novel, that 'confined by the royal mandate, to the Isle of Barra, he had taken up his residence in an old fortress, called the tower of M'Leod, where, could he have forgotten past events, he might have lived happily'.

The 'tower of M'Leod' is a building on a small island in Loch Tangusdale on Barra, called on the Ordnance Survey map 'Dùn Mhic Leòid'. The remarkable thing is that Elizabeth Helme's novel appears to have bestowed names on the loch and the tower which have now become official; Loch Tangusdale is also called Loch St Clair on the Ordnance Survey map, and the tower is called Castle Sinclair in the report of the Commission on Historical Monuments (volume dealing with the Outer Hebrides, p. 129). The tower there is described as having been originally of three stories and measuring 18½ by 18 feet, over walls over 4½ feet thick. There are no fireplaces, and no stairs. The tower may have been secure, but it cannot have been comfortable.

Barra tradition knows nothing of St Clair, and he could hardly have established himself in the island in the way described in the times of the MacNeils. The novel is a work of fiction and Aonghus Beag's version of it is an interesting instance of the adaptation of a iterary work to the Gaelic oral tradition.

[1] a commander in the army, *co-manndair airm.*

[2] secretly with child, *trom gun fhiosd.*

[3] errands, *ceann-turuis.*

[4] he knew very well, *bha fios aige taght'.*

[5] long trousers, *briogais chaol.*

[6] the other lad lost his temper, *leum an nàdur air an fhear eile.*

[7] (he) squeezed him, *thug e plùchadh air.*

[8] visit, *céilidh.*

[9] a sob, *rachd caoinidh.*

[10] rage, *réid.*

[11] a squeezing that hurt, *plùchadh do dhochann.*

[12] a coat of arms, *còta bhairm.*

[13] Did he dare to accuse her of that? *cha robh chridhe stuaghadh rithe-se.*

[14] a commission, *post.*

[15] men-o-wars, English word used.

[16] His brother had the first prize, *bha a' first aige.*

[17] the hall, *hàl.*

[18] a female saint, *bann-naomh.* In a dream, in the original story.

[19] as sure as I stripped you in that field, I'll strip the head off you before the altar, *a cheart cho cinnteach agus a shrip mis' thu an leithid seo a phàirc, stripidh mis' an ceann dhiot ro'n altair.* The reference is to the successful sword duel he had fought with his brother earlier.

[20] like an outlaw, *'nam reubalaiche.*

[21] every sail that was over him, *a h-uile seòl bha os cionn a chlaiginn.*

[22] flag. English word used. A Danish flag in the original story.

[23] below deck, *fo rùm.*

[24] going in disguise, *a' falbh ann an dios-gaidh.* They darkened their eyebrows and hair and went disguised as ordinary Highlanders in the original story.

[25] glove, *miotag.* A dirk in the original story.

[26] Surely you know, *mo làmh-sa gu bheil fios agad.*

[27] Bold, *bould.*

[28] a feast, *banais.*

[29] enlisted, *liost.*

[30] got so excited, *ghabh e leithid a theas.*

[31] he seemed likely to be drowned, *bha e air thuar a bhith bàithte. Air thuar* plus verbal noun, very common expression, means 'looked likely to' 'appeared likely to', not 'on the verge of' as given by the late Dr George Henderson, cp. Fr Allan McDonald, 'Gaelic Words from South Uist,' p. 249. The translation 'on the verge of' would not fit all contexts.

42. WHY EVERYONE SHOULD BE ABLE TO TELL A STORY

Am Fear nach robh Naidheachd aige

Learned by Aonghus Beag from Alasdair MacIntyre, Beinn Mhór.

Recorded on tape at Frobost during the winter of 1958–1959, and again on January 1960.

[1] Walking through Skye, crossing by sea from Dunvegan to Lochmaddy, and then walking south over the Benbecula sea-fords, was the old way of travelling from the mainland to Uist, and the adventures of travellers on this route are often related in Gaelic stories.

[2] away working at the harvest on the mainland, *aig an Lobhdaidh (Loudi).* Apparently Gaelic for 'Lothian', stereotyped in this expression.

In the old days, when the oats were reaped with the sickle, and work was hard to get in the islands, islanders used to go to the mainland to help gather the harvest on the Lowland farms. The term used for this in Gaelic was *falbh gu Lobhdaidh.* Miss Peigi MacRae quoted to me a verse from a song in which the word occurs:

Cò ach Anna mo nighean,
Fuaim orre deasachadh bìdhe,
Cò ach Anna mo nighean,
'S i 'na ruith gu Lobhdaidh!

'Who but Anna my daughter, making a noise preparing food, who but Anna my daughter, rushing off to Loudy'—or to work on the mainland at the harvest.

[3] closet, *clòsaid.* See note on old Island houses.

[4] and clung on to it. Exactly the same incident is described in the Adventure of the Drover, and in practically identical words, although the two stories came to Aonghus Beag from different persons.

GLOSSORIAL INDEX

(The references are to the Notes)

INDEX TO THE STORIES